W9-CZS-802

THE ROMMEL PLOT

JOHN TARRANT

THE ROMMEL PLOT

J. B. Lippincott Company
Philadelphia and New York

**WITH GRATEFUL THANKS
TO KEN NEGUS
AND THE STAFF OF
THE CARNEGIE LIBRARY,
ARNOLD**

First U.S. edition
2 4 6 8 9 7 5 3 1
Printed in the United States of America

All characters in this novel are fictitious, and any resemblance to actual persons, living or dead, who served with the French Section of the SOE is purely coincidental.

U.S. Library of Congress Cataloging in Publication Data

Tarrant, John.
The Rommel plot.

I. Title.
PZ4.E32Ro3 [PR6055.G35] 823'.9'14 77-5731
ISBN-0-397-01235-7

1

Marcel Gilbert left his house in the rue du Docteur Duval and walked toward the river. Born in 1871 just after the Franco-Prussian War, he was now seventy-three and the oldest inhabitant of La Roche-Guyon, although no one would think it to look at him. A tall, lean man with a head of thick iron-gray hair that was only just beginning to turn silver, he carried himself erect like a soldier on parade, as if the fishing rod over his left shoulder was a rifle.

More than an hour had passed since the bell in the church of Saint-Samson had marked the end of the night's curfew, but in most of the red-roofed houses the windows were still shuttered. Gilbert thought the village always looked its best at this time of the morning, but there was no escaping the fact that behind the pastoral beauty La Roche-Guyon was like a concentration camp where the prison staff outnumbered the inmates by three to one. He knew without looking around that there were sentries standing guard inside both gates of the Château Rochefoucauld, in the crumbling ruins of an old tower perched on the hillside above, and by the roadblocks at either end of the village. This was the 1,471st day of the Occupation, and despite the Allied landings in Normandy the Germans seemed as strongly entrenched as ever.

Most villagers managed to ignore the Germans, some tolerated them, a few were willing to cooperate within limits, and there were one or two stupid young women who actually enjoyed their company. But Gilbert was different; Gilbert nursed a smoldering hatred that had been spawned in the summer of

'14. He'd been forty-two then, a middle-aged schoolmaster with a wife and two sons aged fifteen and sixteen to support, but the army had not forgotten that he was still in the Reserve. He had soon discovered that there were thousands of others like him in the ranks of the 87th Territorial Division, elderly men who'd been plucked from the safety of their homes, kitted out, handed a Berthier carbine that could only take three rounds in the magazine, and then sent off to the Front.

In the spring of 1915 his division had been transferred to Ypres and placed in reserve behind the North Africans. The Staff had said that it would be as good as a rest cure for them, but of course the Staff had been proved wrong. The unnatural silence that had been hanging for weeks over the battlefield had been shattered at five o'clock in the evening of Easter Monday. The bombardment had been bad enough, but it was the enveloping, greenish-yellow fog that had made them break and run; no one had expected the Hun to use gas, and the chlorine had decimated the battalion. Gilbert had come through it unharmed and had gone on to survive the war, but not so his sons; they had been sucked into the charnel house that was Verdun and had disappeared from the face of the earth.

In 1920, at the age of forty, his wife had presented him with a daughter whom they christened Yvette. The child grew up to become a lively, attractive, and intelligent girl, and she had filled the gap in their lives. Gilbert had hoped that she would go to the Sorbonne, but shortly after her seventeenth birthday she had fallen in love with Jean Lemmonier, whose father owned L'Hôtel Saint-Georges. His wife, Claudine, had persuaded Yvette to wait a year in the hope that it was merely a passing infatuation, but it wasn't, and their daughter had married Jean Lemmonier in the early spring of 1939.

Gilbert left the road and walked along the towpath, heading downstream until he reached his favorite haunt on the riverbank behind the orchard which lay directly across the road from the château. Leaning the fishing rod against a tree, he then stripped off his raincoat, draped it over the damp grass, and sat down. From the pocket of his tweed jacket that had leather patches on both elbows, he produced a tin of worms and, rather like a nearsighted woman threading a needle, painstakingly baited the hook.

Angling was a fairly recent pastime for which he had no real aptitude, and he thought Claudine would be amused if she could see him now, but she had died of cancer two years back. It occurred to him that his son-in-law might not be quite so amused because the rod belonged to him, but he was scarcely in a position to object since he was behind barbed wire in a POW camp. Gilbert knew that his lack of prowess was something of a joke in the village but he didn't care; what mattered was that the Wehrmacht soldiers patrolling the river had got used to seeing him fish from the same spot every day.

From where he was sitting he could see the inflatable assault boat moored in its usual place near the approach road leading to the suspension bridge which had been blown in May 1940 by French army engineers withdrawing toward Brest. The same tubby little corporal was in attendance, glancing regularly at his wristwatch as he paced up and down the bank like a nervous stage manager who hoped the principal actor would arrive on time. The ritual never varied, and Gilbert, observing him snap to attention, knew that the shooting party was now in sight at the top of the lane. Exactly two minutes later, the corporal whipped up a rigid salute.

There were five of them: a gamekeeper, a signaler with a man-pack radio set, a captain in his late thirties, a lieutenant colonel of engineers, and the Field Marshal, a compact, stocky man with the Knight's Cross of the Iron Cross peeping beneath the collar of his tunic. The Field Marshal exchanged a few words with the corporal and then climbed into the assault boat and sat down in the bow. The others followed in order of precedence, the gamekeeper casting off the mooring line when the outboard motor fired into life. The assault boat nosed out into midstream, picked up speed, and headed toward the far bank.

Gilbert concealed his satisfaction behind a blank face. The pattern had not been broken after all; following his absence yesterday, Field Marshal Erwin Johannes Eugen Rommel had resumed his old habit and was off for an hour's shooting in the forest of Moisson. The short break with established custom had alarmed Gilbert, but now he was glad that he had sat on this conflicting piece of information. Passing a message down the network was always a lengthy and hazardous business, and a second report which appeared to contradict the first would only have confused the Englishman whose code name was Foxhound.

Marcel Gilbert, retired schoolmaster, widower, the oldest lieutenant in the French Forces of the Interior, believed he could help bring the war to a swift and decisive conclusion. Assassinating Rommel would be the means to that end.

The farmhouse on the outskirts of Théléville suited Holbrook because, among other things, the attic made an ideal observation post. A peephole beneath the eaves afforded him a commanding view of the countryside, from Maintenon in the northeast to the twin spires of Chartres Cathedral, which dominated the skyline to the south. Since it was also possible to watch every road leading into and out of the village, Holbrook reckoned that even during the hours of darkness they could count on ten minutes' warning, and that would give them enough time to lift the trap and crawl into the bolt hole under the floorboards.

The bolt hole was just twenty inches deep and about twice the length and width of a normal-size coffin. By trial and error Holbrook had discovered that in order to remain there for any length of time it was necessary for him and Church to lie face to face with the sleeping bags and the wireless transmitter between them. Fortunately, Church was only five foot six, the sleeping bags didn't take up much room, and the radio fitted snugly into an attaché case; so far they had not been obliged to use the hide in earnest, but there was always the possibility to be considered. The fact that there were no longer any field force units in the area didn't mean that they could afford to relax their guard; the Panzer Lehr Division might be fighting in Normandy but the Abwehr and the SD were still in business.

Holbrook raised the binoculars to his eyes and adjusted the focus. The cyclist he'd first noticed some minutes back was no longer a speck in the distance, and he was now able to distinguish her features. He thought the girl looked pale and exhausted, but that was understandable; it was no joke having to pedal a rusty old bicycle all the way from Chartres on such a hot afternoon. Holbrook placed the field glasses on one side and stood up, brushing the dust from his trousers.

"We're in business," he said. "Denise will be here any minute."

Church marked the page he'd reached in the paperback and then slipped it into his bedding roll. "Good. I've been dying for a cigarette."

"Must you?"

"Must I what?"

"Smoke."

Church grinned at him. "Don't worry," he said cheerfully, "I'll be careful."

"You ought to try and give it up. Any SD agent who walked into a supposedly empty room and got a whiff of your stale cigarette smoke would soon put two and two together. He'd sound the walls first, and when he drew a blank there he'd start on the floorboards. How long do you suppose it would take him to find the trap door?"

"About fifteen minutes?"

"Less," Holbrook said angrily. "Take it from me, you wouldn't have time to say your prayers and neither would the Cuviers."

"Jesus, you don't have to make a speech."

"No? Well, just you remember that we're living under their roof and the SD would shoot them out of hand if they found us here. There are only two of us but there are four Cuviers."

Church waved a hand in a resigned gesture. "All right," he said, "if that's the way you feel about it, I won't bother."

Holbrook knew he didn't mean it. The moment his back was turned, Church would crawl over to the peephole and light up. Church was a good wireless operator, the best he'd had, but his addiction to cigarettes made him untrustworthy. His conducting officer at Beaulieu should have spotted this flaw in his character and washed him out of the Special Training School, but somehow he had managed to slip through the net.

Church said, "Do you want me to stand watch?"

Holbrook opened the door and stepped out onto the landing. "It's the usual procedure, isn't it?" he said coldly.

"Yes."

"Well then, why bother to ask?"

The girl was deep in conversation with Madame Cuvier when Holbrook walked into the kitchen. Breaking off, she turned around and smiled warmly as if she were happy to see him again. It was an illusion, of course; much as he found Denise attractive, there was nothing and never could be anything between them. The small emerald ring on her finger was a constant reminder that she was engaged to Philippe Cuvier.

"You're later than usual," he said.

"I was held up at a roadblock."

"Where?"

"On the outskirts of town." She smiled again. "Don't look so alarmed. It was nothing, just a routine snap check by the Abwehr. The Germans were a little suspicious at first when I told them that I was going to visit my fiancé in Théléville, but then I recognized one of the gendarmes on duty and he was able to vouch for me."

Holbrook pulled out a chair and sat down at the kitchen table. "I still don't like it," he said pensively. "Have you ever been stopped and questioned before?"

"Several times."

"When?"

"Twice in January and March of last year, shortly after I joined the network as a courier." She shrugged her shoulders as if to suggest these incidents were of no consequence. "I'm not worried," she said.

"It doesn't pay to be too confident in this game."

The smile faded and was replaced by a petulant expression. "Don't you want to hear my news?"

"You know I do."

"What would you say if I told you that we've located Rommel's headquarters?"

Holbrook searched her face and saw the spark of triumph in her eyes. "I'd say it was one of the biggest intelligence coups of the war."

"La Roche-Guyon," she said briskly. "It's a small village fifty miles west of Paris on the banks of the Seine. Rommel has established his headquarters in the Château Rochefoucauld, and apparently he's in the—"

Holbrook cut her off in midsentence with a peremptory gesture, reached inside his jacket, and brought out a small notebook and pencil. "All right," he said tersely, "first things first. Where did this information come from?"

"The Albert circuit in Paris."

"Is Felix still connected with that network?"

"I wouldn't know."

Holbrook leaned back in the chair and toyed with his pencil, beating a slow tattoo on the kitchen table. It had been stupid of him to ask; Denise was just a courier and for security reasons she would only be allowed to know the names of her most immediate contacts in the chain. All the same, he hoped Felix wasn't involved; René Dufoir, alias Felix, was first and foremost a Gaullist and had scant respect for the French Section in Baker Street. They had quarreled violently back in '42 when Dufoir had insisted he would only take orders from the Bureau Central de Renseignements et d'Action and didn't give a damn for the Special Operations Executive. Holbrook had a nasty feeling that Dufoir had subsequently set him up for the Gestapo, because the SD had almost grabbed him on the steps of the Grenelle Métro station when he arrived to keep an appointment with one of Felix's liaison officers.

"Tell me about the château."

"It's in the center of the village immediately below a cliff."

"Cliff?" he asked sharply.

"A ridge about three hundred feet high; it extends for some two miles in either direction."

Holbrook thought London could check it out, but if she was right about the topography, bombing the château might prove difficult. It would have to be a low-level raid with rocket-firing Typhoons, and they would have to contend with a lot of flak.

"Do we know how many troops are stationed in the village?"

"Between fifteen hundred and two thousand."

Holbrook suppressed a sour smile. If Felix was involved, he could understand why he'd parted with the information. Faced with that sort of opposition on the ground, no one in his right mind would dream of attacking the château.

"It doesn't look good," he said.

"There is a loophole."

"Oh?"

"The Field Marshal regularly goes shooting in the forest of Moisson across the river. There are never more than four or five in the party. It should be possible to ambush him."

It was more than a possibility, and the beauty of it was that the operation could be mounted with no great effort. Given a little more information, even an average shot could pull it off, and he was a marksman. London would have to clear it first, but he didn't think they could possibly object; after all, this was an unique opportunity to shorten the war. He would keep to himself the fact that he also felt a personal satisfaction for the chance to settle an old score.

Holbrook said, "Let's go over the details again. I don't want our people in London raising any queries when they get my signal tonight."

Lewis was sure the doodlebug was coming their way, an opinion which, judging by the tense expression on his face, was evidently shared by the teleprinter operator. Lewis glanced at the warning bell above the door and wondered what the hell the spotters up on the roof were doing. They would have to be blind not to see the tail flame of the jet engine against the night sky; they ought to have sounded the alarm long ago.

The V1 roared on, its engine sounding like a heavy diesel truck with a loose baffle plate in the exhaust. Suddenly and without any prior warning, the engine cut out. Lewis found himself counting off the seconds as he held his breath. The silence seemed interminable and then, just when it seemed his lungs would burst, it was shattered by a deafening explosion and he heard the tinkle of falling glass in the distance.

"Oxford Street," said Newstead without looking up from the file he was reading.

"You think so?"

"Positive."

"We should have gone down to the basement shelter."

Newstead raised his head and peered at Lewis through horn-rimmed spectacles. "Doesn't matter now, does it?"

"I suppose not." Lewis reached out and grabbed the flimsy which the teleprinter operator was clutching in a hand that was still shaking. "Where did this come from, corporal?" he said.

"Bicester, sir, Station Fifty-three A; they received it from Foxhound at twenty-two hundred hours." The teleprinter operator swallowed nervously. "I've sent an acknowledgment."

"And Bicester?"

"They gave Foxhound a QSL to show that his message had been received and understood."

"Thank you, corporal," Lewis said politely. "I'll deal with it."

The signal was longer than most, and Lewis had to read it twice before he realized all the implications. He'd been an instructor at Wanborough Manor before someone had decided that his talents would be more gainfully employed in the French Section at 62/64 Baker Street, but he did not feel sufficiently competent to deal with this particular problem. Lewis had never met Foxhound; he was a Cambridge graduate, a mathematician who, given time, could break any code, but he could no more assess the feasibility of a projected operation than fly in the air.

He cleared his throat to attract Newstead's attention. "What's Foxhound like?" he said.

Newstead closed the file on his desk and clasped his hands together. "Simon Holbrook? Well, let's see. He's twenty-six, dark hair, fairly tall, about an inch or so under six foot, well built —the sort of man women find attractive, so I'm told. He's bilingual—mother's French, you know—grew up in France, but was educated over here: Rugby, I think. His father was a wine merchant, but Holbrook didn't want to follow him into the business."

Lewis tried to interrupt but gave it up as a bad job. Once he was launched into a monologue, there was no stopping Newstead.

"Studied accountancy instead and received his articles a month before war was declared. Anyway, he volunteered on the fourth of September '39, was snapped up by the Intelligence Corps, who were desperately short of interpreters, and of course when the Germans invaded Norway, what did they do?" Newstead's voice dripped sarcasm. "Why, they sent him to Namsos with One forty-six Infantry Brigade, where I imagine his French came in very handy. Fortunately, he came to us in July 1940; otherwise he might well have finished up in Iceland running a NAAFI canteen. Anything else I can tell you?"

"Is he a good agent?"

Newstead looked surprised. "One of the best, a professional right down to his fingertips, but he can be a bit headstrong at times. Why are you so interested in him?"

"Because he wants to take a crack at Rommel." Lewis walked across the room and dropped the teletype on Newstead's desk. "And I don't know whether it's a feasible idea or not."

Newstead removed his glasses and polished the lenses with a handkerchief before reading the signal. His studious appearance reminded Lewis of his tutor at Cambridge, but there the similarity ended. Newstead was ex-Indian Army. A gifted but eccentric soldier like Wingate, he'd retired from the Waziristan Scouts with the rank of major. Recalled to the General List at the outbreak of war, he had been recruited by the SOE, where his expertise in guerrilla warfare had found a natural outlet.

Lewis said, "What do you think?"

"It's risky but feasible; Holbrook could pull it off. I'll brief Parker when he arrives in the office, and if he agrees we'll clear it with the top brass at St. Michael's House." Newstead rubbed his chin. "Did I hear the corporal say that Bicester gave him a QSL?"

"Yes, it's a standard code for acknowledging that a message has been received and understood."

"It's the 'understood' bit that worries me," said Newstead. "If he's a mind to, Holbrook might decide he's been authorized to proceed."

2

Epp hated flying, and his stomach sank as the Feisler Storch began to lose height. There were beads of perspiration on his forehead, his hands were clammy, and he knew that his breath must be foul because the sergeant pilot was quick to look the other way whenever he spoke to him. Epp thought the sergeant should consider himself lucky; no matter how ill he might appear, it was most unlikely that he would be sick at this late stage of the journey. A long, bumpy flight in a JU-52 from Berlin to Le Bourget had taken care of his breakfast, and he hadn't been able to face a haversack lunch.

Epp turned his head and stared out of the side window, forcing himself to ignore the feeling of nausea which threatened to engulf him once more. They were flying parallel with the Seine above the forest of Moisson, and across the river, nestling at the foot of a thickly wooded escarpment, he could see the château of La Roche-Guyon. Perched above it and silhouetted against the skyline were the ruins of a castle which he knew dated back to the ninth century. Time and weather might have eroded the thick stone walls and the circular keep, but much of the grandeur remained. Less obvious were the concrete pillboxes in the chalk outcroppings of the foothills.

The Storch banked, turning through 180 degrees, and Epp braced himself for the landing as they dropped into the grass field, his feet instinctively pressing down on the floor as if that would somehow slow their rate of descent. The meadow which had appeared spacious enough at first sight now seemed ludicrously small, and the embankment at the far end looked menacing. Epp needn't have worried; there was only a slight jolt as the pilot set the plane down and then the Storch came to a halt inside fifty yards.

A Kübelwagen emerged from behind the poplar trees bordering the road and motored slowly toward them. Although the château was less than half a mile away, Epp was grateful that somebody at Headquarters Army Group B had thought to send a car to collect him. His pelvis had never mended properly after a mine had exploded under his half-track on the road to Sevastopol, and even a short walk was enough to bring on every ache and pain again. Clutching a briefcase and a walking stick in his left hand, he opened the door and stepped stiffly down from the aircraft.

The pilot said, "Do you want me to wait for you, sir?"

Epp looked up at him. "Is there any reason why you shouldn't?" he asked sharply.

"No, sir, but we shall have to return to Paris before dark."

"Oh? Why?"

"Because, Herr Major, I'm afraid this Storch isn't equipped for night flying."

The sergeant was polite enough and respectful too, but there was a hint of firmness, and Epp sensed that he was not the sort of man who would bend the regulations for the sake of a mere major. There were still five hours of daylight left and he thought that ought to be sufficient, provided that Rommel wasn't away visiting 7th Army headquarters or one of the forward divisions. The trouble with the Field Marshal was that you could never pin him down when things hotted up. He wasn't content to sit back at headquarters; he liked to command from up front when the battle was raging. At least, that was what he'd been told, but it could be that that habit had died with the Afrika Korps.

Epp said, "If I haven't returned by twenty hundred hours, you may leave without me."

He turned away and limped over to the waiting Kübelwagen, conscious that the pilot was watching him. Acknowledging the salute of the driver, he placed the briefcase on the seat and then, levering himself up with the aid of his walking stick, climbed into the back of the open car and sat down.

The door caused a certain amount of embarrassment because

the catch refused to engage in the lug, but after a bit of a struggle the driver managed to close it. The delay had been negligible but he seemed anxious to make up for lost time; shifting into first, he let the clutch in fiercely and then went up through the gearbox as if he was on a grand prix circuit.

Leaving the meadow, they followed the rue de l'Hospice as far as the mayoral offices in the center of the village, where they turned left into a cobbled road which, curving past the church through an avenue of linden trees, led to the château above. A sentry stopped them briefly to examine their ID cards, and then the wrought-iron gates were opened and the Kübelwagen swept into the upper courtyard.

Epp had been in the army long enough to know that any officer who wanted an audience with the C in C had to observe certain formalities. No one got to see Rommel without first meeting the Chief of Staff, but he was sure that he could rely on Major General Doctor Hans Speidel to smooth the way for him. The staff might think that he had flown in from Berlin to advise them on the reinforcements they could expect to receive from the Reserve Army, but Speidel knew the real purpose of his visit.

The large high-ceilinged room on the ground floor which Rommel used for his office presented a dour and austere appearance. A faded Gobelin tapestry stretched the length of one wall, while from another the haughty face of Duke François de La Rochefoucauld, a seventeenth-century writer and an ancestor of the present duke, looked down out of a heavy gilt frame. Thick draperies hung in the windows, there were no carpets on the highly polished parquet floor, and the furniture simply consisted of a few chairs and a massive Renaissance desk on which there was a small table lamp.

The personal touch was noticeable only by its absence. There were no photographs of the Field Marshal's wife and fifteen-year-old son, no mementos of the North African campaigns, and, even more surprisingly, no map showing the dispositions of Army Group B. Epp thought that if Rommel ever had to leave La Roche-Guyon he could walk out of the room without leaving a trace.

At fifty-two, the Field Marshal looked much older. There was a fine tracery of lines around his eyes, but, although he seemed drawn, Epp had been given to understand that Rommel was still his old self and had lost none of the tireless energy for which he was so rightly famed.

Waving Epp to a chair, he said, "I hope you are the bearer of good tidings, Herr Major; Seventh Army needs every reinforcement it can get. The fighting in Normandy these past few days has been very savage, especially in the Odon sector." He looked down at the desk and frowned. "No doubt Reichsführer Himmler will ensure that the losses sustained by the First and Second SS Panzer Corps are made good, but I'm more concerned about the Wehrmacht formations, particularly the Three hundred forty-sixth Infantry and the Second, Twenty-first, and Lehr Panzer Divisions."

Epp hugged the briefcase to his chest. "I've given your staff all the facts and figures, Herr Field Marshal."

"And?"

"Within the next three months and allowing for normal wastage, units should be at seventy-five percent of their war establishment. I'm afraid that's the best we can do."

"It isn't good enough."

"No, sir," Epp said miserably.

"Normandy will burst open like a festering abscess long before then and the war will be lost."

Epp felt his heart skip a beat. Whether it was intentional or not, the Field Marshal had presented him with the opportunity to bring up the subject of a negotiated peace. Just how to do this discreetly was a problem that had been uppermost in his mind from the moment the JU-52 had taken off from Rangsdorf airport.

"Colonel General Beck is of the same opinion, sir."

"Beck? You've seen him recently? Is he keeping well?"

"He's very sprightly for a man of sixty-four. He asked me to give you his warmest regards."

"Did he now? Of course, Beck always was the perfect gentleman; the army lost a good man when he resigned from Chief of the General Staff in 1938 . . . 1938." he said musingly. "It seems a lifetime ago. Do you know what I was doing then?"

"The Field Marshal was an instructor at the Potsdam War Academy."

"And a mere colonel."

The conversation was not going the way Epp had hoped, and they had strayed from the subject he wanted to discuss.

"Beck"—Epp corrected himself hastily—"the Colonel General believes that Germany will be totally destroyed if this war is allowed to continue. He urges you to consider the possibility of negotiating a separate peace treaty with the Western Allies."

"No one can contemplate such a move while the Führer is still in power."

It was out in the open now. Epp began to sweat. The suggestion had not been rejected out of hand, but there was a condition, and he was aware that he was walking on very thin ice. Despite the fact that Rommel had been lionized in the newspapers and was a folk hero, he remained an enigma. He was said to be contemptuous of the Führer, but like every other German officer he had taken the oath of loyalty in 1935 and had been appointed to command Hitler's personal escort a few days before the invasion of Poland. On the other hand, there were strong grounds for thinking that this close relationship had always been one-sided and that, since El Alamein, Rommel had become one of Hitler's severest critics, at least in private.

"Within a few weeks from now, we may take it that the Führer will find that he's unable to continue as the head of state."

"Are you saying that his health will deteriorate even further?"

The question sounded innocent enough but it was loaded with irony, and Epp found it difficult not to smile. Provided Stauffenberg managed to smuggle his time bomb into the villa at Berchtesgaden, there was every reason to hope that the end result would prove fatal for Adolf Hitler. Although Rommel was known to be strongly opposed to political assassination, Epp felt it was his duty to make him see that Beck and the other conspirators were not prepared to leave things to chance.

"I believe the Field Marshal accepts that when a leader is known to be insane he must be removed from power. Once this has been accomplished," Epp continued firmly, "it will be necessary to replace him with a man who can command both the allegiance of the German people and the grudging respect of our enemies."

Rommel stared at him thoughtfully for a moment. Then, unlocking a drawer, he took out an envelope and passed it across the desk to Epp.

"I suggest you read this," he said calmly. "It's but one example of many I receive in my mail every morning."

The letter was written on lined notepaper in a spidery hand that was almost illegible. There was no address at the top and the author had been careful to sign it under a nom de plume. Yet despite this subterfuge the cry for help rang true, and it was possible to believe the assertion that only the Field Marshal could save the German people now.

Epp folded the letter back inside the envelope and placed it on the desk. "Something must be done," he said quietly.

"Yes. If this were just an isolated case, one could ignore it."

"What shall I tell them in Berlin, sir?"

"I would have thought the answer to your question was obvious. We must take steps to end the war."

It was not the unequivocal commitment Epp had hoped for, but it would have to do. At least it was a step in the right direction, and if the Field Marshal should show any signs of wavering, he could rely on Speidel and General Stülpnagel, the Military Governor of France, to remind Rommel that he owed his allegiance to the German people, not Adolf Hitler.

Epp stood up and clicked his heels. "With the Field Marshal's permission?" he said hesitantly.

Rommel nodded curtly. "Yes, of course, you have a long journey ahead of you."

Epp saluted and then limped out of the room.

Unlike the Storch, the JU-52 was equipped for night flying, and he thought that, with any luck, he would be back in Berlin in time to snatch a few hours' sleep before reporting to Reserve Army Headquarters in the Bendlerstrasse. Stauffenberg and Beck had said that everything hinged on Rommel, and they would be relieved to hear that he was now prepared to join the conspiracy. That he had given no such undertaking was beside the point; if Operation Valkyrie went according to plan, Rommel would find himself President whether he liked it or not.

It might be a deceitful way of doing things, but at least Beck would now alert his contact in Berne and instruct him to get in touch with the Anglo-Americans. Epp tried not to think of what a disaster it would be should anything happen to Rommel before Valkyrie was launched, but the worry nagged at him all the way back to Berlin.

Half an hour before last light, six Mosquitoes of 528 Squadron passed over La Roche-Guyon at an altitude of five hundred feet, homeward bound from a low-level strafing raid on the marshaling yards of the Gare de l'Est in Paris. They appeared on the radar screen too late for the 20mm antiaircraft guns on the grounds of the château to put up much more than a token barrage before they were out of range. No one at Headquarters Army Group B paid much attention to the incident.

The intruders, however, had not strayed over La Roche-Guyon by chance, and their raid on the marshaling yards had been in the nature of a smokescreen. One of the six Mosquitoes was a photo reconnaissance aircraft, and the mission had been mounted at the request of SOE. Newstead didn't expect them to bring back a snapshot of Rommel, but the photographs would provide concrete evidence to show whether or not the château was being used as a headquarters by the Wehrmacht.

3

In Newstead's opinion, St. Michael's House was an indication of how large the "old firm" had become over the years. SOE had begun life in a modest way, but within a few weeks of its inception it had become apparent that it would be impossible to house the organization under one roof, and by courtesy of Messrs. Marks and Spencer the directing staff had moved out of 62 Baker Street into more spacious accommodations. The expansion, once started, had continued to the point where they now had more requisitioned property in West London than any other government department.

Although Parker, the deputy head of the French Section, had told him often enough that he was the best controller in the department, Newstead was aware of his own limitations. There was nothing of the extrovert in his character, and he was apt to become tongue-tied in front of a large audience. He positively disliked the conference room in St. Michael's House because its size permitted far too many people to attend what was supposed to be a select briefing. Parker had led him to understand that it would be an informal meeting, but instead it seemed that half Whitehall had turned up to hear what he had to say.

The rostrum made him feel isolated and conspicuous and he read from notes without once looking at his audience, in case he should dry up when he saw their faces. Newstead was very conscious that he was not doing justice to Holbrook's propositions, but that was scarcely his fault; everyone knew that he was a poor speaker, and yet Parker had delegated the job to him while he sat back and chaired the meeting.

The room was stifling and he could feel the beads of perspiration gathering on his forehead and upper lip. His mouth was dry, too, so that now and then his voice croaked out a word, and he wished that someone had thought to provide him with a glass of water. Finally, he was aware that his listeners were growing increasingly restive, and in the circumstances he thought there was little point in reiterating the principal factors. Coming to an abrupt halt, he stepped down from the rostrum and returned to his seat at the conference table.

"The map," hissed Parker. "You should have pointed to it when you mentioned La Roche-Guyon. That's why it's there."

"Where?"

"On the wall behind the rostrum."

Newstead smiled apologetically. Parker had recently returned from a Methods of Instruction course at Beaconsfield and was keen on visual aids. "I'm sorry," he said. "I didn't notice it."

There was a brief flicker of annoyance before Parker aimed a broad smile at the conference. "Well, now," he said cheerfully, "are there any questions you'd like to ask Major Newstead before we discuss the proposal?"

"I've got one." McCready, the burly American representing the OSS, leaned across the table to grind his cigar into an ashtray. "How good is this guy Foxhound?"

"He's a very experienced agent."

"That isn't what I meant and you know it. Can he do the job if we give him the go-ahead?"

Newstead glanced at Parker and caught his eye. "I think the chairman should deal with that point, George."

McCready smiled. "Just so long as somebody gives me an answer, Dennis."

"I would have preferred not to discuss personalities at this stage," Parker said smoothly, "but I'm prepared to set your mind at rest, George. Our man could handle it all right, but I would like to send in a specialist team."

"We're talking about a team now, are we? I thought Newstead said one marksman would fill the bill?"

"A team would be better."

"Can't Foxhound put one together from his people?"

"I expect he could at a pinch, but if we give him the mission we would have to find another coordinator for his area."

"And just what is he coordinating right now?"

"Supply drops for the Resistance."

"Jesus." McCready shook his head in disbelief. "Look, we ought to get our priorities straight. Foxhound is already on the ground and he's in touch with the group who fed him this information. If we send in another team, they've got to start right from the beginning, which will be one big waste of time."

Parker examined his fingernails intently. McCready was the sort of man who liked to get things moving, but there were times when his abrasive attitude was very irritating. It also occurred to him that they were both acting as if the proposed operation had already received formal approval.

"Before we go any further, George, I think we ought to hear what our friend from the Bureau Central de Renseignements et d'Action has to say." Parker turned to the French naval commander on his left, his face registering an expression of concerned interest that would have done credit to an actor. "I imagine you've considered the possibility that the Germans could make life very unpleasant for the civilian population?"

"If Rommel is assassinated, we can expect reprisals."

"Quite."

"But it is a risk we must accept." The commander pursed his lips. "Providing the operation is successful, it will undoubtedly have a profound effect on the morale and battle efficiency of the Wehrmacht."

"I'm all for that if it breaks the stalemate in front of Caen." McCready leaned forward and smiled across the table at Fawcett. "I guess your people in Military Operations would go along with that, wouldn't they, Alastair?"

Newstead picked up a pencil and drew a series of goose eggs on his scratch pad. McCready could never resist the temptation to deflate one of Montgomery's most ardent disciples. Alastair Fawcett was ex-8th Army; a lieutenant colonel at twenty-seven with a DSO and an MC, he had commanded a company of the Rifle Brigade from El Alamein to Mareth, when he had then been promoted and appointed GSO I (Ops and Plans) on the staff of 30 Corps. Posted home to the War Office in January 1944, he was recognized as one of Monty's bright young men.

"Stalemate?" said Fawcett. "I hardly think that is an accurate description of the situation."

Newstead sucked on his teeth and drew another goose egg. If he wasn't brought to order, Fawcett would launch himself into a long-winded explanation of Montgomery's concept of operations, designed to draw the German armor onto 2nd British Army while the Americans made the breakout from the area of Saint-Lô. His tactics were sound enough, but a lot of people had formed the impression that this had not been his original intention but had developed through force of circumstance. It seemed to Newstead that Montgomery's mistake lay in the various statements he'd made long before D Day when he had attached so much importance to the early seizure of Caen.

Parker said, "We are rather straying from the point, Fawcett. What I'd really like to know from you is whether DMO is in favor of the project or not?"

"We're against it."

"Oh?"

"We would prefer Rommel alive, not dead. We feel we know this man so well that we can read his mind and anticipate his every move. I think everyone here will agree that this gives us an enormous advantage."

Newstead could remember a time when it was a widely held view that Rommel was the best general on either side. Churchill had once said, "Rommel, Rommel, Rommel, Rommel, what else matters but beating him?" Auchinleck had thought it necessary to send a message to his staffs warning them of the danger of Rommel's becoming some kind of "magician or bogeyman," and in November 1941 General Cunningham had landed Colonel Keyes and a commando group by submarine near Apollonia to attack his headquarters in the desert. Now it seemed the army wanted to ensure that he remained in command of Army Group B.

Parker said, "Is this just the view of DMO?"

Fawcett shook his head. "No, sir," he said firmly, "our opinion is shared by Twenty-one Army Group. Of course, it would be a different matter if the Prime Minister gave the plan his blessing—we would then have to accept it as fait accompli."

"You're not prepared to accept a majority decision here then?"

"I'm afraid not."

Parker shuffled his papers together. "We seem to have reached an impasse. The project will be referred to the Cabinet for a final decision, and in view of this the meeting is adjourned." Almost as an afterthought, he added, "Thank you for attending, gentlemen."

They dispersed slowly in twos and threes, leaving ashtrays brimful of cigarette stubs and scattered sheets of scrap paper which would have to be collected and destroyed.

McCready, passing behind Newstead, squeezed his shoulder. "There goes your ball game, Dennis."

"I hate to admit it," said Parker, "but he's right."

"You're not going to take it up with the PM then?"

"Oh, I'll ask for a Cabinet decision, but I can't see Churchill overruling Monty at this stage of the war."

Newstead rubbed his chin. "Holbrook won't like it. He's getting impatient and wants a decision."

"It's less than forty-eight hours since we received his signal, Dennis."

"That's as maybe, but he will still expect a decision tonight. What do I tell him?"

Parker uncapped his gold nib fountain pen and drafted the text of a signal on a scrap of paper which he handed to Newstead. The veiled message was brief and to the point. It read: REGRET MUST FORBID YOU TO GO SHOOTING, YOUR PIGEON WILL BE BAGGED IN DUE COURSE.

Newstead said, "I'd delete the word 'regret' if I were you."

"Why?"

"I have a funny feeling that it could give Holbrook the wrong impression. He may think you are giving him a loophole."

"You're wrong, Dennis," Parker said brusquely. "Even Holbrook couldn't be that obtuse."

Epp left the ugly government building in the Bendlerstrasse which was occupied by the headquarters of the Reserve Army and headed toward the Tiergarten. It had been a long, trying day and he wished he'd been able to scrounge a Kübelwagen out of the motor pool, but the transport officer had flatly refused to let him have one. "There is a grave shortage of gasoline," the lieutenant had said pompously, "and surely the Herr Major must be aware of the standing order which states that anyone using a military vehicle for private purposes will be automatically court-martialed?"

Fromm had been difficult too, but that was not unusual. The Colonel General was renowned for having a quick temper and the news from the Eastern Front had infuriated him. OKW had expected the Russians to launch their summer offensive in the south between the Pripet Marshes and the Black Sea, but they had got it wrong. The attack, which had started five days ago on the twenty-third of June, had fallen on Army Group Center, and now it was beginning to look as if Minsk, the capital of Belorussia, would be captured before long.

The situation was still very confused, but at a conservative estimate it seemed likely that von Busch had lost close to two hundred thousand men. It was quite impossible for the Reserve Army to replace these staggering losses, but Fromm had refused to believe the figures. At his insistence, the staff had gone through every unit strength return to see what they could prize out of the administrative tail. They'd robbed the training schools of half their instructors, reduced the length of recruit training still further, and weeded out the convalescent depots. Their combined efforts had produced an extra ten thousand men on paper, but even so they were nowhere near the required figure. Fromm wouldn't like it, but he had no alternative but to tell OKW that at least twelve divisions would have to be disbanded.

Epp limped across the Charlottenburger Chaussee and turned into Mondelallee. It was one of the few undamaged streets in Berlin, but he was still glad that he had sent Sophie and the children to stay with her parents in Kempten. The flat on the second floor of the Brandenburg apartment building was an empty and lonely place without them, but at least they were safe in Bavaria, safe from the bombing raids and safe from the Gestapo too.

The stern granite face of the Brandenburg reminded him of

a barracks, and, as usual, the elderly janitor behaved like a provost sergeant, opening the door of his room fractionally to peer through the crack as Epp stepped inside the hall. Epp nodded to him and then, transferring his walking stick to the other hand, clutched the banisters and heaved himself up the spiral staircase. Somewhere on the first landing a radio was playing softly and he caught the pervading smell of sauerkraut.

Epp unlocked the door of his apartment and went inside. Leaving his peaked cap on the hall table, he propped the walking stick in a corner and limped through to the bedroom. There was little there to remind him of Sophie apart from the photograph in the silver frame by his bedside, and when he opened the big mahogany wardrobe he thought how empty it seemed now that her clothes were no longer hanging on the rail. Shrugging off his tunic, he draped it over a hanger and then sat down on the bed. The doorbell rang before he had a chance to remove his boots. Anneliese, he thought; it couldn't be anyone else but Anneliese Ohlendorf. Epp pushed himself up from the bed and went back to the hall.

Anneliese greeted him with a friendly smile and held up a carryall. "Your shopping," she said. "I'm afraid I couldn't get any coffee."

Epp stepped to one side to allow her to slip past him into the hall.

"I'll leave it in the kitchen, shall I, Franz?"

"Please," he said. "Can I get you a drink? I have some brandy left, or would you prefer a glass of wine?"

"I could do with a brandy."

"So could I."

"It's been one of those days, has it?"

"Yes," he said. "Nothing went right."

Epp walked into the living room, set out the half-empty bottle of brandy, and searched through the glasses in the cocktail cabinet until he found two that were reasonably clean. The janitor's wife came in twice a week to tidy up, but she never did more than the bare minimum.

"I had tea with Ludwig this afternoon, Franz."

Epp turned about and handed the glass of brandy to her. "How was the Colonel General?"

"As charming as ever."

Anneliese chose the sofa and curled her legs under her body. Although an attractive and fair young woman of twenty-four, she was acutely conscious of her large feet and hands. Distantly related to Beck, she had married unwisely in the opinion of her family and friends. Ohlendorf was the blond, handsome Aryan type whom Goebbels loved to eulogize. An ardent National Socialist whose father was a humble bank clerk, Ohlendorf had joined the Luftwaffe in 1936 and was already something of a hero when Anneliese met him in November 1940. Their wedding the following April had been quite a social event; Goering himself had attended the reception at the Adlon.

Epp raised his glass. "Here's to happier days," he said.

"I'll drink to that." She raised her skirt a fraction and scratched an itch on her knee. "You look tired, Franz."

Epp swallowed his brandy. "I'm not surprised. It's been a frustrating day."

"So I gathered."

"We've had a setback." Epp stared at his empty glass. "Nothing serious but damned annoying all the same. Stauffenberg was supposed to attend a conference at Berchtesgaden tomorrow but it's been postponed until Monday, the third of July. It seems the Führer has summoned von Rundstedt and Rommel instead; no doubt he's angry about the situation in Normandy and intends to make his displeasure known. Rommel will love that, especially if the Leader throws one of his tantrums."

"Well, then, look on the bright side, Franz; it may help to commit Rommel even further to our cause."

"You always were an optimist."

"Whereas you're inclined to be a prophet of doom," she teased.

"No, I'm a realist. This last-minute change of plan means that Stauffenberg will have to wait until the third of July before he can collect his time bomb from Major General Stieff." Epp smiled sourly. "We really are a bunch of amateurs, aren't we? We can't even manufacture our own device but have to rely on one that has been captured from the British SOE."

"Who else but amateurs can save Germany now?"

"You're right. Forgive me, I'm just a little depressed this evening."

Anneliese searched through her handbag and produced a packet of cigarettes. "I have some news that will cheer you up."

"What's that?"

"Ludwig wants you to know that our representative will be seeing 'Mr. Bull' tomorrow."

"Bull?"

"Allen Dulles, the OSS man in Berne. Would you like a cigarette, Franz?"

Epp shook his head.

"You will pass this information on to Stauffenberg?"

"Of course."

Epp watched her light the cigarette and marveled at her serenity. He wondered if she realized how much they all depended on her. She was the essential link between Beck, living in retirement at his house in the suburbs, and the conspirators in the Bendlerstrasse. She was the perfect go-between; as the wife of a Nazi war hero missing in action on the Eastern Front, she was the last person the Gestapo would suspect.

"Bull," he said jokingly. "It's rather an unfortunate code name, don't you think? I mean, in the circumstances. . . ."

She leaned forward and tapped her cigarette over the glass ashtray on the coffee table which stood between them. "I don't see the joke," she said, frowning.

"Bull is Anglo-American slang for an unlikely story."

"That's not very funny, Franz."

"No, I don't suppose it is."

"The Americans have got to believe in us," she said fiercely.

Epp stood up. "Can I get you another brandy?"

"No, thank you, it's getting late and I ought to be going."

"But you only live on the floor above," he protested.

"I have to cook a meal for myself."

"Can't you have supper with me?" Epp, passing behind the sofa, gently squeezed her left shoulder. "Please," he said, "please stay here with me."

"You miss Sophie?"

"Yes; and you, Ulrich?"

"No, it was finished between us long before he was reported missing in action."

"Well, then?"

Anneliese held out her glass. "Perhaps I will have another drink after all," she said.

The rain was falling steadily on the slate roof above their heads, but Holbrook didn't hear it. Sprawled in a battered armchair which the Cuviers had relegated to the attic, he stared at the message that Church had just finished decoding. After forty-eight hours of total silence, he'd expected to receive an indication that Baker Street proposed to take some sort of action on the information he'd given them, but instead they had sent him a noncommittal reply which didn't make a lot of sense.

Holbrook screwed the flimsy up into a tight ball and dropped it on to the floor. REGRET MUST FORBID YOU TO GO SHOOTING, YOUR PIGEON WILL BE BAGGED IN DUE COURSE could mean almost anything. Either they didn't believe his information or else they had some other plan in mind, but if that was the case why didn't they say so? He was offering them Rommel on a plate, and they had turned their noses up as if there was a bad smell in the air.

Church said, "Shall I give Bicester an acknowledgment?"

"How much longer have we got?"

Church looked at his wristwatch. "We're supposed to go off the air in ten minutes."

"That ought to give me enough time."

"For what?"

"To think it out."

There wasn't much to think out. London was sorry but somebody else would take care of the pigeon. Like who? he thought. The Albert circuit? No, that couldn't be right because London was not aware of his source. Perhaps he ought to request Paris to corroborate the story, and then they might listen to him—or better still, he might even persuade the French to help him carry out the operation. After all, this was the opportunity of a lifetime. He was damned if he was going to let a chairborne warrior like Parker stand in his way.

Holbrook said, "Let's have the code book."
"It's best if I encode the message." Church smiled doubtfully. "Just in case there are any queries."
"The code book, please."
"I was only trying to be helpful, Simon."
"I know that."
Holbrook wrote the message down and prefaced it with seven meaningless letters beginning from the key number on the vertical cursor. He then transposed the text in groups of five letters, inserted a second key number, and scrambled the message a second time before handing it to Church.
"Short and sweet," he said.
"So it would seem."
Holbrook grinned. "You'll have to hold the fort tomorrow while I'm in Chartres."
"Going shopping?"
"Sort of. I have to see Denise."
"You lucky dog." Church studied the message and frowned. "Am I allowed to know what I'm sending out?"
"I don't see why not. It says, A NOD IS AS GOOD AS A WINK. WILL ACT ACCORDINGLY."
Church took one look at the determined set of Holbrook's mouth and knew it was useless to argue, but he thought London would have kittens when they received it.

4

The road to Chartres ran straight as a die through an avenue of poplar trees. Holbrook reckoned he'd been cycling for almost half an hour, but still the twin spires of the cathedral didn't seem to be appreciably nearer. The bicycle was old and the links had stretched, which meant that the chain had a tendency to slip unless he was very careful. The brake blocks were uneven on the front wheel and those on the rear didn't function too well either, but he doubted if he would have to make an emergency stop. A couple of buses had passed him going in opposite directions, but apart from a gaggle of cyclists some three hundred yards ahead of him the road seemed empty of traffic. It was, however, a false illusion created by the tunneling effect of the poplar trees in the distance which concealed the oncoming convoy.

Holbrook first became aware of the approaching danger when the convoy was roughly a mile away, but it wouldn't have made any difference even if he'd spotted the vehicles much earlier. There were only cornfields stretching as far as the eye could see in whichever direction he looked, and although there were a number of farm tracks leading off the road, he decided it would only arouse suspicion if he tried to take evasive action.

There were six vehicles in all: a black Citroën, three Morris fifteen hundredweights, and two Bedford troop carriers which he assumed had been captured at Dunkirk if their age and appearance were anything to go by. They were traveling fast, and Holbrook thought they had a lot to learn because the vehicles were bunched too tightly together; a rocket-firing Typhoon would make scrap iron of them in five minutes. But it was a hundred and twenty-five miles to Normandy, and he figured the soldiers were probably replacements from the transit reinforcement camp beyond Chartres.

Few of the soldiers spared him more than a passing glance, but the black saloon worried Holbrook; it reminded him of his previous "outing" late in '42 when all the SD agents in Paris seemed to be riding around in Citroëns. Maintenon was the only town of any consequence in the direction the convoy was going, but he had a prickly feeling that the vehicles would leave Route 906 when they reached the turnoff for Théléville. Between them, the Bedford and Morris trucks could hold about seventy men, and a force of that size was just large enough to cordon and search a small village, especially if the SD was acting on high-grade information.

Church was a good operator, but they had been on the air on three consecutive nights and he thought it was possible that an Abwehr radio direction finding team had managed to get a fix on their transmitter. It might only be conjecture, but Holbrook decided that he would call the farm from a phone booth in Chartres. If Théléville was the target, Cuvier would give him the word when he replied to the test question.

The twin spires of the cathedral were still too far away for his liking; crouching low over the handlebars, Holbrook began to pedal faster.

Church looked up from the paperback he was reading and listened intently. At first he thought he'd been mistaken, but then the distant sound of vehicles on the move reached him again and he scrambled out of the armchair and rushed to the peephole. The convoy was still some way off, but the steel-helmeted figures in the open Bedford trucks were clearly visible to the naked eye.

Church had thought he was equipped to cope with such a situation, but now that it was upon him it was a different matter. All the weeks spent at training school counted for nothing, all the tricks of the trade picked up from Holbrook deserted him as he ran aimlessly back and forth across the attic like a headless chicken.

The moment of blind panic passed, but Church was aware that precious seconds had been wasted and he became frantic to make up the lost time. Everything seemed to be against him. For some inexplicable reason the trap door refused to budge, and in mounting desperation he forced a jackknife into the gap between the floorboards. The blade gave him a certain amount of leverage, and before it snapped in two he managed to get a fingerhold under the rim. Exerting all his strength, he felt the trap begin to yield, and then suddenly it swung back on its concealed hinges. Caught off balance, he sat down heavily.

Madame Cuvier called out to him from below, but he was far too preoccupied to pay any attention to her. Time was running out. He worked feverishly to clear the attic of their belongings. The sleeping bags, the code book, and the paperback followed the wireless transmitter into the bolt hole, and then he lowered himself into the cavity and closed the trapdoor.

Each passing minute seemed like an hour until the brooding silence was broken by the tramp of hobnailed boots on the flagstones in the kitchen. The harsh sound of guttural voices floated up to him, and he lay there in the darkness hardly daring to breathe as a tread on the staircase creaked under the weight of a footstep. The door handle rattled, the hinges squeaked, and he heard a low, tuneless whistle. A match flared briefly, and presently he caught a faint whiff of cigar smoke.

A cheerful voice in perfect English said, "Come out, come out, wherever you are."

Although the intruder was standing directly above him, Church thought he was bluffing until he stamped on the floor. The crack of light which appeared near his feet grew larger as the trap swung away from him and was replaced by the ugly snout of a Walther P-38. The man behind the gun looked deceptively mild and his smile was more amused than triumphant.

"Dr. Livingstone, I presume?" he said with heavy humor.

Church climbed out of the hole, no longer afraid but sullen in defeat. The pistol described an arc and he turned docilely to face the wall, raising both hands high above his head as he did so. Responding to a light touch on the shoulder, he leaned forward with feet astride. The Walther pressed against his spine while the other hand explored his body, probing into every crevice with professional detachment.

Church said, "I am Three-seven-oh-nine-nine-two Captain

David Church; my next of kin is my mother, Mrs. Stephen Church of Twenty-six The Broadmarsh, Kidderminster."

"Quite so, and I am Sergeant Hugo Burghardt. You may stand up and turn round now, Captain Church."

The sergeant, who was an inch or so the taller, was plump and carried an aroma of eau de cologne which even the cigar, now clenched between the stubby fingers of his left hand, was unable to dispel.

"May I lower my hands?"

"You may." Burghardt slipped the Walther into the holster on his belt and regarded him with a tolerant smile. "I imagine you must be feeling a little apprehensive, captain?"

"Apprehensive?"

"Worried. I know I would be in your shoes. As a soldier, you would naturally expect to be treated in accordance with the Geneva Convention, but there are those who would say that you have forfeited that right." Burghardt frowned. "Of course, I do not think it's correct to say that you are a terrorist, but I'm acquainted with others who would."

The scream began with an agonized moan, rose to an inhuman shriek, and then tailed away into a fitful sobbing. Church felt his stomach turn over and thought he was going to be sick.

"Animals," Burghardt said angrily.

"Your people?"

"People? The SD aren't people. Believe me, Captain Church, I will do everything I can to prevent your falling into their hands."

"I am a soldier," Church said huskily, "and I should remain a prisoner of the Wehrmacht."

"I'm in the Abwehr."

"So what? You're still part of the army, aren't you?"

"I don't think you quite understand my position," Burghardt said sourly. "Admiral Canaris was the Director of Military Intelligence until he was dismissed last February, when the Abwehr was then absorbed into the SD. Those pigs downstairs are my superiors, and if they insist on it I'll have to release you into their custody."

"You can't wash your hands like Pontius Pilate; if anything

should happen to me, my people will hold you responsible." Church hoped he sounded more confident than he felt. "You don't want to find yourself on trial as a war criminal, do you, Sergeant Burghardt?"

"I may not have any choice. We're both trapped in a vortex unless we help one another."

"Help one another?"

"Cooperate."

Church licked his lips. "You know I can only give you my number, rank, name, and next of kin."

"I would have been surprised if you'd agreed to do otherwise." Burghardt clucked his tongue. I hope I can persuade the SD to see things my way, but you can never tell with those bastards." He pointed to the open door and then gestured to indicate that Church should walk in front of him. "It's really most unfair," he said.

"What is?"

"We do all the donkey work and the SD insists on claiming the glory."

Church found it hard to sympathize with his point of view.

There were two SD agents waiting for them in the kitchen, hard-faced men who looked as if they enjoyed their work. Madame Cuvier was seated at the kitchen table nursing her left arm, which had been dislocated at the elbow. The bone and several tendons were protruding through the skin, and she had vomited down the front of her dress and apron. One of the SD men spoke to Burghardt in a loud hectoring tone of voice while the other smiled at Church and then smashed a fist into his nose. Thereafter, they both used him as a punching bag all the way to Chartres.

Dust motes swirled and danced in the shaft of sunlight which played on the strip of Axminster carpet in front of Parker's desk. Newstead realized the carpet was a symbol of his status in the Civil Service, but it never ceased to amaze him how much importance Parker had attached to acquiring it. According to the administrative officer, the Axminster had headed the list of priorities which Parker had told him to attend to when he was about to be transferred to the RF Section from the Ministry of Economic Warfare.

Parker said, "What does Holbrook think he's playing at?" His pencil bore down on the message form and drove a hole through it. "A NOD IS AS GOOD AS A WINK, WILL ACT ACCORDINGLY." He looked up sharply. "What the hell is that supposed to mean, Dennis?"

Newstead flexed his legs. Standing there in front of the desk, he felt awkward and ill at ease, much like a prefect summoned to the headmaster's study to explain why the Lower Fourth had suddenly become unruly.

"I think it means that Holbrook understands and accepts your ruling."

"You don't sound very convinced."

"Well, it's certainly the most logical explanation."

"And the most convenient." Parker waved him to a chair. "For goodness' sake, do sit down," he said tersely. "You're hopping about like a cat on hot bricks."

Newstead gingerly lowered himself into a rickety wooden chair that creaked alarmingly even under his slender weight.

"Blast Holbrook," Parker said irritably. "I hardly know him, but I was warned that he could be a bit headstrong at times. In fact, it's possible in this instance that he's decided to ignore my instructions."

"That's rather a large assumption, isn't it?"

"It's not like you to be evasive."

Newstead stared at him thoughtfully. "You've been talking to Lewis," he said slowly.

"Of course; is there any reason why I shouldn't?" Parker leaned back in the armchair, picked up a ruler, and began tapping it against the edge of the desk. The cadence was slow and deliberate like the drumbeat of a funeral march. "Why not admit it, Dennis?"

"Admit what?"

"That right from the very beginning you suspected that he would go after Rommel."

"It was just a hunch and probably a wrong one. Look, he's never disobeyed orders before, even when he disagreed with them." Newstead hesitated and then lapsed into silence. He thought it best not to mention the fact that on at least two previous occasions subsequent events had shown that London should have accepted Holbrook's advice instead of overruling him.

"I believe he ran into a spot of bother in Cannes?" Parker smiled lazily. "In April 1941, wasn't it?"

Parker was better informed than he had thought, but to describe the mess as a spot of bother was a masterly understatement. SOE had sent Holbrook into the Côte d'Azure as a sort of peacemaker with orders to settle the differences between the communist, center, and right-wing elements in the Resistance and find a spokesman who could represent all the various groups. London had been anxious to step up the dispatch of arms and instructors and increase the supply of money to the Underground, and they'd wanted a Frenchman to handle that end of the business. After weeks of patient negotiation, Holbrook had found two possible candidates, but against his advice London had refused to accept his first choice because the man was known to be a Communist and a trade union leader. Newstead suspected that the Foreign Office had been largely responsible for overruling him and, rightly or wrongly, had always blamed them for the repercussions which had followed. The Communists had gone their own way for the best part of a year, and Holbrook had been arrested by the Vichy police, who'd given him a rough time.

Parker tossed the ruler into a filing tray. "Holbrook blamed us for his betrayal, didn't he?"

"Indirectly, but he got over it. After all, we recovered him once he had bluffed his way out of prison."

"And Paris? He advised us to leave the Albert circuit to the Bureau Central de Renseignements et d'Action but we wouldn't listen to him."

Newstead thought he understood what Parker was getting at and felt obliged to set the record straight. "He was wrong about Felix. Oh, it's true the Gestapo almost grabbed him on the steps of the Grenelle Métro, but René Dufoir was not the man who tipped them off."

"That's really beside the point. I think Holbrook has allowed his judgement to be colored by past events."

"So?"

"So I want you to send a message tonight that will make it very clear to Holbrook that he is to back off."

Parker smacked a fist into the palm of his left hand as if to emphasize the point.

Holbrook replaced the telephone, paid the barman for the call, and then left the café. Philippe Cuvier had given him the correct answer to the test question, but there had been a note of fear in his voice which canceled it out. Losing Church was bad enough, but what disturbed him even more was the fact that the SD had obviously cracked Cuvier in record time. He would have to warn the rest of the network and London too, if that was possible; Church was a good operator but even the best could be turned, as SOE had discovered to their cost on previous occasions.

Holbrook crossed the Place Épars opposite the Grand Monarque Hotel and headed toward the town center. He hoped nothing had happened to Denise, because she was the one person who could put him in touch with the Albert circuit and she would also know just how many people would feel the draft now that Philippe had caved in and was talking to the SD.

As soon as he pushed open the swinging door and entered the department store in the rue de Bois-Merrain, Holbrook could see that he had been worrying unnecessarily. Denise was at her usual place behind the handbag counter, looking serene and elegant in a short-sleeved blouse and navy skirt. She was busy serving a middle-aged woman who seemed unable to make up her mind what she wanted from the limited stock on display, and he was forced to circle the ground floor until she was free.

Her eyes mirrored surprise when he walked up to the counter, but she recovered her composure quickly enough and greeted him with a helpful smile.

"May I help you?" she asked.

Holbrook returned the smile. "I want to buy a handbag for my fiancée." He rubbed his chin and looked thoughtful. "I thought something in black might be suitable."

"We haven't many to choose from in that color and they aren't very chic. Have you considered navy blue?" She crouched down, opened the sliding glass panel, and reached inside the display cabinet. "This one is quite a dark blue."

Holbrook examined the handbag just long enough to give the right impression. "May I see it in the light?" he said.

"But of course."

Leaving Denise to bring the handbag, Holbrook walked over to the door.

"Is something wrong?" she asked anxiously, as she drew near to him.

"Smile," he whispered. "Smile, damn it, you look worried stiff."

"It's Philippe, isn't it?"

"And the rest."

"They've been arrested?"

"I think so."

"Oh, my God," she breathed. "What am I going to do?"

"You're getting out."

"How can I?"

"It's easy; you tell the supervisor that you have to go to the staff room for a minute, and then you leave by the back entrance. I'll be waiting for you in the alleyway behind the store."

"When?" The color had drained from her face but she seemed to be in control of herself.

"In five minutes from now."

"All right." She nodded. "I'll do it."

Holbrook pretended to examine the handbag again. Raising his voice, he said, "I'm sorry to have troubled you, but it isn't quite what I had in mind."

"You could always try the Bon Marché in the rue des Écuyers."

She was good, very good. Despite the tension, she had struck exactly the right note. Holbrook thanked her for being so helpful and left the store.

It was a long five minutes and he was just beginning to wonder if Denise had gone to pieces after all when she appeared in the alleyway. There was a fixed, glassy smile on her face, and as he went toward her he could see that she had been crying. As if she could read his thoughts, she stopped to open her handbag and took out a pair of sunglasses.

"That's good thinking."

"What is?" she said listlessly.

"The sunglasses; nobody can see your eyes now." Holbrook took her by the hand. "Come on," he said briskly, "we can't stand around here while we talk."

"Talk? What good will that do? The Gestapo have taken Philippe."

"And maybe he can name the rest of us."

"He'd never do that."

"Even the best have been known to break under pressure, and I'm not taking any chances on Philippe." He felt her recoil and tightened his grasp on her hand. "It may sound brutal to you, but we've got to think of the others now."

"Others?"

"I must know the names of all the people he's met who are connected with the Resistance."

She bit her lip and frowned. "There's Jean Passy and Lise de Létac and I think Philippe has also heard me mention Roger Sapeur."

"Who's the nearest?"

"Passy; he lives with his mother in the rue Félibien near the railway station."

"All right, we'll start with him."

"And then what?" she asked in a subdued voice.

"You're going to introduce me to your contact who knows so much about Rommel."

"He lives in Dreux."

Dreux was twenty miles from Chartres, not an impossible distance to ride, but Denise would have to collect her bicycle from home and he couldn't risk that. The train was out, too, because they would be watching the station. Weighing it up, Holbrook came to the conclusion that a bus was their safest bet. The SD was efficient but they couldn't police every stop.

They had just reached the rue de la Couronne when a black Citroën screamed past them and turned into the rue Félibien.

There was no need for Holbrook to explain anything. Denise could read the danger signs as well as he could.

The network was a busted flush, and Dreux was the only place they could run to.

5

Church rolled over on to his right side, felt a shaft of pain lance through his body, and wondered how long he had been unconscious. Although both eyes were closed to narrow slits, he could just see the tiny window high above his head, and from the sun's position he thought it must be midafternoon. Blood had coagulated around his mouth and broken nose, making it difficult for him to breathe, and he was unable to wipe the muck from his swollen and tender face because his hands were still manacled behind his back. He had lost a couple of teeth, his bottom lip was split, and his ribs felt as if they were badly bruised.

They hadn't broken anything yet, but there was always the next time and he didn't think he could take much more. SOE would expect him to hold out for seventy-two hours, but in this instance he couldn't see the point of it. The SD had the Cuviers and they were bound to go after Denise, and if Holbrook was still with her they'd scoop him up too. It seemed to Church that the network was already in fragments even though he had yet to answer a single question.

A faint scraping noise made his flesh crawl, and instinctively he turned his head in the direction from where the sound had come, convinced that somebody must be watching him through the spy hole. A key grated in the lock, the bolt was drawn back, and then the door opened inward and Sergeant Burghardt walked into the cell.

Church turned over onto his knees and struggled to his feet. The effort taxed his strength to the limit and for a moment he thought he was going to pass out again. He wondered why he had bothered to get up from the floor. Maybe pride had something to do with it. That was stupid; pride would only invite another kicking.

Burghardt said, "I am truly sorry to see you in such a state, Captain Church. Believe me, I am very distressed."

"You're not the only one," Church said hoarsely.

"All this violence is so unnecessary."

"Yes? Well, you'd better pass the word to your friends in the SD then. Not that they will listen to you; they're happy in their work."

Burghardt took a cigar from his silver cigarette case and lit it nonchalantly. "It's unnecessary because they already have all the information they need."

"Really?" Church pressed his thighs together and wished the Sergeant would get to the point of his visit and go. The Gestapo had refused him permission to go to the lavatory because it was part of their technique to humiliate a prisoner, and he didn't want to wet himself in front of Burghardt.

"Your network has been virtually destroyed." The German examined the tip of his cigar. "You see, they have arrested Jean Passy, Lise de Létac, and Roger Sapeur."

"Am I supposed to be impressed?"

"I really don't know."

"You'd best let them go," said Church, "because I've never heard of them."

Burghardt smiled faintly. "I daresay Major Holbrook and Denise Jeanney will be joining you shortly."

"You've got to—" Church bit his lip, starting the blood flowing again.

"Got to what, Captain Church? Catch them? The SD will do that, never fear."

Burghardt was quick, much too quick for his liking. He hated to admit it, but this smooth, paunchy sergeant who bathed his face in eau de cologne was more than a match for him. Where the SD relied on violence, this man would trip him up by skillful and persuasive interrogation.

Burghardt said, "You've become very silent, Captain Church."

"I don't think we've got much to say to one another."

"Actually, I've got a proposition which I'd like you to consider."

Church knew that he ought to tell Burghardt to get stuffed but where would that sort of defiant gesture get him? If the Abwehr sergeant walked out on him now, the SD would be back that much sooner and the stomping would begin all over again. In the circumstances, he thought there was no harm in listening to Burghardt. At least it would postpone the next session and give him time to recover some of his strength.

"What sort of proposition?"

"Well, first of all, the SD have agreed to turn you over to the Wehrmacht."

"They have?"

"On one condition."

"I knew there was a catch somewhere. We're back on the cooperation lark again, are we?"

Burghardt ignored the question. "I want the Foxhound station to continue and of course I need you to run it."

"Because I'm the operator and the home station will recognize my touch on the key, right?"

"Yes."

"And with my help, you persuade SOE to parachute in a few more agents and they walk into a trap."

"It won't be like that." Burghardt flicked his cigar and spilled ash onto the floor. "I know we have lost this war, but I can't take off my uniform. I have to go on doing my job right to the very end, or at least I can give that impression."

"What's that supposed to mean?"

"It means that while I am prepared to feed your people with false information, I will not bait another trap to catch some poor brave fool. Oh, I've played similar tricks on my friends in Baker Street in the past, but not any more. You have my word on it."

"All right," said Church. "I don't see why we shouldn't discuss the idea."

"Good."

"After I've had a pee."

"A what?"

"I want to go to the lavatory. All you have to do is call the guard and he'll take me."

Burghardt poked his head around the door and bellowed into the corridor. It was only a small victory but it meant a lot to Church. He had gained another valuable respite, and he hadn't gone down on his knees to beg for it either.

The guard took Church down to the end of the corridor, unlocked his handcuffs, and then stood behind him while he faced the urinal. His bladder was like a reservoir brim full after the autumn rains, and emptying it was the only good thing that had happened to him that day. The sense of relief was such that he almost felt like a new man, and one moreover who was no longer at a psychological disadvantage.

Burghardt sensed it too when he returned to the cell. "I made a mistake," he said.

"You did?"

"You seem to have recovered your confidence. I think you're no longer interested in my proposition."

"I might still key for you on one condition."

"You English." Burghardt shook his head and smiled ruefully. "You English have all the cheek in the world. However, as you said earlier, we can always talk about it."

"Supposing I do operate the Foxhound station and SOE decide they want to send in another agent for some reason or other. What do we do then?"

"That's easy. We warn them off by saying that the situation has become too dangerous."

The answer was too pat, too glib, and Church knew that he was lying. He had won himself a breathing space, but now it was time to end the game of cat and mouse.

"You know something?" he said. "I think you just overplayed your hand."

Burghardt pursed his lips. "I hope I didn't because, believe me, I want to save you."

"Save me from what?"

"A firing squad."

"Don't give me that shit."

"I'm not lying to you now, Captain Church. Don't you see,

you're no longer of any use to the SD. You can't tell them anything they don't already know. The war may be drawing to a close, but the killing will go on right up to the very last minute, the very last second."

Church remembered the faded photograph of the uncle he had never seen which his mother kept in a silver frame on the mantelpiece in her dressing room at home. Her brother had been killed in action on the eleventh of November 1918 in a futile cavalry skirmish just one hour before the Armistice. Burghardt hadn't overplayed his hand. The ace of trumps had been up his sleeve all the time.

"It seems I'll have to trust you," Church said faintly.

"Do I take it you are willing to cooperate?"

Church nodded his head. The Abwehr might think they had acquired another puppet, but if the opportunity arose he would tip Bicester the wink. All it needed was an unusual signature on the Morse key and a wide-awake operator at the other end who knew him.

The bookshop was hidden away in a cul-de-sac off the Place Capucine and was far enough removed from the town center to lose trade. No chamois leather had touched the plate glass window in months, the shelves inside looked as though they could do with a good dusting, and the sign above the entrance had weathered so much that in some places the letters had disappeared altogether. Holbrook tried to fill in the gaps by guesswork, but the name of the proprietor still eluded him.

Denise said, "The shop belongs to Pierre Racheline now."

"You must be a mind reader. Who's Racheline?"

"The man you wanted to meet."

Holbrook raised a skeptical eyebrow. "You mean he's the courier?"

"Pierre is in the secondhand book trade," she said tersely, "so he's frequently in Paris and Chartres on business. Can you think of a better cover story?"

She opened the door and entered the shop before he had a chance to answer. An elderly woman who was busy cataloguing the stock looked down from her lofty perch on the stepladder, caught his eye as he followed Denise inside, and then hastily glanced the other way. Holbrook closed the door behind him, the bell tinkled for the second time, and the owner finally emerged from a room at the back of the shop.

Racheline reminded him of a bird; he had sharp pointed features and his eyes, though void of expression, darted warily as if sensing danger. An accident of birth had left him with a withered left arm which he hugged to his side, nursing it like a broken wing.

Denise said, "Do you buy as well as sell books?"

"You are a dealer?"

"No, but my aunt left me a first edition of *Candide.* I'm told it's worth a great deal of money."

"You've brought it with you?"

"In my handbag."

"I'd be interested to see it." Racheline stared pointedly at Holbrook. "Perhaps you'd both like to step inside my office."

The office was a glory hole full of bric-à-brac and odd pieces of furniture which had obviously seen better days. There were a couple of armchairs with yellowing antimacassars, a sofa bed, a rolltop desk, and a piano stool. The net curtain in the sash window had a large tear in it, and the linoleum covering the floorboards was beginning to lift in the corners.

Racheline straddled the piano stool and looked from Holbrook to Denise. "Please introduce me to your friend," he said icily.

Denise avoided his cold stare. "I'm sorry, I'd . . ." Her voice faltered and she swallowed nervously. "I'd like you to meet André Thixier."

"Thixier?"

"Or Foxhound," said Holbrook. "Whichever you prefer."

Racheline drew his breath in sharply. "You must be mad." His eyes narrowed to pinpoints of hate. "Why come running to me when you are in danger?"

"Who said we're in danger?"

"Denise did. You don't really think she wanted to sell me a copy of Voltaire's *Candide,* do you?" He reached inside his jacket and took out a packet of Gitanes. "What are you trying to do, compromise me?"

Holbrook watched him fumble with a book of matches and

waited until he had lit his cigarette. "If the SD had grabbed Denise along with the others," he said, "you wouldn't be sitting here now."

Racheline shrugged his shoulders. "All right," he said truculently, "you've earned my gratitude."

"And your help."

"Help?"

"Your name might slip out during the interrogation if they catch either of us."

"That's blackmail."

"You can call it what you like," Holbrook said mildly, "but I don't think you've got any choice."

"So it would seem." Racheline pinched out the cigarette and slipped the stub into his jacket pocket. "What exactly is it you want from me?"

"First, I want a message passed to London, and then I want you to put me in touch with the Albert circuit."

"The message I can handle, but the Albert circuit is another matter."

"London won't like it if they refuse to cooperate."

"Cooperate?"

"With me," Holbrook said calmly. "I'm the man who's going to assassinate Rommel."

Racheline looked as if he was about to say something and then changed his mind. The clock ticking away on the mantelpiece sounded unnaturally loud and the minutes passed slowly. Holbrook wished he could tell what the Frenchman was thinking.

"It will take time," he said presently.

"How long?"

"Two, maybe three days. In the meantime, I can give you the address of a quiet hotel in Évreux where you will be safe enough."

Évreux was a step in the right direction, but Holbrook knew there was an ulterior motive. Like the victims of a contagious disease, Racheline was putting them into an isolation ward. They would be under surveillance the whole time, and if, after seventy-two hours, they were free from infection, somebody from the Albert circuit would get in touch with them.

"We'll need to change our identity cards before we check into your hotel."

"That won't present any difficulty; you'll have new ones within the hour."

"And baggage?"

"That too." Racheline peered at the linoleum as if he had never noticed the floral pattern before. "It might be safer if you were to travel together"—he cleared his throat—"as man and wife."

Holbrook glanced toward Denise, expecting her to object to the idea, but she appeared to be lost in a world of her own. "I don't see any difficulty in that arrangement," he said dryly.

"Good." Racheline slapped his kneecap in evident satisfaction. "And what is the message you wish to send to London?"

"THE MOON IS DOWN," said Holbrook. "And sign it FOXHOUND. They'll know what it means."

Church leaned back in his chair and savored the pleasure of a Lucky Strike. He would have preferred a Gold Flake but it seemed that Burghardt had obtained his supply of cigarettes and cigars from U.S. Rangers captured at Omaha Beach on D Day. His face still looked battered and bruised, but he was feeling much better. The dank cell had been exchanged for a bed with clean sheets, and the fact that the windows of his room were barred and shuttered hardly bothered him at all. The Abwehr headquarters in Chartres was paradise compared to the Gestapo prison.

Of course, Burghardt had already demonstrated that he was determined to make him earn his keep, but Church had persuaded himself that he was also equally determined to throw a spanner in the works at the first opportunity. But not tonight. Tonight he would play it straight because it was necessary to win his trust first, and clearly Burghardt was no fool. Although he had been asked to decode the brief message from Bicester, the portly sergeant was double-checking the text with the aid of his code book. Church thought he was a slow worker and decided that this was as good a time as any to begin needling him. He wanted to establish a moral superiority and make Burghardt feel that he was an inadequate cryptologist.

"At the rate you're going, Bicester will be off the air before we can send a reply."

"I think not. Bicester will listen for nine minutes; we still have plenty of time."

"You are familiar with our procedures then?"

"Naturally." Burghardt looked at the message and frowned. "YOU WILL, REPEAT WILL, LEAVE THE PIGEON ALONE."

"That's what I made it," Church said cheerfully.

"Who or what is this pigeon?"

They had reached the first stumbling block. If he blew the whistle on the plot to assassinate Rommel, he would have to reckon with SOE after the war. It was necessary to survive the peace as well as the war, and he racked his brains trying to think of some explanation that would sound convincing.

"It's short for stool pigeon," Church said slowly. Inspired now, he improvised on the theme. "Holbrook got it into his head that Denise Jeanney was an informer and so he wanted to kill her."

"Why should he think that?"

"Because he discovered that she had been stopped for questioning on three separate occasions and her explanation didn't ring true. He figured she was a double agent. It seems he was right."

"Oh?"

"Well, I'm here, aren't I?"

Burghardt said, "You are here, Captain Church, because we obtained a fix on your transmitter and I walked into a supposedly empty attic and smelled stale cigarette smoke in the air."

Church smiled ruefully. "Holbrook told me to break the habit; I should have listened to him."

"Then why didn't London?"

Church leaned forward and stubbed out the Lucky Strike in a cut-down shell case. "Search me," he said casually. "Maybe they think he's inclined to be a bit too headstrong."

Burghardt read the message again. Holbrook was still at large and that meant the Funkspiel, the radio game, was in jeopardy.

On the other hand, Bicester would smell a rat if the Foxhound station didn't acknowledge the message. Even if Holbrook did manage to evade the SD, it might be weeks or even months before he was able to get in touch with London. The story Church had given him seemed logical enough but he would have to be careful, very careful.

"Your explanation would seem to fit," he said thoughtfully.

Church managed to suppress a smile of triumph. He had told Burghardt a pack of lies, but the story had obviously sounded authentic and the porky bastard had swallowed it hook, line, and sinker.

"What do you want me to do now?"

"Give them a BT break sign and follow it with a QSL to show that the message has been received and understood." Burghardt laid a plump hand on his wrist. "And nothing flashy, please, Captain Church. I just want your normal signature on the Morse key."

Other messages were abroad that night. One, transmitted from Berne and addressed to OSS headquarters in London, ran to three hundred and twenty-five groups, which meant that every six minutes the operator was obliged to change frequency in order to avoid intercept. When decoded, it gave the complete breakdown on Operation Valkyrie and the circumstances in which Colonel General Ludwig Beck thought it would be possible to surrender Germany to the Western Allies.

6

McCready was as much at home in London as he was in New York, Washington, or Paris, where from 1934 until Pétain surrendered France he had been foreign correspondent for the *Herald Tribune.* Arriving in England in June 1940 on one of the last ships to clear Bordeaux before the Wehrmacht rolled into the city, he had stayed to cover the Blitz. Among the host of people he met as a newspaperman was the Special Assistant to President Roosevelt, William J. Donovan, who was destined to become chief of the OSS. Although McCready recalled little of their chance encounter, Donovan had evidently remembered the French-speaking reporter because, some three months after Pearl Harbor, McCready accepted his invitation to join the Office of Strategic Services.

The American organization had been modeled on the lines of its British counterpart, and until 1943 the relationship between SOE and OSS was not unlike father and son, except that, so far as McCready was concerned, the father was a little too damn paternalistic for his liking. The British attitude was characterized by men like James Parker, a product of Winchester and Cambridge, whose patronizing air conveyed the impression that he thought the OSS was a bunch of incompetent but well-meaning, half-witted amateurs. They had crossed swords on a number of occasions and invariably he had been the loser. Today, however, it was going to be different because for once the shoe would be on the other foot. Escorted by a War Department police constable, McCready marched into Parker's office with a broad smile on his face.

There were two telephones on Parker's desk, a black one and a green one which was connected to the scrambler, a large oblong-shaped box on the floor. McCready noticed that Parker was staring at the secure link with a thoughtful expression on his face and guessed that some indication of the purpose of his visit had just come through from the Cabinet Office.

The War Department constable said, "Colonel McCready to see you, sir."

Parker accepted the visitor's pass and waved him to a chair. "Good morning, George," he said brightly. "This is an unexpected pleasure."

McCready smiled. Parker certainly believed in observing all the polite formalities, even though his presence was neither unexpected nor a pleasure. He even contrived to appear affable, which was quite an achievement in the circumstances.

McCready said, "I guess you know why I'm here, James."

Parker stretched his face into another smile. "I was warned to expect a briefing from one of your representatives. I gather it's something to do with Rommel and a coup d'état."

In spite of himself, McCready had to admire him. The Third Reich was about to collapse, but to listen to Parker you'd think this was an event of no great historical significance.

"You don't seem to attach much importance to it."

"I've lost count of the number of times the German General Staff were allegedly on the point of removing Hitler. Before Munich there was some talk of a coup d'état, but it never came to anything."

"This one will."

"You really think so?"

"What do you know about Operation Valkyrie?"

"Nothing, it's just a code name to me." Parker indicated the green telephone. "I heard it mentioned for the first time only a few minutes ago."

"Valkyrie is an internal security operation designed to combat any massed revolt by the millions of slave workers based on German soil. In particular, it calls for the necessary troop movement by units and training establishments of the Reserve Army to occupy the administrative area of Berlin."

"I see."

"I wonder if you do?" McCready unbuttoned the breast pocket of his field jacket and produced a fat cigar. "When the code word is passed, these units will seal off the Foreign Office, the Reich Chancellory, and the Propaganda Department in Wilhelmstrasse, the Air Ministry in the Potsdamer Platz, the radio station and the Gestapo headquarters in Prinz Albrechtstrasse. The soldiers may not realize it, but as a result of their action Goebbels, Himmler, and Göring will virtually be under arrest in their own offices."

"Always providing they are in Berlin at the time and the soldiers don't question their orders."

McCready dropped the cellophane wrapper into the wastepaper basket, trimmed the cigar with a penknife, and then lit it with a Zippo. "I doubt if all three will be absent from the capital. Anyway, Goebbels is the real danger; once he is under lock and key, they've got it made. And don't worry about the soldiers. They always obey orders."

"I wonder."

"Shit, why should they question them? Look, as far as the average Kraut soldier is concerned, he's protecting those SOBs from the mob."

"What mob?"

"The slave workers who might take to the streets when the news of Hitler's death is broadcast over the air."

"Now we're getting to the crux of the matter." Parker clasped his hands and leaned forward. "Just how do they propose to remove him?"

"With a bomb, James, a bomb planted by a guy called Claus von Stauffenberg."

"Stauffenberg?"

"A thirty-six-year-old colonel with a long record of anti-Nazism. He was badly wounded in Tunisia, blinded in the left eye and losing his right hand and forearm, but as of now he is Chief of Staff to Fromm, who commands the Reserve Army. Now, in that capacity Stauffenberg is often summoned to attend the Führer's conferences at Berchtesgaden, which means that he can get really close to Hitler."

"With a bomb, George?" Parker said skeptically.

"He does have a briefcase."

"Yes, that would make a difference, assuming he can get past the guards with it."

"Why don't you wait until you've heard the rest of the scenario before you knock it?"

"I'm still listening," Parker said in a mild tone of voice.

"If Valkyrie is successful, Rommel will be sworn in as president and the new government will be prepared to surrender to the Western Allies."

"If is a very big word in this business."

"Jesus," McCready exploded angrily, "I don't know if their goddamned plan is going to work or not, but they made contact with Allen Dulles in Berne and it sure impressed him. It also impressed Washington and London too."

"So I gather."

"Right, then it's our job to see that nothing happens to Rommel in the meantime because he's the only man who can swing the German people behind the conspirators in the Bendlerstrasse."

"Which brings us to Foxhound."

"That's right. We don't want him fouling it up, James."

"He won't. He's been warned off."

McCready pointed to the desk calendar. "Today is Monday the third of July."

"I'm afraid you've lost me."

"Let's go back to last Wednesday, then. As I remember it, only Fawcett, the boy lieutenant colonel from DMO, was not in favor of assassinating Rommel, and when he refused to go along with the majority you said you intended to refer the project to the Cabinet for a final decision."

"That's correct."

"And how did Foxhound take the news?"

"I imagine he was angry but he won't do anything rash."

McCready rubbed his heavy jowl. "I think you're fencing with me. Look, I can go back to my people, and inside ten minutes that green telephone on your desk will ring and you'll be ordered to produce every incoming and outgoing signal that's passed between you and Foxhound since the twenty-eighth of June." He smiled fleetingly. "Now, that isn't the way business should be conducted between close allies, is it, James?"

Parker studied the American carefully and knew that he wasn't bluffing. Holbrook had been unusually subdued since Newstead had reiterated the stand-fast order, and that was most unlike him.

"Well, to tell you the truth, George, I'm a bit worried about our man."

"Do you think he might jump the gun?"

"It's possible," Parker said reluctantly. His eyes strayed to the green telephone again. "In fact, I'm thinking of sending an emissary over there to have a few quiet words with him."

"Supposing he refuses to listen?"

"Then we shall have to resort to more forceful methods."

Like icing him, thought McCready. Killing your own people was a hell of a way to fight a war, but in this instance it might well be a necessary evil.

"We'd like to send over an observer." McCready leaned forward and crushed his cigar into the ashtray. "I can make it an official request if you wish."

It seemed to Parker that within the space of a year their respective positions had been reversed. It might be a bitter pill to swallow, but there was no getting around the fact that the United States had now become the dominant partner. In approaching Dulles, the German underground had shown that they too were aware of this new relationship between the Western Allies.

"There's no need to do that, George," he said quietly. "How soon can your man be ready?"

"His name is Paul Jackson and he can be ready any time."

"Good. Perhaps you could arrange for him to report to Dennis Newstead this afternoon?"

"Now wait a minute, what I've been saying is for your ears only."

"Dennis happens to be one of the best controllers in the section. You needn't worry; I won't tell him more than he needs to know."

"What about this other guy?"

"Fletcher," Parker said coldly, "is simply a killer. No explanations are necessary. You only have to point him in the right direction."

Holbrook raised his eyes and stared at the stained glass window above the altar. The cathedral, like most he'd seen in France, was a cavernous and somber place and there was a distinct chill in the air. His knees ached from kneeling on the stone floor and he was sick and tired of praying. For nearly four days he and Denise had been cooling their heels in Évreux, never venturing far from the hotel, while they waited for the local Resistance to give them a clean bill of health, and now it was beginning to look as if there was some kind of last-minute hitch.

The note which had been pushed under the bedroom door had been explicit enough, and he had followed the instructions to the letter. They had arrived at ten thirty, lit two candles for the Virgin Mary, and then slipped into the fourth row of chairs down the nave from the main entrance and opposite the confessional box, which he had been told to watch. As near as he could figure it without stealing another glance at his wristwatch, the priest he was supposed to meet was already ten minutes late.

Holbrook crossed himself and got up off his knees. There had been no need to feel the wallet inside his jacket to know just how slim it had become. Racheline had given them a suitcase and a couple of towels to go with the toilet accessories but almost nothing in the way of clothing. An off-the-peg pinstripe in thin gray suiting and a new dress and raincoat for Denise had swallowed most of the folding money, and he was running short of cash. Eating out was expensive too. He wondered how much Denise had in her purse.

She was still praying, her lips mouthing the words silently, a rosary clutched in her neat, small hands. Her face in profile seemed composed, but he knew that she was as nervous as a kitten. Dozing on and off in the armchair, he had heard her tossing and turning in the double bed, whimpering frequently in her sleep. Although they had shared the same hotel bedroom, there was a barrier between them and they were like polite strangers unable to confide in one another. She had never mentioned Philippe Cuvier or the aunt with whom she had been living ever since her widowed mother had remarried and moved away from Chartres, but Holbrook had sensed that she had been thinking about them all the time and he hadn't known what to say to her.

The priest was a ghostly round-shouldered figure in a black cassock who seemed to glide along the aisle. There was not a vestige of color in his face, which looked as if it had been sculptured out of marble, yet despite his frail, almost emaciated appearance he radiated a kind of inner strength that few men possess. The pale eyes flickered in recognition, and then he disappeared into the confessional. Holbrook followed him.

The box was small and dark and the floorboards creaked under his weight. Behind the latticed screen, the priest was no more than a vague ethereal shape.

Holbrook said, "I have been a stranger in a strange land, Father."

"But now you are among friends again."

"That's a relief."

"I imagine these last three days have not been easy for you, but it was necessary, you understand."

"It wasn't a new experience for me; I've been in quarantine before. Just tell me how and when we are to leave Évreux."

"There is a train leaving for Mantes in three quarters of an hour which connects with the two-fifteen to Paris."

"Forty-five minutes," Holbrook said musingly. "That hardly gives us enough time to collect the suitcase from the hotel."

"You will have no further need of it."

"And when we arrive in Paris?"

"You should take the Métro to Abbesses and then make your way on foot to number seventeen rue de la Soussaye. You must tell the concierge that Madame Reyneau is expecting you."

Holbrook waited expectantly, hoping to hear confirmation that Racheline had arranged for the warning message to be sent to London as he'd asked, but the priest remained silent.

"Is there anything else I should know?" he asked quietly.

"I don't think so."

"A signal should have gone to my home station."

"Nothing was said to me about it. Perhaps you should take the matter up with Madame Reyneau?"

Holbrook had a nasty feeling that there had been a foul-up somewhere along the line. The Albert circuit may have thought it unnecessary to inform the priest, but it was also possible that by the time it reached them the original message had become so corrupted as to be meaningless. Alternatively, they might have decided to sit on the damn thing until he came out of quarantine, which would be typical of Felix if he was still around. René Dufoir had broken with SOE a long time ago and he wouldn't lose any sleep if Baker Street was kept in the dark for seventy-two hours; he was a Gaullist, and his first concern would be to preserve the security of the Albert circuit.

"There are other people who need comforting." There was a gentle note of reproof in the priest's voice.

"Yes, of course. I don't know how to thank you."

"It was only a small thing." He dipped his head as if to say good-bye. "I wish you both a safe journey."

Holbrook pushed the curtain aside and stepped out of the confessional box. His eyes immediately went to the row of chairs where he had left Denise, but she was no longer there, and the hair rose on the nape of his neck until he spotted her near the entrance examining the guidebooks on display. He was still some way off when she heard his footsteps and turned in his direction.

Holbrook thought her smile was very brittle and wondered if she was going to crack up.

Newstead folded the map and placed it on the shelf in front of the rear window of the Humber staff car. The suburbs were a long way behind them, and now that they were on the A21 to Tonbridge he didn't think the girl could take a wrong turning. He glanced at the loose-limbed, dark-haired captain who was sitting beside him and thought he was remarkably quiet and reserved for an American. He was not in the least like McCready, but then he wasn't sure that George was all that typical anyway. Nobody was typical; people came in different shapes and sizes. Some were pleasant, some not so pleasant, and he had met a few to whom he had taken an instant dislike.

Numbered among the last group was the man called Fletcher whom they were now on their way to meet. There was a sinister streak to the former schoolmaster that disturbed Newstead. It was nothing he could really put his finger on, but he hoped the situation would never arise where he was forced to share a life raft with him. Fletcher was the sort of man who wouldn't hesitate to push you overboard if he thought his own survival was at stake.

Jackson said, "That's some barrage over there to our left."

Newstead leaned toward the American and craned his neck to peer up at the sky through the side window. They were too far away to hear anything, but he caught a glimpse of a V1 flying straight and level through a curtain of flak.

"I'd say it was beyond Ashford."

"What's so special about Ashford? I mean, you don't seem to have too many guns in London."

"We've changed our tactics in the last few days. All the antiaircraft guns are concentrated in a wide belt inland from the coast. If the V-bomb gets through this first line of defense, the fighters try to shoot it down while it's still over open country."

"And if they fail, what then?"

Newstead shrugged his shoulders. "We just hope for the best. There's no point doing anything once the damn thing is over London. It's going to make a hell of a mess whatever happens."

"That's an oriental sort of philosophy, isn't it?"

"You get fatalistic about these things."

"I guess you do," Jackson said quietly, "but I haven't been here long enough to find out."

"When did you arrive in England?"

"Almost ten weeks ago. I was working out of Naples and Algiers before that, mostly in the south of France, apart from a flying visit to Corsica."

"Ajaccio?"

"Yes, how did you know?"

Newstead looked at him with newfound respect. "Your name just rang a bell."

"Well, don't believe half what you've heard; it was a milk run."

Newstead thought Jackson was being unduly modest. When the OSS team had parachuted into Corsica, the Axis garrison had not been insignificant, especially in the area of Ajaccio, yet Jackson, with the help of the local Maquis, had launched a simultaneous attack on the harbor and the airfield on the outskirts of the town. From aerial photographs taken the following day, it was evident that the ferry and four merchantmen had been sunk at anchor and the airfield had been littered with the burned-out skeletons of fifteen JU-52M transports.

"What sort of Joe is this guy Fletcher?"

"He was a schoolmaster before the war, lived in Saint-Malo and taught English at the lycée."

"I was in the IRS."

"What's that?"

"Inland Revenue Service," Jackson said tersely. "And you haven't answered my question."

"Fletcher is ruthless, efficient, and very experienced. He kills without compunction."

"You make him sound like a difficult man to get along with."

"People respect him for what he has done, but I've yet to meet anyone who actually likes him."

"I reckon I can handle him."

Newstead thought he probably could. The OSS screened their people with infinite care to ensure that they conformed to the personality structure of the ideal agent, a catalog of ten groups of character traits which had been drawn up by their psychiatrists. SOE had their share of head shrinkers too, but their advice was not always taken. He fancied the OSS would have rejected a man like Fletcher out of hand.

The girl driver said, "It's the next turning on the left, isn't it, sir?"

Newstead sat up. For a moment, the countryside seemed unfamiliar but then he recognized the pub ahead. "Next left it is, Fay," he said cheerfully.

Jackson leaned forward, resting his arms on the back of the seat in front of him. "Fay. That's a nice name."

"Thank you, sir."

"How long have you been in the ATS, Fay?"

"I'm a FANY."

"You're a what?"

"First Aid Nursing Yeomanry," said Newstead. "They're a very superior crowd."

The girl laughed. "That's right," she said. "We get to meet all the best people."

Jackson noticed that they had turned into a private drive flanked on either side by towering rhododendrons. The road snaked through an S-bend and he caught a glimpse of a huge pond covered in water lilies, and then the house was upon them and he whistled softly.

"Crompton Manor," said Newstead, "the home of Number Four Special Training School. It belonged to Lord Faveringham before we requisitioned it. If you're interested in history, Cromwell is supposed to have knocked it about a bit in 1643."

"Who's that square-shaped guy in battle dress waiting for us in the courtyard?"

"Fletcher."

"He looks a hard man."

"Oh, he's a hard man, all right. There's a café in Pont Rémy which used to be popular with the Luftwaffe fighter pilots based at Abbeville back in '41. Fletcher walked in there one night and shot six of them dead."

"Jesus Christ."

"No," Newstead said dryly, "just Harry Fletcher."

7

They arrived in the rush hour, and as he steered Denise toward the exit it seemed to Holbrook that half Paris had traveled to Abbesses on the Métro. Elbowing his way through the crowds, he looked up the rue de la Soussaye on the street map and memorized the route before leaving the station. The Métro had been stifling but the atmosphere above ground was no less sultry; black thunderclouds were building up over the city and, realizing that the storm would break at any minute, he set off for the Place du Tertres at a brisk pace.

War or no war, the artists were still there, braving the weather to paint the same old view of the tiny square, invariably from the same aspect because it was almost de rigueur to include Sacré Coeur in the canvas. In the same quarter of Montmartre back in '42, Holbrook had come across a weedy, bespectacled German infantryman who had artistic pretensions, but of course, as a representative of the Wehrmacht, he had contrived to retain a soldierly bearing. Palette in one hand, brush in the other, he had been standing to attention in front of the easel as if painting, like foot drill, was something you could learn to do by numbers. Had the German been a Nordic type and more photogenic, the scene would have made a good propaganda picture for *Signal Magazine,* but instead he had provided a brief moment of comic relief on a somber winter's afternoon.

Forked lightning ripped through the leaden sky and a thunderclap broke overhead as they left the square to descend a long flight of steps into the narrow alleyway which connected with the rue de la Soussaye. A few isolated spots of rain began to fall;

anxious to avoid a soaking, Holbrook grabbed Denise by the hand and started running.

Number 17 rue de la Soussaye was one of three large, gloomy houses tucked away in a courtyard off the street. There was no sign of the concièrge, but Madame Reyneau appeared among the tenants listed on a board inside the vestibule. A cardboard arrow pinned to the wall pointed the way to a dimly lit spiral staircase with worn steps and a rickety handrail which corkscrewed up to her flat on the fourth floor.

Holbrook checked the name plate above the buzzer and then pressed the button. A few moments later the door was opened by a homely looking woman in her early fifties who greeted them with a blank stare.

"Madame Reyneau?" he asked inquiringly.

"Yes."

"I believe you are expecting us." Holbrook cleared his throat. "We're friends of Father Soustelle in Évreux; he gave me your address and said to look you up when we arrived in Paris."

The blank stare was replaced by a welcoming smile. "Oh, yes, your other friend is here waiting for you."

"What other friend?"

"He's in the living room; perhaps you'd like to have a word with him while I show Madame to your room."

The suggestion was put in a polite enough manner, yet it also carried an air of authority which made it sound more like a command. As if determined to forestall any further argument, she opened a door off the hall and ushered him into a room cluttered with Second Empire furniture. A familiar figure rose from the wing-backed chair in the far corner.

Holbrook wasn't too sure, but he thought Felix had shed a pound or two, and certainly the light brown hair had receded at least another inch, but otherwise he had scarcely changed at all in the past two years.

"Hullo, René," he said awkwardly. "It's good to see you again."

René Dufoir clasped his outstretched hand with a noticeable lack of enthusiasm. "And you, Holbrook." The greeting was less than cordial, but then they had never seen eye to eye. "I hear you've run into another spot of trouble?"

"The Abwehr got a fix on our transmitter. One of the occupational hazards of the trade."

Dufoir smiled bleakly. "First Nice, then Paris, and now Chartres; bad luck seems to follow you everywhere. How long have you been in France this time?"

"We arrived in April to coordinate Resistance operations for D Day."

"Successfully, I hope?"

Dufoir might feign ignorance, but word of their activities must have reached somebody in the Albert circuit. Early on the sixth of June, the entire railway network in the Chartres area had been disrupted, every major road cratered, and the telephone lines cut. Censor or no censor, news of that kind was bound to filter out.

"We did all right," Holbrook said stiffly.

"And now you plan to go after Rommel?"

"With a little help from you."

"I'm afraid that's quite out of the question."

"Then why did you feed me the information?"

"Because we assumed SOE stood a better chance of persuading the RAF to bomb the château than the Bureau Central de Renseignements et d'Action."

"Your man in La Roche-Guyon suggested an alternative method."

"Yes, he did, but then the Ancient One is an incurable optimist."

"Ancient One?"

"Marcel Gilbert. We included all his observations because we thought it would add substance to the information."

Dufoir was only one voice on the Central Committee of the FFI, but Holbrook formed the impression that he had done most of the talking when the committee had met to discuss Gilbert's proposal. It would be typical of René to suggest the message should include the fact that Rommel was in the habit of shooting game in the forest of Moisson because he realized just what effect that tidbit of information would have. And he was also right in thinking the RAF would listen to SOE.

Holbrook said, "We don't think bombing is the answer."

"No?"

"Well, Rommel could easily be away visiting his forward units when the château was attacked. That's why we favor Gilbert's plan."

"Your people must be mad." Dufoir wagged an admonishing finger. "You may think it's worth committing suicide to get Rommel, but we don't. Whether the Field Marshal lives or dies is of very little interest to us."

"You have other plans, is that it?"

"Yes."

"Like what?"

"The liberation of Paris from within."

"You need an army for that."

"We've got one."

"Things must have changed an awful lot since 1942."

"They most certainly have. I venture to suggest that after the war you won't be able to find one Parisian who was not in the Resistance."

Holbrook smiled. Dufoir's acid sense of humor was as sharp as ever. "Then you can afford to lend me a helping hand."

"I've already told you—"

"I only want to get in touch with your Marcel Gilbert."

"Impossible. La Roche-Guyon is like a fortress."

"If Gilbert can get a message out, surely you can pass one to him?"

"Is that all the assistance you require?"

"It's a one-man job, but I'd like to brief the courier myself."

Dufoir stared at him thoughtfully. Knowing Holbrook as he did, he guessed it wouldn't end there, but that was a problem which could be dealt with as and when it arose. In the meantime, he saw no harm in agreeing to his request.

"All right," he said, "I'll let you know the time and RV tomorrow."

"Good. While you're at it, you might do something about Denise Jeanney too; she's becoming a problem."

"Don't tell me you're tired of her already?"

"I'm tired of sleeping in an armchair."

"You must be slipping."

Dufoir had always seized on any opportunity to needle him, and he hadn't changed. The old enmity was still there. As coldly as he knew how, Holbrook said, "Did London acknowledge my message?"

"If they have, no one told me. I can find out if you like."

René was just a little too glib for his liking, and he was prepared to bet that the suspicious little bastard had sat on the message until he was satisfied it was genuine.

"You do that, Felix."

"You're out of date, old friend; I'm known as Pierre now." Dufoir walked across the room and peered out of the window. "The storm seems to be passing over," he murmured.

Holbrook had an uncomfortable feeling that an altogether different and more violent storm was about to break in London.

Epp pulled back the shirt cuff and turned his wristwatch toward the light of a flickering candle. As he had suspected, no more bombs had fallen in the past ten minutes, and he thought they would soon get the all clear. From a purely selfish point of view, this raid had been the worst yet; on several occasions the basement shelter had been rocked by a near miss and he wondered how many houses were now left standing in Mondelallee.

Everyone around him seemed half paralyzed with fear; the janitor couldn't stop biting his nails and Anneliese looked as white as a sheet, but that was only natural in the circumstances. In all probability, something in the region of eight hundred Lancasters had unloaded their bomb bays over the city in the space of an hour and a half. Not for the first time, Epp was glad that he had persuaded Sophie and the children to leave Berlin.

A siren wailed in the distance and others quickly joined in rapid succession to swell the discordant orchestration of noise. As if awakening from a deep slumber, the residents of the Brandenburg apartment building slowly came to life. The tension melted away and their faces gradually became more animated. Responding to the relaxed atmosphere, the janitor wondered vocally if Göring had finally got around to changing his name to Meyer; it wasn't a very funny anti-Jewish joke and it had grown whiskers over the years, but it raised the usual caustic laugh. Like a ticket line patiently shuffling toward the box office, people began to leave the shelter.

The hall was covered in broken glass and Epp wondered if his own apartment had been similarly damaged. If it had, the velvet curtains in the living room which were Sophie's pride and joy must be hanging in shreds. He supposed they might have been saved if he had remembered to fit the blackout screens over the windows, but he rarely used the sitting room these days.

Anneliese said, "I expect we shall be without gas or electricity for the next day or two."

"And water."

"I do hope not."

"Fortunately, I still have a few bottles of wine left." Epp unlocked his door. "You can help me drink one now."

"Not tonight, Franz, I'm very tired. Another time, perhaps."

"It's not entirely a social invitation."

"Oh?"

"There have been certain developments which I think Beck should know. I promise not to keep you more than ten minutes."

Anneliese stifled a yawn. "I'll hold you to that," she said.

Epp began to feel his way down the passage, forgetting that there were some candles in the drawer of the hall table, but in any case he had no need of them. Opening the door, he walked into the living room to find it bathed in the glare of a huge fire which was raging out of control in the Moabit District beyond the Spree. It was some moments before he realized that the room was undamaged.

"Oh, my God," whispered Anneliese.

"Yes, you could read a newspaper in this light."

"Draw the curtains."

"What?"

"For God's sake, Franz, please draw the curtains. I don't want to look at that fire."

Epp limped across the room and tugged the heavy drapes across the windows, leaving just a small chink.

"Is that any better?"

"A little." She swallowed nervously. "I know I'm being silly, but I don't think I can take much more of this."

"You need a stiff drink," he said firmly. "I'm afraid I'm out of brandy but there's a bottle of schnapps." Epp crouched beside the cocktail cabinet and struck a match. "Knowing the janitor's wife, I don't guarantee the glasses will be particularly clean."

"It doesn't matter," she said listlessly. "Nothing does any more."

He had never known her to be depressed before and he found it disturbing. Anneliese had always appeared indestructible, but now it seemed she was vulnerable like everyone else.

"We matter: you, Beck, me, Stauffenberg, and the rest." Epp handed her a glass of schnapps and sank down into the sofa. "You can tell the Colonel General that we've moved a step nearer our goal. Stauffenberg collected his time bomb from Major General Stieff today."

"He did?" Anneliese was close enough for him to see the sudden blaze of excitement in her eyes. "That's marvelous news, Franz."

"It gets even better. Stauffenberg has also been warned that he will be required to attend the next Führer conference at Berchtesgaden on Tuesday the eleventh of July. Unless Beck has any objections, we think we should seize this opportunity to launch Operation Valkyrie."

"I'm sure Ludwig will agree." A frown wrinkled her forehead. "Of course we haven't heard from the Americans yet, but there's still time."

Time, he thought, was one thing they didn't have; within the next fortnight, a glut of posting orders would remove a large number of officers commanding Reserve Army units and training establishments stationed in and around Berlin. Their replacements were an unknown quantity, but it was too much to hope that the majority would be opposed to the regime. If there were any dedicated Nazis among them, Operation Valkyrie might well end in total failure. Whether the Amis were prepared to negotiate with the provisional government or not, it would have to be the eleventh of July.

"Think of it, Franz," she said breathlessly. "In just over a week from now, Germany will no longer be ruled by a madman."

Her lips were parted, moist and inviting. Sophie intruded for a brief moment, but then Anneliese whispered an endearment and Epp gently prized the glass from her fingers and placed it on the carpet. Their mouths fastened hungrily, and she made no attempt to stop him when he began to unbutton her blouse. Patiently he eased the bra straps over her shoulders until he was able to cup her small breasts in both palms. The nipples hardened under his touch and he thought he heard a contented sigh. Like children indulging in a secret pleasure, they toyed with one another while all around them the city burned.

Newstead was a light sleeper, and the strident jangle woke him instantly. Alert but resentful, he lay in the camp bed shielding his eyes from the glare of a seventy-five-watt bulb in the ceiling while he waited for Lewis to answer the telephone. As was their usual practice when their names appeared together on the duty officer's roster, they had arranged to split the night watch between them, but now it was beginning to look as if this longstanding agreement had broken down. Somewhat irritably, Newstead threw the blankets to one side and sat up on the edge of the bed. He was still groping for his spectacle case under the pillow when Lewis, who was slumped over the desk, woke up with a start and reached for the telephone.

Newstead lit a cigarette. The conversation was entirely one-sided, but he noticed that Lewis was frowning and without knowing why he had an intuitive feeling that it was bad news. After what seemed an eternity, Lewis finally replaced the telephone and leaned back in his chair.

"How odd," he said laconically.

Newstead closed his eyes and counted up to ten. There were times when Lewis tried his patience to the limit, and this was one of them.

"Suppose you let me in on the secret."

"De Gaulle's people have received a message from the Albert circuit which they claim was originated by Foxhound."

"Holbrook?" Newstead said incredulously.

"Yes. It reads THE MOON IS DOWN. I don't like the implications, but I'm afraid the message must be authentic. That's one of the exclusive codes we allocated to Holbrook for use in an emergency."

Newstead didn't like the implications either. Earlier that evening, the Foxhound station had called Bicester on schedule to report that elements of the Hitler Jugend SS Panzer Division had been observed in Chartres, yet Holbrook had now sent a message from Paris to the effect that they were in danger of being arrested by the Gestapo. No matter which way he looked at it, there was no avoiding the distasteful fact that in all probability, Church had been turned around and was working for the Abwehr.

"I suppose we ought to inform Parker?"

Newstead looked up. "Why?" he asked sharply.

"Well, after all, Dennis, he is the deputy head of the French Section."

"Yes, of course you're right. I'll call him as soon as I've had a word with the operator at Bicester."

For one moment he'd had a nagging suspicion that somehow Lewis knew about the liaison mission which Parker had in mind for Fletcher and the American, Jackson, but it seemed he was mistaken. Not that it made any difference now, he thought; that particular scheme was dead and buried along with the rest of the Foxhound group.

8

The WT operator from Bicester impressed Parker. It was obvious that she had been on duty all night, but, although tired, she answered his questions intelligently, occasionally volunteering additional information which she thought might be helpful. Clare Russell-Jones was so very calm, poised, and self-assured that he had a disquieting feeling that she was interviewing him instead of the other way around.

Parker consulted his notes again and wondered if he had missed anything. Presently, he said, "How long have you been listening to Captain Church, Miss Jones?"

"Since the tenth of April, sir, the day after he and Major Holbrook were parachuted into the Chartres area."

She sounded faintly annoyed that they were going over the same ground again, but Parker was unrepentant.

"I believe you also work to eleven other out-stations?"

"That's correct, sir, but I know his touch, just as I can recognize all the others." She smiled briefly. "It's not easily explained to a layman, but each operator has an individual signature on the Morse key which is like a voice to me. I can even sense when they are excited or nervous."

"And has Captain Church been nervous or excited of late?"

"Oh, he's been nervous since the day he landed."

"I see. Did you notice any idiosyncrasies last night? An unusual way of signing off or anything of that nature?"

"No, I didn't, but you see Captain Church is a stickler for correct procedure." She lowered her eyes. "Correct me if I'm wrong," she said quietly, "but I have a feeling you suspect he's been turned round."

Parker exchanged glances with Newstead and frowned. The girl was sharp, a lot sharper than he had given her credit for.

"What makes you say that, Miss Jones?"

"Because this is not the first time I've been summoned to Baker Street."

"I don't remember having met you before."

"It was early in 1941; I don't think you were in SOE then. Anyway, I was working to the Dolphin cell in Angers in those days, and your predecessor discovered that the station was being operated by the Abwehr. We fed them false information for six months before they tumbled to it."

"How very interesting."

"Yes, it was quite fascinating. Will you use the same ploy again, sir?"

"We might," Parker said cautiously. "Of course this is all highly classified, you understand?"

"Perfectly."

"Well, I'm sorry we had to drag you all the way from Bicester, but you've been most helpful. I really can't thank you enough, Miss Jones."

Parker smiled and half rose from his chair to indicate that the interview was over. Taking the hint, she stood up and gave him a decidedly feminine salute; Newstead, interpreting his glance correctly, then escorted her out of the office.

Parker could see that it was going to be one of those days where he ended up with a splitting headache and precious little to show for it. Holbrook had never disclosed his source of information, but he was now willing to bet that it had reached him via the Albert circuit. It would certainly explain how and why Holbrook had made his way to Paris. In one important respect it was a damn good job he had made contact with de Gaulle's people; but for his warning message, the Abwehr would have been in a position to manipulate SOE. At the same time, he couldn't help feeling that Paris was more than just a safe haven.

The more he saw of his personal dossier the more Parker was convinced that Holbrook would find Erwin Johannes Eugen Rommel an irresistible target. Somebody had once asked Mallory why he wanted to climb Everest and the mountaineer had replied, "Because it's there." In much the same way, he believed

Holbrook would regard Rommel as the supreme challenge he couldn't ignore.

Understanding his motivation was one thing; solving the problem which Holbrook had created was quite a different matter. Parker supposed he could always go cap in hand to André Dewavrin, "the Colonel," even though relations between the French Section and de Gaulle's Central Bureau in Duke Street had never been exactly cordial. Part of the trouble stemmed from the fact that they believed SOE had been in the habit of recruiting French nationals despite the assurances they had received to the contrary from Churchill. In the early days they had also regarded the activities of British agents in their native land as an infringement on the sovereignty of France, meaning de Gaulle, but on reflection he thought this was just so much water under the bridge. The situation had changed radically since those far-off days, and now they might even find it amusing that SOE was obliged to ask for their help.

A gentle tap on the door disturbed his train of thought, and he looked up to find Newstead hovering in the entrance.

"I'm not intruding, am I?" Newstead asked tentatively.

"Not in the least." Parker smiled and waved him to a chair. "As it happens, I wanted to have a word with you. By the way, I hope you managed to wangle a car to take Miss Jones to the station?"

"There was no need to. Bicester sent her up here in an Austin Utility." Newstead removed his spectacles and polished them with a silk handkerchief. "Did she guess right? I mean, are we going to try the same ploy again?"

"Yes, I think so, Dennis. Of course, Twenty-one Army Group may want to partake in the deception plan, so you'll have to liaise with Military Intelligence to see if they have any bright ideas."

"Couldn't Lewis take it on?"

"I'd like you to handle it. He's not sufficiently experienced."

"I see," Newstead said thoughtfully. "What about Fletcher and our tame American?"

"Jackson?"

"Yes. Do you want me to stand them down in view of what's happened?"

"No, I think they'd better move into Orchard Court."

"You want them brought to Portman Square?"

Parker could understand why he was bewildered. Orchard Court was the place where SOE agents received a final briefing on the eve of their departure for France. Now that the Foxhound group no longer existed, it was only natural for Newstead to assume that Fletcher's mission would be canceled.

"We've got to recover Holbrook."

"Why should we? Surely the Albert circuit can look after him?"

"It's not that simple, Dennis."

"Why isn't it? Is there something you haven't told me?"

"Yes, I'm afraid there is. I'd like to take you into my confidence, but unfortunately my hands are tied."

"Don't tell me it's Top Secret," Newstead said sarcastically.

"Put the word Ultra in front of it and you might be nearer the mark."

"Is there such a classification?"

Parker ignored the question. The French claimed they could get in touch with Paris whenever they liked because they had an out-station on permanent listening watch. The system had its faults—messages transmitted in daylight hours were never acknowledged—but even so it was better than nothing. At least he could set the wheels in motion by asking the French to detain Holbrook.

"Can I leave you to telephone Crompton Manor, Dennis?"

"Of course."

"Good." Parker got up from his desk, collected an umbrella from the hatstand, and moved toward the door. "I'll be off then. Should anybody want me in the next hour or so, I'll be in Duke Street conferring with Dewavrin."

Jackson placed the figure targets against a bank in the rose garden and walked back to the firing point where Fletcher was crouched over a box of .38 ammunition. McCready had led him to understand that there was some sort of emergency, but as far as he could see the British were in no great hurry to get this particular mission off the ground. Newstead had been singularly evasive, and it was obvious that Fletcher too was totally in the dark. If it was a no-go situation, he wished somebody would tell them so.

Fletcher stood up and handed him a Smith and Wesson. "Six rounds, six targets," he said crisply. "Let's see how many you can hit in four seconds."

Jackson hefted the revolver in his hand, trying to get the feel of it.

"Is something bothering you?" asked Fletcher.

"What gives you that idea?"

"Oh, I don't know; you look pissed off to me."

"Yes, well I can think of a better way to celebrate the Fourth of July."

"Remind me to buy you a drink in the mess at lunchtime."

"I might just do that." Jackson faced the targets and planted his feet astride. "I'm ready when you are."

"Go," said Fletcher.

Jackson raised his right arm, took aim, and squeezed the trigger. The pistol cracked and kicked up; traversing from left to right, he emptied the remaining five chambers, holing each wooden figure in turn.

"Five out of six," said Fletcher. "The last one didn't count."

"Why not?"

"You ran out of time." Fletcher reset the stopwatch to zero and waited for Jackson to unload the Smith and Wesson. "Still, it wasn't a bad effort for a pianist."

"Pianist?"

"Wireless operator. You are a WT man, aren't you?"

"I can work a radio."

"That's a relief." Fletcher exchanged the stopwatch for the revolver. "I thought you were just coming along for the ride."

"Do you know something I don't?"

"Not a damn thing."

Fletcher deftly loaded six rounds and snapped the cylinder home. He looked down at his feet and then loosened up in the way swimmers do before they step up to the mark.

"What's all that in aid of?" asked Jackson.

Fletcher didn't hear him. The rose garden no longer existed: He was in a different place, at a different time. . . .

It was evening and there was a light drizzle falling, and he could see the vague outline of the café farther down the road, and someone with a heavy touch was playing the piano. A buzz of conversation greeted him as he drew near, and a woman laughed raucously. He opened the door, pushed the blackout curtain aside, and stepped into the light, blinking his eyes. The room was L-shaped, with a balcony above it, and there were half a dozen or so tables in a semicircle near the tiny floor where three couples were dancing to a slow foxtrot. He counted ten fliers with sidearms: young men in jackboots, riding breeches, and leather jackets who were relaxing with the local talent. A girl sitting on the lap of a towheaded captain to his right shot him a dirty look and tugged the woolen dress down over her knees in a belated attempt to hide the white garters. A pilot leaning over the balcony threw him a mocking salute and called out *"Vive La France."* Fletcher drew the revolver from his raincoat pocket and shot him in the chest. The pilot folded over the banisters and dropped head first to cannon into a crowded table under the balcony. Turning half right, he blew a hole through the skull of the towheaded captain before taking the pianist in the back. The melody ended in a harsh discord and the couples stopped dancing and broke apart as he backed toward the door, the pistol jerking in his hand. From beneath the bodies lying on the floor, three separate pools of blood slowly inched toward one another, and then one of the girls found her voice and started screaming.

He was out of the café now and running hard toward the motorcycle which he'd left a hundred yards down the street. Vaulting into the saddle, he closed the choke, advanced the ignition, and slammed a foot down on the kick start. Somebody took a potshot at him, but then the engine caught and he roared away into the darkness.

The Luftwaffe buried their dead with full military honors on the very day when the SS chose to execute one hundred and twenty hostages in the prison yard at Abbeville. Suddenly, just as Fletcher had intended, the occupation became a harsh reality and a burning hatred was kindled. . . .

A cool voice behind him said, "You're wanted on the telephone, sir."

Fletcher turned his head and stared at the girl.

"It's Major Newstead," she said anxiously.

"Did he say what he wanted?"

"Not really, but he muttered something about Orchard House."

Fletcher smiled, creasing his hazel-colored eyes. "All right," he said cheerfully, "tell him I'll be there in a minute."

The pistol in his hand came to life and it was impossible to distinguish the sound of one report from the next, but as the echoes died away Jackson could see a neat round hole in the forehead of each figure target.

"Is that how it was in the café at Pont Rémy?" he asked softly.

"Oh, no, I've improved since then."

There was a wolfish grin on his face which Jackson found disturbing.

Holbrook left the Métro at the Pont de Clichy station in the seventeenth arondissement and turned into the rue Émile-Level. The café on the street corner was exactly as Dufoir had described it, an eyesore in sun-blistered chocolate-brown paint.

The midmorning trade was slack, just a workman in blue overalls, a middle-aged shapeless woman in black, and two pensioners, one of whom was blind. A pimply-faced boy took his order and brought him a cup of substitute coffee and a Pernod. Folding his copy of *Le Monde* in three, Holbrook made a space for the newspaper between the glass and the coffee cup. As a final touch, he placed a half-empty packet of Gitanes on the table.

The courier arrived ten minutes later. Glancing around the café, he spotted the recognition signal and joined Holbrook, smiling broadly as if they were old friends.

"Mine?" he asked, pointing to the glass.

"Yours." Holbrook moved the Pernod toward him. "Help yourself to a cigarette."

"No, thanks." The man smiled again, showing nicotined-stained teeth. "I gave them up during Lent."

"Really?"

"Well, you know how it is with the bus company, André, they don't like you smoking behind the wheel."

Holbrook pocketed the Gitanes. "What run are you on now?" he asked casually.

"The same as before; La Roche-Guyon and back." He dropped his voice to a low murmur. "I ran into your grandfather when I was in the village the other day."

"Oh? How's he been keeping?"

"Marcel's sprightly enough, but I think he's lonely."

"That's the trouble," Holbrook said quietly. "I don't see him as often as I should."

"Well, André, the way things are in La Roche-Guyon, it can't be easy for you."

"No, but I have some business in Mantes on Friday; perhaps he could meet me there?"

"Mantes is a big place."

"I could pick him up from the station around noon. He could wait for me in the buffet."

"I think that can be arranged." The man tossed back the Pernod. "I'll see you when I come off work at five."

"Where?"

"What's wrong with this place?"

"Nothing; you can wait here until you get a telephone call from me."

"It's like that, is it?"

Holbrook smiled. "I'm just naturally cautious."

"So am I. You'd better ask for Cheval." The man pushed his chair back from the table and stood up. "It's been nice meeting you again, André."

"And you, old friend," said Holbrook.

Dufoir left his office in the Prefecture, crossed the boulevard, and entered the Palais de Justice by a side door. He thought Maître Paupal knew better than to send for him during working hours, but the lawyer had been very insistent and he could only assume it was a matter of some importance. Turning left inside the entrance, Dufoir walked to the end of the corridor and knocked on the door of his chambers. A voice from within said, "Enter."

Paupal looked up from the brief he was reading. "Ah, René," he said. "Good of you to drop by."

"My pleasure, *maître.*"

"Do sit down."

Dufoir glanced about him, looking for a chair which was not encumbered with files. Paupal was easily the most untidy and disorganized advocate he'd ever met, but it never paid to judge a man by his appearance or the surroundings. The office might be in a total shambles, but the lawyer seated on the high stool behind the old-fashioned desk possessed a mind sharper than any razor.

"I think I'd better stand."

Paupal followed his gaze. "Perhaps you're right," he said. "We do seem to be a little crowded. Still, never mind, this won't take a minute." He clasped his hands together and leaned forward on his elbows. "We've just had a message from our Central Bureau in London concerning Holbrook. It would appear that SOE are very anxious we should not go out of our way to help him."

"It's a bit late in the day for that; I've already put him in touch with one of our couriers."

"He hasn't left Paris, has he?"

"No, *maître.*"

"Well, that's all right then. London has asked us to detain him, so you'd better get moving."

"You know how it is between Holbrook and me. Why pick on me?"

"Because you're a policeman," Paupal said coldly. "Now go out and arrest him."

9

Detective Édouard Tambour heard his stomach rumble and glanced longingly at the delicatessen on the opposite side of the road. Food was short in Paris, but there were still a few loaves, some camembert, and a smoked sausage in the window which made his mouth water. He looked into the rearview mirror again and wondered if he should chance it. There was no sign of the Englishman yet but, knowing his luck, he thought the bastard would show up the minute he left the car and went into the shop.

Tambour loathed and despised the English almost as much as he hated the Germans. A native of Toulon, his younger brother had joined the navy in 1936 and was serving on the battleship *Dunkerque* when a British squadron under Vice Admiral Sir James Somerville had attacked the French fleet while it lay at anchor at Mers-el-Ķebir. In the space of two short hours, twelve hundred officers and men had been killed, among them his twenty-four-year-old brother, Paul. Today was the fourth anniversary of his death, and none of the bitterness had evaporated with the years.

His eyes flicked to the mirror once more and narrowed. The man who had just entered the street bore a close resemblance to the description given by Inspector Dufoir; he was about the right height, had close-cropped dark hair, and was wearing a rumpled-looking gray pinstripe suit. Tambour watched him turn into the courtyard of number 17 rue de la Soussaye and was convinced he hadn't been mistaken.

Dufoir had warned them that Holbrook was a hard man, and that suited him down to the ground. Tambour patted his shoulder holster and smiled grimly; just let the swine get past Herriot and Vallin, who were waiting for him inside number 17, and he would stop him cold. Still smiling, he started the Citroën and backed up the road, reversing slowly into the courtyard.

Vallin checked the door to the sitting room to satisfy himself that it opened inward and then stood to one side with his back to the wall. The plan was simple yet effective and, providing Denise Jeanney stayed in her bedroom and Madame didn't muff it, he could see no reason why it shouldn't succeed. When the Englishman rang the bell to her apartment, Madame Reyneau would answer the door and usher him into the lounge cluttered with Second Empire furniture and that would be that. He might wonder where Denise Jeanney had got to, but the gun would be pressing into his spine before he sensed that something was wrong. Vallin unbuttoned his jacket and closed his fingers around the butt of the revolver in the shoulder holster. It wouldn't be long now: two, perhaps three minutes at the most. He wondered what was so special about this man that Dufoir had thought it necessary to send three of them to arrest him.

Holbrook entered the apartment house and walked toward the spiral staircase. Tailing Cheval after he'd left the café to check out his story had seemed a good idea at the time, but it hadn't worked out in practice. There was no way you could shadow a man without his knowing it once he boarded a single-decker bus, and Cheval had caught one at the junction of the Boulevard de Clichy and the rue des Maines, leaving him high and dry.

Holbrook rounded the first curve of the staircase and stopped abruptly, half convinced that he'd heard a sound of movement in the hall below. At first he thought it was only the concierge being nosy, but as he continued upward he was almost certain that someone was following him stealthily. It was then that he remembered seeing a black Citroën parked by the curb down the street from number 17, and everything suddenly fell into place.

It was a typical stakeout, which meant there was probably a third man waiting for him in the flat. There was no telling whether they belonged to the SD, the pro-German French Secret

Police, or Joseph Darnand's neo-Nazi militia, but that was academic. He was boxed in, the meat between the sandwich, whichever way he moved.

The odds were three to one and they were almost certain to be armed, which tipped the scales even more in their favor. Faced with a similar but hypothetical situation, the instructors at Brockhall would probably advise him to catch the enemy off balance by doing the unexpected. It was one of their favorite maxims and, like most, it was easier said than done.

The idea was so simple that he wondered why it hadn't occurred to him before. He remembered now that there was a blind spot between each floor where he could lie in wait, ready to strike without fear of being spotted from above or below. All he needed was a diversion, and that wasn't difficult to arrange. Without stopping, he rang the doorbell of the flat directly beneath Madame Reyneau's and slipped past the landing.

He needed an element of luck. If no one was at home in the flat or if they were slow to answer, the ruse would go off at half cock. The footsteps came nearer, a floorboard creaked, and then a door opened on the landing below and a truculent woman said, "I'm very busy, what do you want?"

Holbrook flew down the stairs and the detective hesitated just long enough to make all the difference before he turned away from the woman. The shoulder charge caught him off balance and he fell backwards into space, one arm flailing wildly to seek a handhold on the railing. He somersaulted twice, cannoned into the wall, and was still struggling to push himself up into a sitting position when Holbrook kicked him in the face. The woman standing in the entrance to her flat on the third floor began to scream.

Detective Édouard Tambour saw the man running toward him and reacted instinctively. Determined to intercept him, he drew the automatic from his shoulder holster and pushed open the door. He was half in, half out of the car when the door slammed against his right arm and leg to send a wave of pain shooting through his body. The door hit him a second time and he dropped the pistol on to the cobblestones. Almost passively, he allowed himself to be dragged out of the Citroën, and then a knee went into his groin and a hand chopped down on his neck as he doubled up. Before he became unconscious, Tambour had a nightmarish feeling that he was plunging head first into a bottomless pit.

Holbrook reached inside the car, grabbed the ignition key, and ran.

Dufoir closed the file, tossed it into the out-basket, and then answered the telephone.

A breathless voice said, "Is that you, *patron?"*

"Yes, who's that?"

"Vallin." The detective cleared his throat noisily. "I'm afraid we lost him."

Dufoir stared into space, unable to believe his ears. Just how three of his best men could make such a hash of a simple job was beyond his comprehension. If Holbrook had spotted them before he walked iinto the trap, he was either incredibly observant or else they had been damned careless.

"What happened?" he asked harshly.

"I'm not too sure, *patron.* I was waiting for him in the apartment when I heard this woman screaming on the floor below. By the time I got down there, he'd vanished."

"Into thin air like Houdini, I presume?"

"Like who?"

"Forget it." Dufoir clenched his teeth. "Why didn't Tambour and Herriot stop him?"

"They tried to and got half killed in the process. I found Herriot lying on the staircase with his face bashed in, and Tambour looked in a bad way too. I think his arm's been broken."

"You've sent for an ambulance?"

"They're already on their way to the hospital." Vallin cleared his throat again. "I'd like to get my hands on that bastard, *patron,* I really would."

"And I'd like to see you in my office in twenty minutes from now."

"That might be difficult." Vallin sounded more than a little embarrassed. "You see, I can't start the engine."

"Why not?"

"The ignition key is missing; he must have stolen it."
"Do you know how to bypass the switch with a piece of wire?"
"I'm not a mechanic, *patron,*" Vallin said plaintively.
"Then for Christ's sake find somebody who is."

Dufoir slammed the phone down and reeled off a string of four-letter words. He could imagine what Paupal would have to say when he learned that Holbrook had slipped through their fingers. It was too late to catch him in the office, but the lawyer usually lunched at Chez Louis on the Boulevard Saint-Michel, and he supposed that that was as good a place as any to break the bad news to him. At least Paupal wouldn't dare to blow his top in public.

Dufoir half rose from his chair and then had second thoughts. Holbrook was a singularly determined man, and despite what had happened it was just conceivable that he might try to get in touch with the courier again. At best, it was no more than a faint possibility, but short of launching a large-scale manhunt which was bound to attract the attention of the Gestapo, it was the only lead they had to work on. Paupal had been quite specific; he wanted Holbrook under lock and key. But he hadn't set a time limit for his arrest, an omission which Dufoir thought would give him some room for maneuvering.

Holbrook left the cinema on the Boulevard des Capucines and slowly made his way toward the Gare Saint-Lazare. The main feature had been a frivolous comedy about the adventures of a young girl up from the provinces who was determined to become an actress. The story line had been practically nonexistent, the dialogue banal, and the situations farcical, but nobody in the audience minded. The star had been a shapely blonde who, like Jane in the *Daily Mirror,* had contrived to lose most of her clothes at the first opportunity. The critics had probably hated it, but it was the sort of escapist entertainment which drew large crowds to the box office.

The cinema had been a temporary refuge, a hiding place where he could think things out without constantly looking over his shoulder. He had been on the run before but there was a subtle difference between then and now; in '42 the SD were the hunters, but this time it looked as if he was up against Darnand's militia.

Holbrook was quite sure that the driver of the Citroën had not been a German. It might be an old adage, but he believed that in moments of great stress or intolerable pain even the best undercover agents were apt to revert to their native language, and the driver had certainly said a mouthful in French. They had also known exactly where to find him, and that meant that either Madame Reyneau, Denise, or René Dufoir must have tipped them off.

Dufoir was the most likely candidate of the three, but it didn't make sense. If René was cooperating with Darnand's people, why did they wait until he'd arrived in Paris when they could have picked him up in Évreux? The business with the courier didn't add up either, unless they had intended to arrest him at the café and the plan had misfired.

Holbrook crossed the Boulevard Haussmann and entered the rue du Havre. The evening rush hour was under way and long lines were beginning to form at the bus stops. There were more cyclists on the road than he remembered seeing two years ago, but that was before an increasing shortage of gasoline had forced the authorities to make cuts in the public transport service.

For some people, however, the working day had only just begun. In the narrow side streets off the Gare Saint-Lazare the prostitutes were already looking for trade. From the phone booth opposite the railway station, he watched a dark-haired girl in a tight dress promenading with a white French poodle. Reaching the end of her beat, she about-turned and walked off in the opposite direction, her skirt swaying like a pendulum in time with the exaggerated movement of her pelvis. The girl didn't know it but she was about to become an ally.

Leafing through the telephone directory, Holbrook found the number he wanted and started dialing. He jabbed the pay button with his thumb a few seconds before the purring tone ended with a tinkle.

A man with a harsh voice took the call and said, "Hello."

Holbrook said, "Is that the Café la Villette?"

"It is."

"I believe a Monsieur Cheval is expecting me to phone him."
"Who?"
"Cheval," said Holbrook. "I was told I could reach him at this number."
"We're not an answering service."
"It's urgent."
"It always is."
The phone clattered and he could hear a faint buzz of conversation in the background. Leaning against the glass partition, he noticed that the girl had about-turned again and was accosting a middle-aged man who looked decidedly ill at ease. There was a bright smile on her face but it failed to have the desired effect; the man, thoroughly alarmed, backed away, tipped his hat, and hurried off. Somebody with heavy breathing picked up the phone.
Holbrook said, "Cheval?"
"Yes; who wants me?"
"André. Remember me?"
"As if I could forget. Where are you calling from?"
"A room with a view of the Gare Saint-Lazare."
"Oh, yes?" said Cheval.
"Why don't you take the Métro and join me?" Holbrook focused his eyes on the street sign across the square. "My friend will meet you in the rue de Roma."
"What friend?"
"A brunette with a white-haired poodle."
"She sounds like a tart to me."
"That's just what she is," said Holbrook. "Play it her way and she'll lead you to me. Got it?"
"Sure. I'll be there in twenty minutes."
"You do that small thing." Holbrook broke the connection and left the booth.
There were a number of vantage points in the neighborhood, but after some deliberation he thought the coffeeshop near the bus terminus afforded the best view of the rue de Roma. It also had a side entrance, which was a distinct advantage if he had to leave in a hurry. The coffee, however, was terrible; it looked weak, smelled of acorns, and tasted lousy.

The girl with the French poodle wasn't having much luck; a corporal in the Wehrmacht turned her down in favor of a red-head with slimmer legs. In the next fifteen minutes she approached three other men, turning away with a characteristic shrug of her shoulders when it became apparent they weren't interested. At precisely ten minutes past six, Holbrook saw René Dufoir arrive to keep the appointment which he'd made with Cheval.

Suddenly he felt naked and alone. To stay on in Paris was madness now; Dufoir and Madame Reyneau were the only two contacts he had who could put him in touch with the other members of the Albert circuit, and clearly they were on the opposite side of the fence. It seemed the old advice still held good: if you were a hunted man, Communists and priests were the only people you could afford to trust. He didn't know any priests in Paris, and he remembered Newstead telling him that the Communist cell people who'd helped him in '42 had been rounded up by the Gestapo, but there was a girl in Saint-Germain who'd sheltered him before and might do so again. Gabrielle Marsac had never held a political opinion in her life, but she was an old friend and there was a time when they had been very close.

Holbrook pushed the cup and saucer to one side and walked out of the café.

Dufoir didn't like it; the girl was too natural, too self-possessed. She'd picked him up just like any other man, and he was beginning to suspect that either she had missed her real vocation or else she wasn't play acting. Despite a nagging seed of doubt, he followed her into a shabby-looking tenement and climbed three flights to reach a two-roomed flat in the garret. The girl, who said her name was Paulette, led him into a bed-sitting room which was furnished in bad taste. As soon as his lead was slipped, the poodle jumped onto the bed and bared its teeth at him.

Dufoir eyed the dog warily and moved back a pace. "Does he bite?"

"Yes, but only if he thinks you're going to attack me." Paulette smiled coquettishly. "Or if you forget to give me a present."

Dufoir opened his wallet, removed two ten-franc notes, and slapped them into the palm of her outstretched hand. The money disappeared into her bra. Lifting the dog off the bed, she walked across the room and opened the intercommunicating door.

"Make yourself comfortable," she said gaily. "I won't be a minute."

Dufoir waited until the door had closed behind her before he drew the automatic from his shoulder holster. As he stood there with his back to the wall, he wondered what the hell was keeping Vallin. A few moments later, the girl returned alone and he whipped the pistol out of sight a split second before she turned around to see where he was.

Her eyes widened. "What on earth are you doing?" she said. "There's no need to be shy." She smiled, cocking her head on one side like a mechanical doll. "Would you like to undress me? No? Well, perhaps it's best if I do it." She reached behind her, unzipped the dress, and tugged it down over her hips, allowing it to fall about her ankles. "I expect you're like all the other men," she said archly. "You want to see me in my stockings and shoes."

Dufoir sidestepped, tried the door knob with his left hand, and found that the key had been turned on the inside. Backing off, he aimed a savage kick at the door. It was only then that she realized what he was up to, and noticing the gun in his right hand she let out a piercing scream.

The lock splintered and gave way. The pimp in the small back room fell back into his chair and stared at the intruder, his mouth opening and closing like a stranded fish.

Dufoir said, "I'm a police officer."

The pimp looked disgusted. "Oh, shit," he said. "Something told me when I got out of bed this morning that this wouldn't be our lucky day."

Dufoir could almost sympathize; it wasn't his lucky day either.

Parker sat up and groped for the telephone on the bedside table. He lifted the receiver and answered the call in a whisper, anxious not to disturb his wife, who was still sleeping peacefully in the other twin bed.

A businesslike voice said, "Copping here, sir, duty officer.

You left word that you were to be informed immediately if we heard anything from our friends in Duke Street."

"That's correct."

"Well, I'm afraid it's disappointing news, sir. It seems they failed to bring home the bacon."

"I see."

"Do you want me to send a follow-up?"

"No, that won't be necessary."

Parker quietly replaced the telephone and lay back. In his opinion, detaining Holbrook should have been a simple enough job, but somehow or other the French had managed to bungle it. The whole affair had suddenly become much more complicated, and he realized that it would now be necessary to be completely frank with de Gaulle's people in order to resolve the situation. Reluctantly, he also came to the conclusion that Holbrook had shown that he was not open to peaceful persuasion.

10

The springs creaked as she rolled over in the bed and reached out for the inevitable cigarette. A match flared briefly and Holbrook waited expectantly, knowing that Gabrielle would start coughing as soon as she inhaled. The smoke drifted toward him and then he heard her splutter and catch her breath before the paroxysm gripped and shook her body.

"Oh, God," she wheezed, "that's better."

"You could have fooled me."

She turned over onto her stomach, the quilt sliding from her back as she propped herself up on both elbows. "Did I wake you, Holbrook?"

Her smile was mischievous, and he thought how lovely she looked. Her long chestnut hair with its natural auburn tint was silky to the touch and her eyes, green and set wide apart, were the most fascinating he'd ever seen. Slipping an arm around her neck, he drew her face close to his and kissed her lips.

"That was nice," she murmured. "Do it again."

"I knew you were a hussy the first time I laid eyes on you."

"And you only a schoolboy?"

"I was pretty advanced for my years."

"You were gauche." She traced a finger down his chest. "But very nice and so English."

It had been the summer of '35 and he was seventeen, and his father had taken him to Paris on a sales trip hoping it would spark an interest in the family business. His father had been a likable man, but even then Holbrook had realized that he would never have amounted to anything but for the fact that he'd married well. His in-laws had little regard for him, but he was family and so his job was secure.

They had met Gabrielle and her father for lunch at the Lucas-Carton in the Place Madeleine, and his father had been both surprised and a little disconcerted to see her. Her presence had certainly queered any hopes he had entertained of combining business with pleasure. But she had captivated the younger Holbrook, and somehow he had found the courage and the opportunity to ask if he might see her again.

"Why are you smiling, Holbrook?"

"I was remembering the first time I took you out to dinner."

"And you didn't have enough money to pay the bill."

"Well, it was Maxim's and I wanted to impress you."

"You looked so embarrassed that I couldn't be angry with you." She leaned across the bed and stubbed out her cigarette. "What became of those two young people?"

He turned his head and saw the wistful expression on her face. "You married Charles Marsac, remember?"

"It was a mistake. You should have talked me out of it."

He thought Gabrielle had a convenient memory. He had tried to do just that, but she had refused to listen to him. There was only a difference of eighteen months between them, yet he remembered her telling him that he was behaving like a stupid adolescent because he was jealous of Charles, and there had been more than a grain of truth in that remark. Consequently, she had laughed at him when he'd declared that Marsac was a shallow, good-looking man with too much money and too few brains whose life-style was one long round of cocktail parties. Women and horses had been the only two subjects that interested him, and in the end there had been too many women. Their marriage had lasted three years. That had been the only surprising thing about it.

"Have you seen him recently?"

"Who? Charles? Only in passing at Auteuil Race Course last year. He had a woman on either arm." The recollection seemed to amuse her. "He was always a philanderer; sometimes I think you must be two of a kind, Holbrook."

"I'm not like Charles."

"No? You take what's offered you but you never allow yourself to become involved."

"I care about you."

"Perhaps you did once but that was a long time ago."

"There's never been anyone else."

It wasn't strictly true. There had been a WAAF at Tangmere but she had turned him down in favor of a flight lieutenant with a smooth line who claimed he'd flown with Bader in the Battle of Britain. Subsequently it transpired that he'd spent the summer of 1940 with 26 Operational Training Unit in the north of England, which tarnished his image a bit but not fatally so.

"Never?"

He could see that she wanted to believe him. "Never," he said firmly.

"I wonder. Would you have come to me if you hadn't been in trouble?"

It was the sort of loaded question which was impossible to answer. If he said yes, Gabrielle would know it was a lie, and if he told her the truth, she would think he was only using her.

"I'm here, aren't I? Isn't that enough?"

"I can't help you to escape this time, Holbrook." There was a hard edge to her voice. "The priest died of cancer last October. He was my only contact with the Resistance."

"Can't I stay here, at least until Friday?"

"And then where will you go?"

She had a point. He didn't know if Marcel Gilbert had received his message or, if he had, whether he would still keep the rendezvous in Mantes. And there was Dufoir to consider too; he might use the old man as bait to set another trap.

"I'm not sure," he said.

"I can let you have some money, if that's any help." She saw him frown and placed a finger across his lips. "You won't be taking it from me."

"I won't?"

"No. Can you guess what my father did when he knew there was going to be a war? He bought gold and buried it all over Paris like some ignorant peasant. There's some of it here in the garden of this house. We could dig it up if you like."

He could just picture her father shoveling away for dear life in the dead of night. It was probably the only time he'd raised blisters on his hands.

"That really must have been a sight worth seeing."

"What?"

"Your father." His body shook with silent laughter. "How many gardeners did he employ before the war?"

"Three."

"Three. And he couldn't trust one of them to do the job for him when it came to the crunch."

The smile was hesitant at first, but then she saw the funny side of it too and started to giggle. "Poor Papa," she said, "hard work never did agree with him."

Her father might be a figure of fun, but he knew the gold was no laughing matter. It could buy help, even from someone like Marcel Gilbert.

"Shall we?" she asked.

"Shall we what?"

"Dig it up tonight?"

"It's an idea."

"You sound doubtful."

"I'm trying to think how I can make the best use of it."

"I could sell some of it on the black market."

"There's always that possibility." Holbrook rubbed his jaw. "On the other hand, I may know somebody in Mantes who might take it off us."

"Who?"

"A man called Marcel Gilbert. But I would have to make the deal—providing, of course, that I can recognize him if he shows up."

Her eyebrows met in a puzzled frown. "I don't understand a word of what you've said."

"He's an old man who lives in La Roche-Guyon, and although I've never met him there is a chance he will be waiting for me in the station buffet on Friday. He's supposed to be in the Resistance, but I could be walking into a trap if I show up at the rendezvous." He grimaced. "It's all very complicated and I don't know who to trust."

"You can trust me, Holbrook. I'll go in your place."
"No, I couldn't let you do that; it's too risky."
"Please," she said fiercely. "I must."
She was the most mercurial woman he'd ever met—her moods could change like quicksilver—but this sudden note of desperation puzzled him.
"Why must you?"
"I have my reasons." She rolled over onto her back and stared up at the ceiling. "You see, I'm afraid."
"Of what?"
"There are some people here in Saint-Germain who know that I've had a German lover, and I'm frightened what they will do to me." There was a brief silence and he could see her throat working as if she found it difficult to swallow. Her voice was husky when she spoke again. "We met each other in the Louvre one dreary, wet afternoon in November last year and he asked me if I would have tea with him. He was gentle and kind and I was lonely and I can't explain it, Holbrook, but it happened, it just happened, that's all." She turned her head away, blinking her eyes rapidly. "I suppose I must be a whore."
"And the German?" he asked quietly.
"He was posted to the Eastern Front a month later."
Well, that was typical of Gabrielle, he thought. She never did have any luck with the men in her life. There were twenty something million Frenchmen to choose from, but she had to go and fall in love with a German, and they would make her pay for that. As soon as Saint-Germain was liberated, she would be rounded up along with all the other girls who'd fraternized with the enemy, and they would cut off her hair and shave her head with a razor, and like as not some brave man would daub the word 'harlot' on her forehead before she was paraded around the town for everyone to jeer and spit at.
"You must hate me," she whispered.
"No, you're wrong. I feel sorry, very sorry."
"Then you've got to let me help you." She turned to face him again. "Please, Holbrook," she implored. "Don't you see, it's my only chance to put things right."
Maybe she was right that by helping him there was just a

chance that it might square things with the local Resistance. So what if she had slept with the enemy? He knew he could trust her; Gabrielle had risked her neck for him in '42 when most people refused to lift a finger, and when he'd come knocking at her door last night she had taken him in without any hesitation. They needed one another now. Perhaps they always would.

"All right," he said, "let's talk about it."

The apartment at Orchard House boasted a black-tiled bathroom with an onyx bidet and a cheerful butler whose welcoming smile made every agent feel at home in Portman Square. There was also a WAAF officer with an encyclopedic knowledge of work permits, travel restrictions, police registration, food rationing, and curfew regulations which were relevant in wartime France. A veritable magician, she appeared to have an unlimited supply of genuine tailors' name tabs, family photographs, old love letters, French matches, and Métro tickets with which to support the forged documents produced by the SOE laboratory. Fletcher had been through it all before and was familiar with the procedure; the only thing that puzzled him was the fact that Parker had decided to conduct the final briefing session instead of Newstead.

Fletcher supposed the atmosphere was intended to be informal. They were both reclining in comfortable armchairs, facing one another over a gin and tonic, but Parker seemed ill at ease and was behaving like a fussy old woman.

"You want me to go over my cover story again?" he asked incredulously.

"Yes."

"How many more times?"

"Until I'm satisfied you know it off by heart."

"All right," said Fletcher. "My name is Jean-Claude Arnaud. I'm twenty eight, single, and I'm rooming in a lodging house at six-oh-six Émile-Zola, which is within walking distance of the Renault works in Boulogne-Billancourt, where I'm employed as a welder. I've been given a day's leave of absence to visit my mother in Beauvais who is sick."

Parker opened a worn-looking imitation-leather wallet and took out a photograph. "Who is this girl?"

"My fiancée, Françoise Savy; we're to be married in October."

"But you also have a love letter from a woman signing herself 'your loving Nicole.' How do you explain that?"

Fletcher smiled. "Well, it's like this—Françoise is in Beauvais and I don't get to see her very often, so I've got this bint on the side who lives in Montparnasse. Nicole is married but her husband's away in Germany and she gets lonely, if you know what I mean."

"Try winking when you say that, Harry."

"Try winking," Fletcher repeated with heavy emphasis. "I really must remember to do that."

"Now tell me about the arrangements for your reception."

"Oh, we've finished with the mock interrogation, have we?"

"We have."

Fletcher shrugged his shoulders to show that, although he thought Parker was wasting valuable time, it was no skin off his nose. "Very well," he said with mock deference. "The dropping zone is on the outskirts of Laversines, a small village five miles east of Beauvais and thirty-eight miles due north from Paris. It will be marked by three green lamps laid out on the ground in the shape of a triangle, and the reception committee will consist of two men and a woman answering to the name of Michèle. The challenge is 'Caen,' answer 'Carentan.' After burying our chutes we'll be guided to a safe house in the village, where arrangements will then be made for me and Jackson to travel by separate routes to Paris. When I reach Paris, I take the Métro to Voltaire and make my way on foot to eighty-three rue Keller in the eleventh arondissement, where a Madame Mortier will be expecting me. Jackson will arrive later the same day, and we are to wait there in her apartment until we are contacted by a man code-named Pierre."

Parker pressed both hands together and raised them to his lips. "That's very good," he said primly. "Most satisfactory."

Fletcher snorted. "Perhaps now you'll tell me what I am supposed to do in Paris."

As he leaned forward to reach for the gin and tonic, an identity card was pushed across the table.

"Do you know this man?" Parker asked casually.

Fletcher stared at the small head-and-shoulders photograph in the top right-hand corner. "No." He pursed his lips thoughtfully. "Who is he?"

"Simon Holbrook, otherwise known as Foxhound. Do you think you can remember his face?"

"Is it a good likeness?"

"Yes."

"Then I'm sure I'd recognize him."

"Good. He's your target."

Fletcher examined the photograph again and then dropped it back on the table. "Is he a traitor?"

"Not exactly, but we are unable to make him see reason. Despite orders to the contrary, we believe he intends to assassinate Rommel, and that would be most inconvenient."

"Why?"

"Because it would interfere with our plans."

"And you want me to kill him, is that it?"

"When you've found him," Parker said impassively.

"How does Jackson fit into the picture?"

"This is a joint SOE-OSS venture; he will be your radio operator. Do you have any other questions?"

"Only one. When do we go?"

"Tonight," said Parker. "From Tempsford at twenty-two fifteen hours."

The garden had been neglected. The flower beds were choked with weeds, and molehills sprouted in the long grass of a lawn which had been her father's pride and joy before his death early in 1940. There was also a foul smell coming from the ornamental pond opposite the arbor, and as he drew nearer Holbrook saw that it was full of rotting vegetation. The summerhouse looked dilapidated; most of the paint had weathered away and the wood was infected with some sort of fungus which he thought might be dry rot. The door was warped and was difficult to budge; putting a shoulder to it, he eased it open a few inches at a time. The grating noise set his teeth on edge and alarmed Gabrielle.

"For God's sake," she whispered vehemently, "you'll wake the dead with the racket you're making."

The door gave a few more inches and he squeezed through the gap sideways, tearing a path through a latticed screen of cobwebs. The moon was partially obscured, and in the poor light he blundered into a solid object.

Holbrook swore under his breath and rubbed his knee. "What the hell have you got in here?"

"Garden furniture."

"That figures. I think I've just found a bench seat with my leg."

"I'm afraid you'll have to move it out of the way and lift the floorboards underneath."

"And then what?"

"You start digging."

Holbrook leaned the spade against the wall and then stood the bench seat up on one end before lifting it into a corner.

"Do you know the exact spot?" he asked.

"My father said he'd left the nailheads protruding so that I would know which boards to raise." She knelt down and brushed a hand across the floor. "Damn," she muttered angrily, "I've just broken one of my fingernails."

Holbrook removed the hammer from his belt and, crouching beside her, inserted the claw under the nail and yanked it out. He moved a fingertip slowly across the plank, located another head, and extracted it. He repeated the process, drawing a dozen nails before he was able to lift a section of the floor. The cavity measured four by two feet, and the earth six inches below the foundations felt as hard as a rock.

"How deep do I need to go down?"

"About a meter," she said.

Holbrook whistled softly; her father must have been a lot tougher than he supposed. A meter was roughly thirty-nine inches, and excavating a cubic yard of earth in such a cramped space would take some doing. Removing his jacket, he rolled up his sleeves and stepped down into the hole.

It was hard going at first, but once the chalky topsoil had been removed he struck clay and from then on made better progress. Twenty minutes later, the spade struck metal, and digging around the obstruction he gradually unearthed a strongbox wrapped in burlap. Levering one end up with the shovel, he was then able to lift it out with surprising ease.

"Is it heavy?" she asked.

"No, it's pretty light. I doubt if it weighs more than three or four pounds." He stepped out of the hole and looked at the mound of earth on the floor of the summerhouse. "What about this lot?"

"Leave it; you can fill it in tomorrow night." Gabrielle hugged both arms around her waist. "I'm cold, Holbrook."

"All right," he said, "you take my jacket and we'll get out of here."

Curious to know how much gold it contained, he hefted the box onto his left shoulder and followed her back to the house. As soon as he was inside, he placed it on the kitchen table and slashed the burlap with a clasp knife. Despite the protective covering, both the box and the padlock securing the staple and hasp were in a rusty condition and the key refused to turn in the lock. Taking a carving steel from the drawer, he broke the hasp and raised the lid. Packed between layers of straw were eighteen two-ounce blocks, each bearing the assay mark of the Bank of France.

The port wing dipped and the Dakota executed a leisurely 180-degree turn. The red light was still showing, but the dispatcher had already moved aft to unclip the hatch. Responding to a nudge from Fletcher, Jackson hooked up his static line and shuffled toward the exit. A cold blast of air whipped his face as the dispatcher opened the door. The RAF sergeant gave him a cheerful grin, checked their lines, and then saw to the supply container.

The light changed to green. Jackson, standing in the door, felt a tap on his shoulder and went out; caught up in the slipstream from the Dakota, he tumbled over and over until the canopy opened and checked the rate of descent. He spotted the markers on the DZ and just had time to correct the drift before the earth rose swiftly to meet him. For once, he landed in the approved style, folding sideways to break the fall.

He was still gathering his chute in when he found himself being warmly embraced by a large enthusiastic Frenchman in a trench coat. The girl with him was less demonstrative but infinitely more practical. She insisted Jackson give her the password before she consented to shake hands.

11

Epp inspected his appearance in the full-length mirror of the wardrobe. The uniform was not such a good fit as it had been in the old days, and it was obvious that he had lost a considerable amount of weight. He knew Sophie would be upset if she could see his gaunt face, and he supposed that, if only for her sake, he ought to look after himself better; unfortunately, a staff officer attached to Fromm's headquarters in the Bendlerstrasse worked irregular hours, and cooking dinner for one when he returned home late at night was just too much trouble, even allowing for the fact that his culinary expertise only extended to boiling an egg.

Epp frowned at his reflection. The medal ribbon of the Iron Cross First Class was beginning to look decidedly grubby and would have to be replaced before long. There was a spare piece of ribbon in the chest of drawers, and he wondered if Anneliese would sew it on for him. He also noticed that he had forgotten to transfer the Crimean Campaign badge from his best uniform, and that was the sort of oversight old Colonel General Fritz Fromm was bound to jump on. It was only a simple bronze shield depicting the Crimean peninsula in relief below an eagle clutching a laurel-wreathed swastika in its claws, but it was the one thing he had to show for a deformed pelvis.

He remembered that day late in April 1942 when Fedor von Bock had awarded him a bar to the Iron Cross he'd earned the previous summer at Kiev and had jovially remarked that he would soon get a badge to go with it. The presentation had taken place in a forward observation post overlooking Sevastopol, and the Field Marshal's veiled reference to a new campaign medal had not been lost on him. Everyone in the 11th Army from Manstein, the commander, down to the latest batch of reinforcements to join them from the infantry training depots had known that a major offensive was in the offing. Even the Russians knew it; they had erected huge signs in front of the fortifications guarding the ancient port which, printed in both Russian and German, had read, "Come ahead, fascist dogs! We are waiting!"

Six weeks later, on the eighth of June, to the accompaniment of a massive artillery bombardment, Epp had found himself in the forefront of that attack and his half-track had been blown up by a small aerial bomb planted under a culvert less than a thousand yards from the starting line.

The doorbell interrupted his reminiscing; without undue haste, he closed the wardrobe and left the bedroom. The caller rang a second time before Epp was halfway down the hall, and in an irritated voice he called out that he was coming. He thought it was probably the milkman after his money, or else the janitor's wife had forgotten her key and was too lazy to go back and get it. In fact, Anneliese Ohlendorf was the very last person he expected to find on his doorstep at that hour of the morning.

"Hello, Franz," she said. "Can I come in for a few minutes?"

"But of course." He opened the door wider.

"I promise not to keep you long."

"Oh, that's all right, I'm not in a hurry. I was on duty all night at the Bendlerstrasse."

"I see."

"Stauffenberg was kind enough to lend me his staff car so that I could run home to change my uniform. Would you like a cup of coffee? There's some percolating on the stove."

"That would be nice." She followed him into the kitchen, which looked as if it could do with a good cleaning. "Shall I get the cups and saucers, Franz?"

"If you wouldn't mind. You'll find them in the cupboard."

"I saw Ludwig again yesterday afternoon."

"Oh, yes?" Epp fetched a bottle of milk from the larder and poured some into a jug. "And what did he have to say for himself?"

"He's heard from Switzerland."

"Was the news good or bad?"

"I'm not sure. Adam told him that Dulles inferred the Americans would be favorably disposed toward a democratic German government."

Epp presumed that the Adam she'd mentioned must be von Trott Zu Solz, who had been seconded to the Abwehr from the Foreign Office. Certainly, with his diplomatic experience, Trott would be the ideal man to approach Dulles.

"Were you hoping for a more positive commitment from the Americans?" he asked.

"Ludwig was."

"Well, I think he was expecting a lot." Epp lifted the percolator from the ring and turned off the gas. "I imagine the Americans want to be sure the coup d'état is successful before they get down to business. After all, if you look at it from their point of view, the whole thing could be a trick to drive a wedge between the Western Allies and the Russians."

"That's ridiculous, Franz."

"No, it isn't. You can just imagine how Stalin would react if Goebbels was able to show that the Anglo-Americans were prepared to negotiate a separate peace treaty."

"I hadn't thought of it like that."

"You should be thankful they haven't turned us down flat. Frankly, I think it's a mistake to court the Americans at this stage. What if they rebuffed us? Would Stauffenberg then abandon his plan to assassinate the Führer? You know he wouldn't." Epp poured out the coffee and pushed a cup toward her. "I've forgotten, do you take sugar or not?"

"I've given it up," she said in a listless voice.

Her forehead was creased in a worried-looking frown and he guessed that something was bothering her.

"Do you want to tell me about it?"

"What?"

"There's obviously something worrying you."

She bit her lip. "It's probably my imagination working overtime."

"Suppose you let me be the judge of that."

"Well, if you must know, Franz, I think I was followed when I left Ludwig's house in Goethestrasse yesterday."

"You think?"

"I first became aware of this man when I turned the corner into Königsberger. By the time I reached the station at Lichterfeld East, I was convinced he was following me."

"So what did you do about it?"

"I got off at the Anhalter terminus and took the U Bahn from Gleisdreieck, hoping I could shake him off. I went all the way out to Kottbusser Tor, took the Gesundbrunngh line to Alexanderplatz, doubled back to Stadtmitte, and finally ended up at Rehberge. Thankfully, he left the train two stops down the line at Leopoldplatz. Anyway, to be on the safe side, I stayed the night with my cousin in Wilmersdorf instead of coming back here. Did I do right, Franz?"

Epp wished she hadn't asked him. If the Gestapo were watching Beck's house in Goethestrasse, her suspicious behavior had only succeeded in arousing their interest. Had Anneliese gone straight back to the Brandenburg apartments, the Gestapo agent might have supposed that she had nothing to hide, but he thought no useful purpose would be served by airing his opinion. It was impossible to put back the clock, and in any case Anneliese needed reassuring if she was to keep her nerve.

"My dear, don't you realize that you're a very attractive woman?"

"What's that got to do with it?" she snapped.

"Everything. Hasn't it occurred to you that this man was probably trying to pick you up?"

"No, it wasn't like that, Franz."

The denial meant nothing. He could tell by the expression in her eyes that she wanted to believe him.

"I don't think you should dismiss the idea out of hand. Let's face it, if the SD have been keeping Beck under surveillance for any length of time, they would know all about you by now. God knows it wasn't your first visit to Goethestrasse."

"I suppose there could be something in what you say." The doubt was still there but slowly evaporating.

"Oh, you were followed all right, but not by a policeman."

"Do you honestly think somebody was trying to pick me up, Franz?"

"I'm positive that was the case," he said emphatically.

"Oh, God, you don't know how relieved I feel."

It was as if a heavy weight had suddenly been lifted from her shoulders. There was a broad smile on her face and her eyes were bright again. Epp smiled back at her and wished he could believe in his fairy tale too, but he had a strong premonition of impending disaster.

Dufoir left the train for the Pont de Sèvres at Madeleine and followed the directional signs for the Château de Vincennes line where he knew Paupal would be waiting for him on the platform. Caught up in the rush hour, he zigzagged through the crowded subway only too aware that he was already late for his appointment. A log jam at the head of the staircase delayed him even further, and by the time he reached the foot the commuters were lined up five deep on the platform. Despite the crush, he knew exactly where to find the lawyer; just as they had arranged, Paupal was standing at the far end within a few feet of the tunnel.

Paupal said, "You're late."

"There was a holdup on the line between Belleville and Goncourt." Dufoir gesticulated and became more garrulous with his excuses. "The lights were against us for a good ten minutes. I think there must have been a temporary power failure."

"An apology would have sufficed. After all, it was you who made the appointment."

"I'm sorry."

Paupal nodded. "Let's get straight to the point. This is going to be a very busy day for me, and I can only spare you a few minutes of my time."

"I'm not happy about the new arrivals; I don't like the idea of them being attached to my department."

"We've been over that ground before."

Paupal felt a warm breeze on his face and fell silent. A few moments later, a train roared into the station and squealed to a stop. The doors opened; the crowd in front of him surged forward and, assisted by a platform attendant, squeezed into the compartment until they were packed inside like sardines in a tin. The doors slammed under a hiss of compressed air, and the train pulled away leaving half the passengers still standing on the platform with them.

"Anyway," Paupal continued softly, "your objections were

noted, but the Central Committee decided that there was no alternative. The hunters will be issued with police identity cards and you will place a car at their disposal."

"I only have eight detectives working under me."

"So what?"

"Well, isn't it obvious? When two new faces suddenly appear, somebody is almost bound to ask a few awkward questions."

"Now you're being stupid, Dufoir," Paupal said irritably. "God in heaven, man, nobody is suggesting that they should meet the rest of your squad. If you use Vallin as a go-between, there's no need for them to go anywhere near the Prefecture."

"I still don't like it."

"Your job is to locate the renegade and then stand back out of the way so that they can deal with him. Now that shouldn't be too difficult with the resources at your disposal."

"Why go to all this trouble when it isn't necessary?" Dufoir moistened his lips. "Look, we've been in touch with Marcel Gilbert again and warned him to stay clear of Mantes. We've locked and bolted the door and there is nothing our man can do about it."

"I wish I could believe that. Unfortunately, your friend is very resourceful. I wouldn't put anything past him." Paupal glanced to his left and saw that the signal had changed from red to green. "I'm afraid your time is up," he said brusquely. "There's another train on the way, and I intend to catch it."

"Now wait a minute, this just isn't good enough—" Dufoir caught a warning side glance from the lawyer and was suddenly aware that a number of people were staring at them. Still in a loud voice, he said, "I know there's a war on, but you'd think the trains would run on time just once in a while."

A buxom woman standing next to him nodded her head vigorously. "You're so right," she complained bitterly. "Traveling to work becomes more of a nightmare every day. Somebody ought to do something about it."

A loud voice from the back of the line said, "What do you suggest we do, madame? Invite Mussolini to take over the Métro?"

A train swept into the station, drowning the titter of laughter.

Dufoir looked around for Paupal and found that he had disappeared into the milling throng.

Marcel Gilbert walked into the café, propped his fishing rod against the wall, and sat down at the corner table in the window which, as usual, Thérèse had reserved for him. Although they had known one another for over thirty years, she still treated him with the same deference she had shown as a pupil at the village school. Thérèse, he thought, was a nice, pleasant woman but not very bright; it simply never occurred to her that by laying claim to this particular table he was not merely exercising an old man's prerogative. Without moving from his chair, he could watch the whole of the Grande Rue from the Church of Saint-Samson to the hospital beyond the Château Rochefoucauld.

Thérèse approached him with a shy smile. "Good morning, Monsieur Gilbert," she said, "and how are you keeping?"

"I'm very well, thank you." Her bedside manner annoyed him today. She knew very well that he'd never had a day's illness in his life, yet she always made a point of inquiring after his health. "There's still a spark of life left in the old body. I'd like a cup of coffee, please."

"Large?"

"Small."

"Small," she repeated. Her eyes strayed to the fishing rod. "Did you have any luck this morning?"

"No," he said tersely, "the fish weren't rising."

Gilbert stared out of the window at the bus which was still parked outside the mayoral offices, hoping that some sort of telepathy would induce the driver to join him. There were a number of questions he wanted to ask Cheval, but it was beginning to look as if he was determined to avoid him. Obviously something must have happened to the Englishman for the Resistance Committee in Paris to cancel the rendezvous, but the message he'd received from them had not explained anything. If the Gestapo had arrested Foxhound, he knew Paris wouldn't lift a finger to help him and there was nothing he could do except sit tight and hope for the best. Right from the very beginning, the Albert circuit had never been keen on the idea of assassinating

Rommel and they had been quick to unload it onto the British. Perhaps, with any luck, SOE would send another man to do the job.

A plume of gray smoke escaped from the exhaust, and then the bus moved off to make a U-turn around the fountain in the center of the village square. Gilbert thought it significant that Cheval should look the other way as he drove past the café and took the road to Mantes.

Thérèse said, "Your coffee, Monsieur Gilbert."

"Thank you."

"It's a lovely day, isn't it?"

"Yes, I suppose it is, Thérèse."

The sun was shining out of a clear blue sky, but so far as he was concerned it was a lousy day. Cheval undoubtedly had his orders, but the fact remained that an old friend had cut him dead, and that hurt. Gilbert reached into his pocket and produced a tin of tobacco; slowly and methodically, he began to fill his pipe.

"Do you think they are going to bomb the château?"

Gilbert looked up. "What are you talking about, Thérèse?"

"Those low-flying aircraft in the distance. Can't you hear them?"

Gilbert listened attentively and then smiled. "It's just a couple of motorcycles."

"Never."

"You wait and see if I'm not right."

A few seconds later, a small cavalcade swept through the village. Preceded by two outriders on BMWs, the Mercedes staff car turned off the Grande Rue and disappeared into the avenue of linden trees behind the church.

"Well, I must say that's a relief." Thérèse smiled. "Thank goodness it's only some bigwig visiting the château."

No one at Headquarters Army Group B, least of all Rommel, had any illusions about their visitor. A new messiah had been appointed to clean up the temple, and the messiah was Field Marshal Günther von Kluge. Von Rundstedt had gone, compulsorily retired like so many other generals who dared to speak their mind. Perhaps Rundstedt had been indiscreet to advise

Keitel that their only option was to sue for peace, but at least he was a realist, unlike his successor, who seemed to think that sheer willpower alone was enough to push the British and Americans back into the sea.

The war map in the operations room showed that the German 7th Army had been forced to commit over five sixths of its available armor against the British and Canadians, leaving just one and a third panzer divisions to bolster the infantry formations holding the line from the Cotentin peninsula to Saint-Lô. In the last forty-eight hours, this dangerous imbalance between the two wings had become even more critical with the arrival of several fresh American divisions as yet unidentified. Sooner or later the bubble would burst and then 7th Army would be in serious trouble.

"We are fighting a losing battle," said Rommel. "We must change our tactics."

"In what way?"

"We should conduct a limited withdrawal—"

Kluge shook his head. "You must know that is completely unacceptable, Herr Field Marshal. We have to make them fight for every meter of ground."

"I beg to disagree. We should draw them on until they are out of range of their naval gunfire support and then strike against their left flank with our armor. If we adopt this course of action, there is a slim chance that we may be able to roll them up like a carpet."

Kluge decided the Führer was right after all: Rommel was an insubordinate pessimist, the old snap and fire had evaporated, and he had obviously lost his grip on the situation.

"We stand and fight."

"We will be inviting disaster."

His dour manner irritated Kluge. "You may have had a free hand in North Africa," he snapped, "but times have changed. You will now have to get accustomed to carrying out orders."

Rommel clenched his hands. For one field marshal to address another in such a manner in front of the staff was unforgivable. Without visiting the front, how could von Kluge know what the conditions were like in Normandy? He had been campaigning in Russia since 1941 and had yet to face an enemy with such overwhelming supremacy in the air.

"With respect, Herr Field Marshal," Rommel said coldly, "I think the time will come when you will be forced to revise your tactical concept."

He had never really seen eye to eye with Gerd von Rundstedt, but at least they were agreed that Germany had already lost the war. He wondered how long Kluge would take to reach the same conclusion.

Jackson turned into the rue Keller and quickened his stride. The sun was warm on his back, but the memory of the freight train was with him still and he felt cold inside. It had been shunted off into a siding to make room for them, so he had been able to count the boxcars as they crawled past. Each wagon had been padlocked, but it was the armed sentries facing inward at ten-yard intervals down the track who'd first led him to suspect that it was not an ordinary supply train. Although they had been deployed in a way which suggested that men and not materials were locked inside, he had refused to believe it until he noticed a hand protruding through the slats under the roof of the last wagon. What had disturbed him more than anything else was the fact that the fingers had belonged to a child who was obviously perched on the shoulders of an adult.

Jackson walked into the hallway of number 83 rue Keller, checked the list of tenants, and discovered that Madame Mortier lived on the ground floor. The woman who answered the door eyed the large attaché case at his feet, inquired after his aunt in Caen, and looked relieved when he replied that she had just been evacuated to Carentan. Fletcher was waiting for him in the living room with the contact, a compact, athletic-looking man who had tufts of dark hair growing on both cheekbones.

"You're late," said Fletcher.

"So it would seem." Jackson placed the attaché case on the dining table. "Aren't you going to introduce me to our friend?"

"Sure, this is Pierre."

Dufoir acknowledged the introduction with a curt nod.

"Now tell me what kept you."

"We had to wait outside Paris until a prison train had been shunted into a siding."

"A prison train?"

Jackson scowled. "That's what I said."

"I'm sorry I asked."

"There were women and children among them."

"They were probably Jews on their way to a concentration camp."

Both men looked at Dufoir. "How would you know?" Fletcher asked softly.

"Because it's my business to know these things."

"My mother is Jewish."

Fletcher raised his eyebrows. "Now I know what makes you tick, Jackson. It's a shame we can't go after the Germans, but that's life, I guess. Isn't that right, Pierre?"

"There is no freedom of choice in a war."

"Holbrook wouldn't agree with you."

"That would appear to be his trouble."

"And ours," said Fletcher, "if we don't find him in a hurry."

"You may get a chance to grab him in Mantes tomorrow. He's arranged to meet the Resistance leader for La Roche-Guyon in the station buffet at noon. Naturally, our man won't be there but he's not to know that." Dufoir examined his fingernails. "Of course, Holbrook may decide not to keep the appointment, but it's worth a try."

"Maybe it is but we can't touch him in broad daylight."

Jackson pulled out a chair from the dining table and straddled it, resting his chin on the back rest. "We could always tail him, Harry, find his hiding place, and wait until dark before we make our next move."

"With the necessary papers, you can arrest him whenever you like," Dufoir said calmly.

"What papers?"

"Ones that will identify you as police officers."

A broad grin appeared on Fletcher's face. "You know what?" he said cheerfully. "I think we're in business."

"There is just one thing." Dufoir pointed to the attaché case.

"If, as I suspect, you've got a transceiver concealed in there, you can hand it over now."

Jackson uncoiled himself from the chair and stood up. "Give me one good reason why we should."

"Because you will get no help from us unless you do." Dufoir smiled. "Orders from the Central Committee; any messages for London will go through me."

12

The morning had started badly for Newstead with an entry on the duty officer's log which read: *From BCRA to SOE. Your hunters have established base in Paris and made contact with Albert circuit.*

De Gaulle's intelligence service had professed to be equally perplexed to know why Fletcher had used the Free French radio net instead of his own set. They did, however, offer a possible explanation; perhaps, they said, the SOE transmitter had been damaged in the drop. Parker, who'd thought this theory sounded unconvincing, had become even more suspicious when his opposite number in Duke Street subsequently offered to seek further details from the Albert circuit. Since it was impossible for SOE to check the facts, it had become painfully obvious that, whether by accident or design, Fletcher and Jackson would be controlled by the Bureau Central de Renseignements et d'Action in future.

The Funkspiel was also running into difficulties. Both the War Office and 21 Army Group remained unconvinced that the tactical deployment of the Wehrmacht in Normandy could be influenced by feeding the bogus station in Chartres with false information. Newstead could see they had a point. It had required a vast and elaborate deception plan before D Day to convince the German High Command that the major landings would take place in the Pas de Calais, and SOE simply didn't have the manpower or the resources to stage a repeat performance on that scale.

Reluctantly, Newstead had come to the conclusion that, in the circumstances, it would be difficult if not impossible to hoodwink the operations staff at Army Group B and no useful purpose would be served by continuing with the farce. Although he was tempted to send the Abwehr a sarcastic message to inform them that the game was over, he knew that Parker would insist on a more dramatic and vicious ending. Blood would have to be spilled before honor was satisfied.

"We must give them an unpleasant surprise," he said, voicing his thoughts aloud.

Lewis looked up from the file he was reading. "Who are you referring to?"

"The Abwehr detachment in Chartres. Our little game with them has got to end with a bang, not a whimper." Newstead leaned back in his chair, suddenly pleased with himself. "That's it," he said.

"What is?"

"We end it with a bang."

"Well, I suppose if we knew the exact location of their headquarters in Chartres, we could always go and drop a bomb on it."

"I've got a better idea. Why not tempt them into a target area of our own choosing?"

"What are we going to use for bait, Dennis, a supply drop?"

"No, that isn't tempting enough. We need to come up with something which will make their mouths positively water. Something like a troop of SAS. I think they would lay on quite a show if they thought we were going to send in a party of twenty-five men. They'd have at least a company on the ground to meet them."

"I wonder if they really would buy it?"

"Well, we're not going to spring it on them just like that," Newstead said irritably.

Lewis had a fine analytical mind, but there were times when he showed little or no imagination. The situation in Normandy was hardly fluid, and there had been some ill-informed criticism of Montgomery's tactics in the press which would certainly have reached the Abwehr through neutral sources. From the German point of view, therefore, it would be logical for the British to step up the level of Resistance activity behind the lines. Newstead reckoned he could count on the support of the Overseas Service of the BBC to create this impression by broadcasting a flood of messages. If the volume equaled the peak number transmitted on the eve of D Day, the Abwehr station at Chartres might be deceived into thinking that SOE was planning a large-scale operation.

There was, however, one snag. Unless Church had kept his mouth shut, which seemed unlikely, it was reasonable to assume that the German Intelligence Service had started the radio war in the full knowledge that Holbrook was still at large. It had been a calculated risk on their part but it was vital that SOE took advantage of their eagerness before they assumed that London knew that the Foxhound station had been turned around.

Newstead pushed his glasses up on to his forehead and rubbed his eyes. "How good are you on nursery rhymes?"

"I had a very deprived childhood," Lewis said dryly. "Nobody ever read me a story in bed."

"Now's your chance to fill a gap in your life. You can trot round to the London Reference Library in St. James's Square."

Lewis wondered if Newstead had suddenly taken leave of his senses. "You're pulling my leg, aren't you?"

"I'm certainly not joking. I want a list of phrases—the cow jumped over the moon, Jack and Jill went up the hill, the little dog laughed to see such sport, Old King Cole was a merry old soul—that sort of thing."

"You don't need my help, Dennis, you're doing all right on your own."

"I've given you four but we need at least two hundred. You'll have to do a lot of checking to ensure that not one single quotation has already been used in a broadcast message to the Resistance."

"How long have I got to produce your list?"

"Oh, there's no great hurry," Newstead said airily. "First thing on Monday morning will do. You can spend the weekend on it; that ought to give you plenty of time. Provided Parker has no objections, I'll start the ball rolling tonight with a directive addressed to the Foxhound cell."

Lewis leveled an accusing finger. "You haven't cleared this project with him yet, have you?"

"No, but I'm about to." Newstead adjusted his glasses and

stood up. "Don't give it another thought," he said crisply, "Parker will go along with the idea because he hates to be defeated. You mark my words, he will see this as a way to even the score."

Gabrielle Marsac walked into the crowded station buffet at Mantes, saw at a glance that every table had been taken, and, not wishing to appear obvious, decided to join the line which had formed at the self-service counter. By the time she had collected a cup of watery-looking coffee, there was a vacant chair near the entrance. A harassed, poorly dressed woman with two small children gave her a wan smile when she asked if she might share their table.

A high-pitched, nerve-grating screech coming from the public address system preceded a message that was almost unintelligible. Gabrielle caught the words ". . . train, Rouen, delayed for . . ." and glanced inquiringly at the woman seated opposite her.

The woman shrugged her shoulders in a resigned gesture. "Another half-hour delay, Mademoiselle." She sighed. "The way things are going, we will be lucky if we get to Rouen today."

"How long have you been waiting?"

"Since nine o'clock, almost three hours." She glanced at her children. "It's very hard on them, they're so looking forward to staying with their grandmother. I don't know what I'm going to do if the train is canceled."

"I'm sure it won't be."

"You never know in wartime." Her face crumpled without any warning, and the tears began to stream down her face. Opening the handbag on her lap, she took out a handkerchief and dried her eyes. "I'm sorry, it's just that I'm so dreadfully worried." She sniffed and somehow managed to stifle a sob. "You see, my husband's just been taken to the hospital. The doctors say he has a duodenal ulcer but I think it's cancer."

"You mustn't distress yourself like this." Gabrielle reached across the table and squeezed her hand. "The doctors wouldn't lie to you, would they?"

"You don't know them like I do." She searched through her handbag and found a crumpled packet of cigarettes. "I watched him wasting away until he was nothing but skin and bone before they decided it was an ulcer."

She rambled on, describing her husband's symptoms in minute detail, pausing only now and then to puff nervously on the cigarette before continuing with the monologue. With some relief, Gabrielle realized that there was no need for her to say anything; the woman just wanted somebody to listen while she unburdened herself. Talking about her husband was a kind of therapy that made her feel better.

For the third time in the space of half an hour, Gabrielle looked around the buffet hoping to spot the contact from La Roche-Guyon. There were three oldish-looking men that she could see, but they were not alone. She thought the whole business verged on the ridiculous because Holbrook had been unable to describe Marcel Gilbert in any detail, and when he'd arranged the rendezvous Cheval had omitted to point out that there were two railway stations in Mantes. It was just conceivable that Gilbert was waiting patiently at Mantes-la-Jolie for somebody to get in touch with him.

The public address system clicked into life again with a harsh discord and then settled into a low-pitched hum. The same nasal voice made a further announcement which, although garbled, led to a sudden exodus. The woman smiled at Gabrielle, tucked her handbag under an arm, and, clutching a battered suitcase in one hand and a shopping bag in the other, herded both children toward the exit. Within a few minutes, the buffet was half empty.

Jackson couldn't take his eyes off the girl with the long chestnut hair and shapely legs who was now sitting alone at a table near the entrance. He had noticed her the moment she had walked into the crowded buffet because he'd always had an eye for an attractive woman and she was positively striking.

"She's getting anxious," he muttered.

Fletcher stubbed his cigarette out in a saucer. "Who is?" he growled.

"The dish over there near the door. Who do you suppose she's waiting for?"

"How would I know? Maybe the boyfriend has stood her up."

"Would you?"

Fletcher studied the girl thoughtfully. "She must be pushing thirty, but I'd still make room for her in my bed."

"I suppose she could be having an affair with a married man who's suddenly developed cold feet, but somehow I doubt it."

"For Christ's sake," Fletcher said irritably, "does it matter who's screwing her? We're here to pick up Holbrook, not some fancy-looking tart."

"I haven't forgotten." Jackson rubbed his jaw. "It's just that her behavior seems odd to me. You may not have noticed it, but until that woman with the two small children left the table she kept looking around the room."

"So what? She was probably hoping to find her boyfriend."

"I don't think so. She would have recognized him at a glance if he'd been there. I've got a hunch that the man she is expecting to meet is a complete stranger."

"You and your hunches," Fletcher said scathingly. "Look, for all we know, she could be a bloody tart on the make."

"With a liking for old men?"

Suddenly it all began to make sense and there was no need for Jackson to elaborate. Holbrook was no fool; knowing the Albert circuit had tried to grab him before, he would naturally assume that they could be waiting for him at the rendezvous. Since Paris had become too hot for him, it was only logical to suppose he must have looked up an old friend who was both willing to hide him and act as a go-between.

"Are you thinking what I'm thinking?"

Jackson pursed his lips. "I reckon he could be using that woman."

"So do I." Fletcher picked up a teaspoon and tapped it against the saucer. "Tailing her shouldn't be too difficult if we ring the changes and pull in Vallin."

"Okay, who's going to take first crack?"

"Looks like you are," said Fletcher.

Gabrielle glanced at her wristwatch, saw that it was past one o'clock, and decided it was time she left. Holbrook had said to give it no more than an hour, but she had hung on longer hoping that Gilbert might show up at the last minute.

There were still quite a few passengers milling about in the concourse, but the station was not nearly as crowded as it had been. Pausing only to buy a magazine from the news vendor, Gabrielle strolled into the ticket office, found an empty pay phone, and dialed the number Holbrook had given her.

A woman said, "Hôtel Nid du Mage. May I help you?"

Gabrielle pushed the button and waited until the coins had dropped into the box. "I believe you have a Monsieur André Beauvais staying with you," she said.

"That's correct."

"May I speak to him, please?"

"Who shall I say is calling?"

"Madame Marsac."

"One moment, please."

The moment stretched into several minutes. Two military policemen wandered into the ticket office and almost immediately picked on an inoffensive-looking private whom they stopped and searched. Out of the corner of her eye, Gabrielle watched the taller of the two corporals going through the contents of the soldier's kitbag while the other examined every document in his possession.

Holbrook said, "Gabrielle?"

"Yes."

"How did you get on?"

"I'm afraid I didn't have any luck. I could try elsewhere if you like."

There was a longish pause and she could picture him frowning at the telephone, annoyed because she had departed from their simple code.

"I don't think you will find anything in Mantes-la-Jolie," he said pointedly. "At least, not anything you can't get in the shops here in town."

"You don't have to lay it on so thick," she said. "I can take a hint."

"Of course, if you still draw a blank, you can always write to the manufacturers, but I wouldn't bank on getting an early reply."

In a roundabout way, he was warning her that he might have to lie low for a while if things looked bad.

"I won't," she said. "I know only too well how unreliable the post can be these days."

Gabrielle replaced the phone and left the booth. The MPs were still questioning the unfortunate soldier.

Jackson followed her at a discreet interval, hanging well back until she had crossed the yard in front of the station. As he came down the steps, Fletcher, who was waiting on the approach road with Vallin, signaled that she had turned left on the Boulevard Calmette. Apparently unaware that she was being followed, Gabrielle then turned left again at the next intersection, crossing the railway bridge to head southeast on the rue de Verdun. As they approached the shopping center, Vallin overtook them in the Citroën and dropped Fletcher off at the junction with the Avenue Jean Jaures.

Holbrook adjusted the net curtains and moved the chair closer to the window until he was satisfied that he could watch the marketplace without being seen by anyone from the opposite side of the square. There was still a blind spot directly below the hotel bedroom, but he thought that wouldn't matter so long as Gabrielle remembered to steer clear of it.

A black Citroën turned off the Avenue Jean Jaures, drove slowly around the square, and then parked outside a furniture shop opposite the Nid du Mage. A few moments later, Gabrielle turned the corner and strolled into the marketplace. A dress in the window of a boutique next door but one to the furniture store appeared to catch her eye, and she stopped to examine it more closely. Some twenty yards farther back, a heavily built man wearing a dark navy blue suit suddenly turned about and wheeled into a tobacconist's.

Gabrielle stepped back from the window, hesitated just long enough to give the impression that she was sorely tempted to buy the dress, and then moved on. The man in the navy blue suit left the tobacconist's and walked diagonally across the square. Craning his neck to get a better view, Holbrook saw that he was keeping pace with her on the opposite side of the marketplace. Moments after she had walked into a hairdressing salon, the

Citroën pulled out from the curb, made two left turns, and crawled past the hotel.

Holbrook stood up and moved away from the window. The pantomime wouldn't end until Gabrielle returned to the boutique and bought a dress, but he had already seen enough to know that she was being followed. There were at least two of them, but since the driver was no great help he thought it likely there was a third man. If Gabrielle wasn't aware of it yet, she would know for certain when he failed to show up at the bus terminal on time.

They had discussed what she should do in such a situation, and, providing she adhered to his advice, there was a good chance that she could bluff them into thinking they had made a mistake. Unfortunately, by her behavior at the railway station, Gabrielle had shown a tendency to ignore his instructions and rely on her own judgment.

They had rung the changes twice and Fletcher thought it was about time they stopped kidding themselves, because Jackson's hunch wasn't getting them anywhere. For more than two hours the bitch had led them on a wild goose chase all over town, and while she might be quite innocent Fletcher was determined to put the fear of God into her. Nudging him in the ribs, he told Vallin to pull out from the curb and overtake her.

Jackson saw both men leap out of the Citroën and wondered what the hell they were playing at. By the time he caught up with them, Fletcher had already grabbed the woman and bundled her into the back seat of the car while Vallin seemed ready to take off without him. Wrenching the door open, he scrambled into the front seat a split second before Vallin shifted into gear and gunned the engine.

Fletcher leaned forward and dropped a handbag into Jackson's lap. "Here," he growled. "Go through this and see if you can find her papers. I think she's telling us a pack of lies."

"You've no right to arrest me," Gabrielle said defiantly. "I haven't done anything. I keep telling you, I'm Madame Charles Marsac. My maiden name was Estaing and my father was a minister of state under Édouard Daladier."

Fletcher moved his elbow, winding her with a sharp blow under the heart. Gabrielle retched and doubled up, her eyes watering as the pain stabbed through her body. Slowly, she regained her breath and sat up, her face distorted with anger.

"You pig," she screamed, "you dirty rotten pig!"

Fletcher saw her lips purse; before he could turn his head away, a gob of spit landed on his cheek. Lashing out, he caught her a vicious backhander across the mouth.

Jackson twisted around, grabbed Fletcher by his shirt, and slammed him back against the seat. "For Christ's sake," he snarled, "what's got into you?"

"The bitch spat at me."

"Well, you asked for it. Here, take a look at this." Jackson shoved the identity card under his nose. "Her name is Madame Gabrielle Marsac and she lives at 32 rue des Loges, Saint-Germainen-Laye."

"Then what's she doing here in Mantes?"

Jackson relaxed his grip on Fletcher and smiled at Gabrielle. "There's no need to be frightened," he said. "Just answer his questions, and I promise you I won't let him hit you again."

Gabrielle explored her split lip with the tip of her tongue and winced. "Why should I?" she asked faintly. "I haven't done anything wrong."

"Didn't my friend show you his warrant card?"

"He did, but I'd like to see it again."

"Why?"

"Because I intend to report him to the prefect of police."

Fletcher stretched out a hand and dug his fingers into her thigh. "What did I tell you?" he said. "She's a troublemaker."

"And I told you to leave her alone." Jackson smiled at her again. "Come on," he said. "Why be difficult?"

Gabrielle hesitated. The story Holbrook had concocted for her had sounded convincing at the time, but now she wondered if it would hold up.

"I'm divorced," she said nervously.

"Yes?"

"Well, I met this man in Paris a few months ago and we formed an attachment."

"You mean you've got a lover," Fletcher said harshly.

"Yes." She stared at her lap to avoid his gaze. "I knew he was married but I always understood they were separated because he told me he was going to get an annulment."

"On what grounds?"

"He said their marriage had never been consummated."

"But he never had any problems with you, did he?" Fletcher squeezed her thigh again and she thought she was going to be sick. "I bet you couldn't wait to drop your pants."

"I think I'm pregnant." Gabrielle drew her breath in sharply. There had been no need to embroider the original cover story, but it was too late now to have any regrets because the damage had been done. "That's why I came to Mantes," she said huskily.

"To see an abortionist?" Jackson suggested quietly.

"Yes. I mean, no."

"What do you mean?"

She stared at Jackson, her heart thumping against her ribs. She had made another foolish mistake. She couldn't understand why she had fallen in with his suggestion so readily. Committed now, she stumbled on. "He said he knew a doctor here in Mantes who might be able to help me. I was waiting for him at the station but he never showed up."

"Who? The doctor?"

"No, my friend," Gabrielle said weakly. "I telephoned his office in Paris, but he said something had come up and he couldn't get away."

She glanced out of the window and wondered where they were taking her. Mantes was a long way behind them now and they were heading into open country.

"And then what did you do?" Jackson asked softly.

"I went into town and bought a dress to cheer myself up."

"This friend of yours?" said Fletcher. "Does he have a name and address?"

They had arrived at the moment of truth. If she lied to them now they would know where to find her again. Gabrielle thought she had perhaps a minute in which to think of someone among her many acquaintances who would be prepared to back up her story, someone who was married and could be taken for her lover.

"What will you do to him?" she muttered.

"Nothing. We'll just ask him a few questions about you, that's all."

"De Neury. His name is Roland de Neury."

Fletcher took out a notebook. "And the address?"

"Four twenty-eight rue Saint-Honoré, Paris."

"For your sake, I hope you're telling the truth."

"You've got my name and address," she said in a dull voice.

"That we have." Fletcher leaned forward and tapped Vallin on the shoulder. "Make a U-turn," he said, "and then stop so that we can drop her off."

"Here?" said Gabrielle. "How will I get back to town?"

"Try catching a bus."

Fletcher opened the door, placed a hand on her shoulder, and shoved Gabrielle out of the car before it had stopped moving. Grabbing the handbag from Jackson, he tossed it into the road along with the dress and then slammed the door.

"All right," he said, "what are we waiting for?"

"This," said Jackson and punched him in the mouth.

Gabrielle heard the Citroën drive off and struggled to her feet. The fall had skinned her hands and knees and the grazes were already beginning to smart. For a moment she was unable to grasp what had happened, but then she noticed that the contents of her handbag were scattered all over the road and she began to tremble. It also slowly dawned on her that Holbrook would steer clear of Saint-Germain until he was satisfied that she was not being watched by the police. And then she started to cry.

Church decoded the message and handed it to Burghardt. Prefixed URGENT, it read:

FOR FOXHOUND. PRESENT SITUATION IN NORMANDY DEMANDS THAT WE SHOULD STEP UP LEVEL OF RESISTANCE ACTIVITY IN REAR AREAS IN ORDER TO PIN DOWN MAXIMUM NUMBER OF TROOPS ON INTERNAL SECURITY. EVERY MILITARY INSTALLATION AS WELL AS ALL CONVOYS MOVING THROUGH YOUR SECTOR MUST BE ATTACKED AT EVERY OPPORTUNITY. APPRECIATE FORCES AT YOUR DISPOSAL MAY

NOT BE EQUAL TO THESE TASKS. PROPOSE THEREFORE TO REINFORCE YOU WITH ONE TROOP SAS. PLEASE ADVISE SOONEST WHEN YOU ARE IN POSITION TO RECEIVE THEM.

"Don't you want to check it first?" asked Church.

"It isn't necessary." Burghardt smiled. "You see, I've learned to trust you, Captain Church."

"I wonder if I can trust you."

"What is that supposed to mean?"

Church cleared his throat noisily. "I'd like to know what you intend to do about this directive?"

Burghardt scratched his head. Church had voiced the question that was uppermost in his mind, though he doubted if they were thinking along the same lines. The Funkspiel had always been a calculated risk, and it was possible that SOE had heard from Holbrook and were wise to his little game. On the other hand, the message from Bicester made a lot of sense in view of the present stalemate in Normandy, and there was no reason, as far as he could see, to suppose it wasn't genuine. It would certainly be the coup of a lifetime, but he would need to play it carefully in case the British thought he was a little too eager.

"Well," he said, "for the time being, I think we ought to give Bicester a QSL."

"For the time being?"

"Until we have had time to consider what our next move should be." Burghardt saw the strained expression on his face and guessed what Church was thinking. "Compose yourself, captain," he said harshly. "I don't want your hand to tremble on the Morse key."

13

Vallin wondered how much longer the storm would last. Opening the glove compartment, he found a duster and wiped off the condensation that was fogging up the windshield. The rain was still coming down in torrents, and he supposed Dufoir was probably waiting for it to ease up a little before he left his office in the Préfecture. Vallin opened the side window to let in a cool draught of air and then lit a cigarette.

A few minutes later, Dufoir emerged from a side entrance with a raincoat over his head and ran toward the Citroën, swerving frequently to avoid the puddles lying on the uneven surface of the parking lot. Vallin opened the door and he scrambled into the car, shucking the raincoat onto the back seat.

Vallin said, "I thought you would wait for a break in the weather, *patron.*"

Dufoir grunted and brushed a palm over his hair, smoothing it back into place. "You left word that you wanted to see me urgently."

"That's right."

"Well, then, what's your problem?"

"I'm not happy about this assignment, *patron.*" Vallin removed a shred of tobacco clinging to his lower lip and flicked it on to the floor. "The American is all right, but the Englishman is dangerous."

"In what way?"

Vallin tapped his temple with a finger. "He's crazy. He beat up a woman in Mantes yesterday for no good reason. The American tried to restrain him; as a matter of fact, he punched him in the mouth." He shook his head as if still unable to believe what had happened. "You'd think they would save their energies for the Boche."

Dufoir gritted his teeth and wished Vallin would get on with it. "Who was this woman?" he asked impatiently.

"According to her papers, she's a Madame Gabrielle Marsac. I don't know whether it's true or not, but she claims her father was a minister of state under Édouard Daladier. For what it's worth, she lives in a pretty classy area of Saint-Germain." Vallin opened the ashtray in the dashboard and stubbed out his cigarette. "She threatened to report the Englishman to the prefect of police, but I think she's bluffing."

"Suppose you give me the story from the beginning."

Vallin knew he deserved the mild rebuke. He had been with the patron long enough to know that he expected to be given the facts without any verbal frills. Dufoir was a good detective, one of the best; given the right breaks, he could be commissioner of police one day.

"The American had a hunch that Holbrook was using her as a go-between, so we followed her all over town and I must say she led us on a wild goose chase. Anyway, the Englishman was convinced she was up to something and he grabbed her off the street."

"Were there any witnesses?" Dufoir asked sharply.

"No, I don't think so. We were well off the beaten track at the time." Vallin lit another cigarette and slowly exhaled. "We asked her what she was doing in Mantes, and she spun us a yarn about some lover who'd arranged for her to see an abortionist. She insisted she had no idea which doctor was going to perform the operation but in the end she gave us the name and address of her lover, a Roland de Neury of four twenty-eight rue Saint-Honoré."

"De Neury?"

"You know him, *patron?*"

"The name seems to ring a bell somewhere." Dufoir scratched an itch on his cheek. "You'd better watch your step with him."

"If it's all the same to you," said Vallin, "I'd rather not interview him. I mean, suppose he denies everything?"

"Then the American could be right, perhaps Holbrook was using her as a go-between."

"That's what worries me." Vallin drummed his fingers on the steering wheel. "If the Englishman discovers that she has been lying to us, there's no telling what he would do to her, and we might not get away with it next time. Like I said, *patron,* he's a madman."

There was an anxious expression on his face which disturbed Dufoir. Vallin was not the worrying kind and he was a good man to have at your side in a tight corner, but it was evident that the Englishman made him feel very nervous. It was all very well for Paupal to make light of their difficulties, but Dufoir thought there was a very bad smell about this whole business with SOE.

"I think you had better call me after you've seen de Neury. I'll be in the office until one; after that you can reach me at home."

"Yes, *patron.*" Vallin peered through the windshield. The rain had eased off a lot and he thought he could see a break in the clouds. "It looks as if the weather is beginning to clear up," he said diffidently.

"Good. That means you won't get wet." Dufoir grabbed his raincoat and opened the door. "Don't look so surprised," he said. "The walk will do you good; a little exercise might even reduce your waistline."

"But I've just drawn this car from the transport pool," Vallin protested.

"Return it and save the gasoline." Dufoir smiled grimly. "Don't you know there's a war on?" he said.

Gabrielle stared at her reflection in the mirror. The lower lip had swollen up like a balloon and no amount of makeup would hide the fact that both eyes were bloodshot. A nerve ticked on the left lid. It was almost as if the tense, pale face belonged to a stranger instead of herself. In the stillness of the house, the sudden jangle of the telephone startled her and she knocked a silver compact off the dressing table, spilling face powder onto the carpet. Roland, her mind raced, it had to be Roland; his wife, Céline, must have passed on her message and he was telephoning at last to see what she wanted. No longer apprehensive, she rushed downstairs and ran into the study to answer it.

The operator said, "Saint-Germain six-six-five-five-four-three?"

She frowned, knowing that it couldn't be Roland after all.

"Yes, this is six-six-five-five-four-three," she said listlessly.

"You're through, caller."

Holbrook said, "Gabrielle? It's me—André."

"Oh."

"You sound surprised."

"I am. I didn't expect to hear from you again."

"Are you all right?"

"More or less." Her voice was brittle. "I'm touched you should ask."

"You're angry."

"Do you blame me?"

"No," he said quietly, "I don't blame you."

"Where are you?"

"In a phone booth."

"I see, it's like that, is it?"

"Now you know I'll come home as soon as I can."

"Do I?" Her eyes began to blink. "I need you so much, André."

"I need you too."

"I wonder. Sometimes I think you just make use of me."

"You're wrong." She heard him clear his throat. "Look, if nothing comes up in the meantime, I'll see you on Tuesday."

"Promise?"

"I'll do my best; I can't say more than that, can I?"

"No," she said miserably. "No, I can understand there may be difficulties."

"Well, then. . . . Take care of yourself, Gabrielle."

And you too, she wanted to say, but there was a purring tone on the line and she realized he had already hung up. She started to replace the receiver but then, abruptly changing her mind, she flashed the operator.

A different woman said, "Can I help you?"

"Yes." Gabrielle swallowed hard. "I've been cut off," she said nervously.

"What number were you calling?"

"It was an incoming call. My friend was ringing from a pay phone and . . ."

"I see. One moment, please."

Gabrielle picked up a pencil and drew a series of question marks on the memo pad.

"Are you there, caller?"

"Yes."

"The number you want is Pontoise seven-four-eight-two-one. I've tried ringing but I'm afraid there's no answer. Perhaps your friend will call back later."

"Yes, I expect he will. Thank you for trying anyway."

Gabrielle replaced the telephone and looked at the number she had written on the pad. Pontoise was only a few miles north of Saint-Germain. She guessed that Holbrook had doubled back on his tracks because he was afraid to move south of Mantes to Dreux or Évreux where he might be recognized. He couldn't afford to spend more than one night in the same hotel either, because he was still using the identity papers supplied by Racheline, but he didn't have an inexhaustible supply of money, and sooner or later he would have to stop running.

Gabrielle looked at the telephone number again and decided she ought to burn it while it was still fresh in her mind and before she made another attempt to get in touch with Roland de Neury.

Deep in thought, Holbrook strolled toward the town center. Gabrielle had sounded on edge, as if her nerves were stretched to breaking point, and he wondered if she was being watched. Certainly the opposition had been tailing her in Mantes yesterday, and it was quite possible that, tired of being led on a wild goose chase, they had picked her up for questioning. Gabrielle had never been an accomplished liar; one slip of the tongue and a good interrogator would have her tied up in knots. First demolish the cover story and then let her go? It made sense, good sense. Dufoir had probably guessed that there was no one else he could turn to for help. Gabrielle was to be the tempting morsel on the hook, and it didn't matter that he could see and smell the trap because Dufoir knew that in the end he wouldn't have any choice but to swallow the bait.

Trouble came sooner than Holbrook had anticipated, and it arrived in the shape of two men who stepped out of an alleyway to block his path. One was about five foot six and moon-faced, the other lean but wiry and a good head taller. The small man snapped his fingers and asked to see his identity card and work permit. There was no "please" or "may I," just a terse command delivered in an accent that wasn't French.

"My papers? Yes, of course." Holbrook stretched his face into a sickly smile, knowing that this was the sort of nervous reaction the Gestapo would expect from most Frenchmen in these circumstances. Reaching inside his breast pocket, he produced a leather wallet that had seen better days. "I think you'll find they're in order," he said ingratiatingly.

The small German riffled through the contents and extracted the identity card which Racheline had forged. "You're André Beauvais?"

"That's right."

"You're a long way from Dreux, aren't you?"

"I'm here on business." Holbrook moistened his lips. "If you look at my work permit you'll see that I'm an insurance agent."

"Yes?"

"For the Mutual Life Guard; their head office is in Paris and I work for them on a commission basis, selling everything you can think of: auto, third party, fire and theft, death benefit, endowment policies, that sort of thing."

"Are you staying in a hotel?"

"Yes, the Floréal on the rue de Saint-Ouen."

The tall silent man took out a notebook and wrote down the address. Looking over the shoulder of his companion at the identity card, he laboriously copied out Holbrook's physical description.

"When are you returning to Dreux, Monsieur Beauvais?"

"Before lunch or early this afternoon, depending on how long it takes to complete my business here."

"You're on your way to see a client now, is that it?"

It was only a snap check, one of the hazards of wartime France, but they were probing a lot deeper than was usually the case. Holbrook wondered if they suspected that his identity card and work permit might be forgeries. His mind raced. Should he kill them, chop and break the small man's neck and then jab his friend in the throat to sever the vocal cords before he had time to drop the notebook and propelling pencil? In broad daylight, in a small town with a population of twenty thousand which could be sealed tighter than a drum before he even reached the bus depot? No, that was stupid. Put your trust in Racheline's pen and ink artist and remember what they taught you at the Special Training School. You've been through it all before and you can do it again.

"Yes, I am, as a matter of fact."

"Without a briefcase? What if your client asks to see a brochure?"

"I have a booklet on me." Holbrook produced a small, dog-eared pamphlet from his inside pocket and gave it to him. "There is an actuary table in the back, a sort of guide which enables me to frame a policy to suit the particular needs of the investor. Of course, I do have some more literature back at the hotel but as it happens I don't need any brochures this morning." He smiled in a way that suggested he was eager to be helpful. "The man I am going to see wants a tailor-made policy."

"Does he have a name?"

They were pushing him into a corner, pressing for details that could be verified. He had taken the precaution of going through the telephone directory shortly after he'd checked into the hotel, but this interrogation was a lot shrewder than he'd bargained for. Contingency planning was all very well, but once he gave them a name they would ask for an address, and then, if things really went sour, it might only be a question of time before his cover was blown and André Beauvais appeared on the Gestapo's wanted list.

"Tanant," Holbrook said slowly. "Dr. Pierre Tanant."

"And the address?"

"Seventeen Place du Petit-Martroy."

The small German returned his wallet and papers with a condescending smile and stepped to one side. There was no explanation, no apology, but Holbrook knew that he was free to go, free to go where he liked within limits. He had gained a breathing space of one or perhaps two hours if he was lucky. One thing was certain: he would have to leave Pontoise, find another hiding place, and change his identity. Change his identity? How? He was alone, cut off from all contact with the Resistance, the only people who could supply him with the necessary papers. Perhaps he could steal them—yes, that was it—find a man who had roughly the same physical characteristics and then lift his wallet.

Holbrook turned the corner into the rue Thiers and lengthened his stride. The solution wasn't that simple. Only a skilled pickpocket could lift a wallet on the street, extract an identity card, and return the damn thing without the victim's being any the wiser. To have any hope of success he would have to catch the man in an unguarded moment when he was preoccupied. Preoccupied with what? A woman? His eyebrows met in one long furrow. So now we're looking for two people, are we? A man and a woman so wrapped up in each other that they're lost in a dream world. And just where are you going to find a pair of lovers at this time of the day, except maybe in a brothel. A brothel? Hell, yes, a man would take off more than his jacket in a brothel and he would be preoccupied, all right.

The euphoric feeling lasted all of a minute before he realized that the plan was impractical. It involved too many risks, too many people, and even if he did manage to pull it off, the identity card would still defeat him because he would have to switch the photographs, a task which even a good forger would be reluctant to tackle. Whether he liked it or not, he was stuck with André Beauvais. It was a bit of a Hobson's choice, but at least his papers had withstood one close scrutiny and that was something to be thankful for. With any luck, he wouldn't be in Pontoise by the time the Gestapo got in touch with the good doctor. And then the answer came to him in a flash of blind inspiration, a plan that was both foolproof and yet simple to execute.

Looking for a pay phone, he found one in a bar across the street and dialed Tanant's surgery. The receptionist was reluctant to put him through at first but he managed to talk her around. The good doctor wasn't so amenable, but that was all to the good since the phone call was likely to make a lasting impression on him.

Holbrook said, "Dr. Tanant? My name is Beauvais, André Beauvais. I believe I have an appointment to see you at twelve thirty this morning?"

"Are you one of my patients?"

"No, I represent the Mutual Life Guard. I understand you received a letter from them."

"The Mutual Life Guard?" Tanant sounded very puzzled. "Who are they, Monsieur Beauvais?"

Holbrook smiled; the name had been planted and now he could build on it. "An insurance company," he said smoothly.

"In that case, I'm not interested."

"Well, how very odd." Holbrook cleared his throat noisily. "The head office led me to understand that you had asked for more information. They did send you some of our brochures, didn't they?"

"They did not."

"But I was told to call on you. You are Dr. Pierre Tanant of Seventeen Place du Petit-Martroy?"

"I am, and I'm still not interested in buying an insurance policy from you. Now if you don't mind, Monsieur Beauvais, I am a very busy man—"

"Of course. Please accept my apologies, Monsieur le Docteur. There seems to have been some mistake."

"I'm inclined to agree with you," said Tanant.

Holbrook put the phone down and left the bar. One loophole had been closed, and he now had a good excuse to check out of the hotel. He would collect his suitcase, go to the station, and buy a ticket to Dreux which would take him via Paris. To be absolutely safe, he would get the booking clerk to look up the timetable to make sure the man remembered him.

Everything fitted together like a neat jigsaw; his cover was still intact and the Gestapo would get nowhere. Once in Paris, he would lie low for a few days and figure out a way to get in touch with Gabrielle again.

Vallin had always thought that the rue du Faubourg Saint-Honoré was one of the longest streets in Paris. By the time he had walked from the Avenue de Wagram northwest of the Arc de Triomphe, past the haute couture fashion houses in the vicinity of the Élysée, to de Neury's apartments near the Place Vendôme, he was convinced of it. He also wished he'd had the foresight to look up the address in a street directory before taking the Métro out to Ternes. It was too late now, but it was galling to think that he could have saved himself a long hike if he'd caught a train to the Palais Royal.

Vallin could see that de Neury had not allowed the war to interfere with his way of life. Despite compulsory direction of labor, he still managed to retain a butler and two footmen. The number of leather gloves, swagger canes, and dress hats belonging to senior officers of the Wehrmacht which were on the hall table showed where his sympathies lay. But nobody put out the welcome mat for Vallin; a footman examined his identity card and then swiftly ushered him into the library in a manner which clearly suggested he was unwelcome.

Earlier in his career, Vallin had spent two years with the Art Squad, and although he was no great reader he knew enough about books to realize that there were some rare first editions among the leather-bound volumes crammed on shelves which reached almost to the ceiling. Even though he had never met him, he was prepared to bet that, as with the Persian carpet which covered the huge floor and the Gauguin over the fireplace, de Neury merely regarded them as an investment.

"Sergeant Vallin?"

Vallin turned about. "Monsieur de Neury?"

"Yes. What is it that you want?"

De Neury bore no resemblance to the mental picture Vallin had conjured up. Instead of being small, fat, and pompous, he was a distinguished-looking man whose direct manner suggested he wouldn't stand for any nonsense.

"It's rather a delicate matter, sir."

"Yes?"

"I believe you are acquainted with a Madame Gabrielle Marsac?"

"That's correct. I've known her since she was a child." De Neury sat down at his desk. "Is she in some sort of trouble?"

"She was picked up in Mantes yesterday for questioning."

"Mantes?" de Neury repeated, frowning. "What was she doing in Mantes?"

Vallin thought it curious that he hadn't asked why Gabrielle Marsac had been detained by the police, but he let it pass.

"She said you were supposed to be making arrangements for her to have an abortion."

"Me?" de Neury said incredulously. "Why, that's absolutely preposterous, sergeant."

"Madame Marsac would have us believe that she is your mistress."

"I presume she was able to substantiate her story? Love letters —photographs—that sort of thing?"

"No, sir."

"And yet you believed her?" De Neury looked astonished at first but then became angry and contemptuous. "Well, let me tell you about Gabrielle Marsac, sergeant. She may be an attractive, wealthy young woman but she is also very spoiled. Her parents separated when she was quite a small child and she remained in the custody of her father, which in my opinion was most unfortunate because he was foolish enough to indulge her every whim. He allowed Gabrielle to make a disastrous marriage at the age of nineteen and she has been in and out of trouble ever since. What has she been up to this time?"

Vallin didn't bat an eyelid. "We think she's been dealing in the black market, sir," he said calmly.

"I can't say I'm very surprised." De Neury pushed back his cuff and glanced pointedly at his wristwatch. "Do you have any other questions, sergeant?"

"I'd like to clarify one point, sir, if I may?"

"Yes?"

"Are you her lover?"

Vallin saw his face darken and knew he had gone too far.

"You forget yourself, sergeant," he said coldly.

A warning note had been sounded, but Vallin was damned if he was going to allow himself to be intimidated by a smooth-talking, well-heeled collaborator.

"With respect, sir," he said doggedly, "you've avoided my question."

De Neury reversed the photograph on his desk so that Vallin could see it. The woman was quite magnificent but the camera had captured a glitter of spitefulness in her eyes.

"My wife, Céline," he said flatly. "Does that answer your question?"

"Yes, sir."

"Good. Then perhaps you will allow me to rejoin my guests."

He saw de Neury move his knee under the desk; a few moments later a footman answered the summons and escorted him to the door. It was all very polite. No one laid a finger on him, but Vallin felt as if he had been forcibly ejected from the house.

He was still burning with anger when he called Dufoir from a pay phone in the rue de Rivoli.

Dufoir, however, was not sympathetic. He said, "Well, how did you make out?"

"It was hard going; I thought he was going to turn very nasty." Vallin lit a cigarette and leaned against the booth. "Take it from me, patron, he's a real shit."

"You don't have to go into details. I've done my homework and I know he's got friends in high places."

"And they wear field gray."

"Never mind that," said Dufoir. "What did he have to say for himself?"

"He dropped the girl right in it."

"I thought he might."

"So what do I tell my new colleagues?"

"Nothing, you just stall them. Try and give the impression that he neither denied nor confirmed her story, and if they're not satisfied you can pitch them some yarn about Denise Jeanney. Let them question her if necessary; that ought to keep them happy."

Vallin smiled to himself. The patron was smart; they would get a fat lot out of that little mouse, but they weren't to know that. She had been on the run with Holbrook, and he thought it wouldn't be too difficult to plant the idea that there was a chance Holbrook might have confided in her. With any luck, they'd waste a lot of time before they tumbled to the fact that she couldn't tell them a damn thing.

"Do I find her at the same address?"

"No, she's had to move."
"That figures," said Vallin.
"She is now living at ninety-two rue de Cailloux."
"Where's that?"
"Near the cemetery in Clichy; you can't miss it."
Dufoir broke the connection before Vallin had time to think of a suitable reply.

Gabrielle moved the curtain a fraction and peered out of the study window. The man, who was standing with his back toward her, rang the bell a second time and then suddenly turned around, smiling broadly, as if he'd known all along that she had been watching him. Taken by surprise, she hastily released the curtain and backed away from the window.

It was easy enough for her to put two and two together and come up with the right answer. The police had obviously spoken to Roland, and either he or that bitch of a wife of his had refused to corroborate her story. Holbrook had always said she was a lousy judge of character, and, as in so many other instances, it seemed he was right again. Gabrielle supposed she ought to be grateful they had sent a different officer to question her instead of the pig who'd cut her lip; putting a brave face on it, she marched through the hall and opened the front door.

Dufoir smiled. "Madame Marsac?"
"Yes."
"I'm Inspector Dufoir."
"Oh, yes, you'd better come into the study." She stood to one side and then closed the door behind him. "I've been expecting you."
"You surprise me."
"I should have said that I knew a policeman would be calling on me."
"I admire your candor, madame." Dufoir followed her into the study, removed his raincoat, and draped it over a chair. "I must say it makes a refreshing change after all the lies you've told."
"I thought I could rely on an old friend like Roland de Neury."

"That was your unfortunate mistake, madame; one should never trust the de Neurys of this world. Didn't you know he was a collaborator?"

"I knew he was on good terms with the Occupation authorities."

"A masterly understatement."

Dufoir wandered around the room, restless as a caged animal. He picked a book at random from one of the shelves which took up the whole of one wall and leafed through the pages before returning it to its rightful place.

"Are all these volumes your father's?" he asked.

"Yes."

"He must have been a widely read man. Everything from reference books to the sensational erotic novel."

"His tastes were catholic, inspector."

"Quite so." A pile of albums on the bottom shelf caught his eye and he crouched down to examine them more closely. "Family photographs?"

"Yes. Do you have a search warrant?"

"Do I need one?" he countered.

They had hidden the gold under the floorboards beneath the gas stove in the kitchen. Whether Dufoir found it or not would depend on how thoroughly he intended to search the house.

"I wouldn't know, I'm not a lawyer." She shrugged her shoulders. "Feel free to look around; you won't find anything here."

"That remains to be seen," Dufoir said idly. "Many years ago when I first joined the Police Judiciaire, a very wise old detective told me that you can always find some interesting pointer at the scene of the crime if you look hard enough."

"What scene of what crime?" she snapped.

"A figure of speech, madame." Dufoir stood up. "Photograph albums have always fascinated me. You've no idea how useful they can be in my line of work." He placed the album on the desk, opening it at the page he'd marked with a finger. "I see we have a mutual friend," he said.

The snapshot had been taken in the garden of the villa in Cap d'Antibes. They were posed together, she in the middle, Charles Marsac on one side, Holbrook on the other.

"Of course he was much younger-looking then," said Dufoir.
"Who was?"
"Your friend Holbrook."
"I haven't seen him in years."
Dufoir closed the album with a flourish. "You were with him yesterday in Mantes." He placed a hand on her shoulder and gently pushed her toward a chair. "Now, you sit down and listen to me," he said.
"Why should I?"
"Because your friend is in serious trouble and you are the only person who can help him. I can't, because he doesn't trust me."
"I don't blame him."
"I still think of him as a friend. That's why I'm here." Dufoir paused, wondering how much he could safely tell her. He didn't care for her friends, but it was evident that Holbrook trusted Gabrielle Marsac. They had known one another for a long time. It was even possible that she had sheltered him when he'd been on the run in '42.
"Look," he said, "Holbrook has got this fixation; he wants to assassinate Rommel. Now, a few weeks ago everyone would have agreed that this was an admirable idea, but for some reason the situation has changed and now it's the very last thing anyone wants. He has been officially warned off, but since he refuses to take any notice, London has decided to eliminate him."
"Eliminate him?" she echoed incredulously.
"They've sent a couple of gunmen to kill him." Dufoir leaned over her. "You've already met these men; one of them is responsible for the state of your lip. Believe me, madame, if they catch up with him before I do, they won't hesitate to squeeze the trigger. That's why I need your help."
"How can I possibly help you," she said despairingly, "when I don't even know where he is?"
"I have a hunch that Holbrook will come back here when he thinks it's safe to do so." Dufoir reached inside his jacket and brought out a card. "When he does, I want you to persuade him to ring this number. If Holbrook will surrender to me, you have my word that no harm will come to him."
He had a feeling that Paupal wouldn't approve, but they could

argue about that afterward. If they weren't careful, the SOE agents could stir up a hornet's nest and jeopardize the entire Albert circuit. Offering Holbrook asylum was a practical solution to their difficulties.

Gabrielle made no move to pick up the card which Dufoir had left on the arm of her chair. "You know something, inspector?" she said. "I think you're looking for a Judas to save you the trouble of keeping this house under surveillance."

"And I thought you were an intelligent woman. If I had this house watched, the Gestapo would soon get to hear about it. Holbrook has got enough problems without the SD breathing down his neck. If nothing else, at least you could try persuading him to lie low and forget Rommel." Dufoir picked up his raincoat. "Don't bother to get up," he said curtly. "I can see myself out."

The door closed behind him with a loud bang.

14

Epp had been tempted to circle the date on his desk calendar to mark this turning point in history but had resisted the impulse in case some lynx-eyed staff officer or inquisitive clerk asked what was so special about Tuesday the eleventh of July. A crowded in-basket awaited his attention but he felt unable to tackle it, which in the circumstances was scarcely surprising. His experiences on the Eastern Front had taught him that the time spent in the final assault position was often the worst part of any operation. You were keyed up, ready and waiting for the word to go, and it was impossible to think of anything but the battle which lay ahead.

The minute hand jerked forward with an audible click, and his eyes instinctively flicked to the electric clock above the door. Two more clicks and it would be 1200 hours; two more clicks and the Führer's conference in the Berghof at Berchtesgaden would start to assemble. He could picture Stauffenberg walking into the conference room with his briefcase, perhaps exchanging a few words with Field Marshal Keitel before casually placing it under the heavy oak table . . . Hitler entering the room with Göring and Himmler, and then the scrape of chairs on the polished floor as they took their places: Keitel and Colonel General Jodl of OKW, Gruppenführer Fegelein representing the Waffen SS, Rear Admiral Voss, and General Schmundt, Adjutant to the Führer . . . Stauffenberg reaching under the table to extract the files he wanted from the briefcase and surreptitiously crimping the detonator at the same time with a tiny pair of pliers . . . the vial broken and the acid slowly eating its way through the cardboard plug to ignite the fuse . . . Stauffenberg murmuring an excuse to Keitel that he would have to check certain details with Berlin which the staff had omitted to include in his brief and then tiptoeing out of the room, anxious to be clear of the villa before the bomb exploded at ten past twelve.

Epp opened the file which lay in front of him and made a determined effort to ignore the clock. He read the memo attached to the top folio, glanced at the mass of figures the chief clerk had penciled in, and hastily placed the file on one side. Today of all days, he was in no mood to check the accuracy of the consolidated strength return of the Reserve Army. Sifting through the basket, he unearthed a "Fitness for Role" inspection report on the 648th Jaeger Regiment which was easier to digest.

The 648th, he discovered, was a hodgepodge of sixteen-year-old youths and middle-aged men leavened with German expatriates recruited from the Baltic states. The Inspector General, a man with an acid sense of humor, was of the opinion that, like Napoleon, they should be sent to Elba where they would be out of harm's way.

His eyes went to the clock again and he was surprised to see that it was eight minutes past twelve. Stauffenberg would telephone the Bendlerstrasse from Reichenhall, and that was only a twenty-minute drive from Berchtesgaden. Colonel General Olbricht, the head of the Supply Section, would be the first to hear the news, but Mertz von Quirnheim, Stauffenberg's assistant, was hovering at his elbow and he wouldn't waste any time in spreading the word. Epp removed the Walther PPK automatic from the pistol holster on his belt and pulled the slide back to chamber a 7.65mm round and then put the catch on safe. No one could be certain how Fromm would react, but if he attempted to halt Operation Valkyrie it would be Epp's not altogether pleasant duty to arrest the Commander in Chief of the Reserve Army.

Epp returned the pistol to its holster and wondered what he could do to pass the time. One obvious answer was to buckle down and clear the in-basket, but he'd already tried that and it hadn't worked. He glanced at the enlarged snapshot of his wife and children that graced a cheap wooden frame on his desk and supposed he could always write to Sophie, except that he didn't really have the inclination to do so. Sophie had become a distant figure and he no longer missed her because Anneliese had filled the gap in his life.

Epp knew of several officers who kept a woman on the side, but he could not bring himself to think of Anneliese as a mere plaything to be discarded when he grew tired of her. Although she excited him in a way that Sophie never had or ever could, there was more to their relationship than just sex. He thought the word love was a much debased expression of endearment which all too often was used to convey satisfaction and enjoyment in the heat of coitus, but he loved Anneliese in the sense that he could not imagine what life would be without her.

The sound of heavy footsteps in the corridor alerted him. He hoped it wasn't the chief clerk with another batch of files for his already overladen in-basket. Moments later, he could have wished otherwise when he saw the despondent expression on Quirnheim's face as he slouched into his office.

"Don't tell me," said Epp. "I don't want to know."

Quirnheim closed the door with a vicious kick as if to relieve his feelings. "Wouldn't you just know it," he snarled. "Goering and Himmler were absent."

"So?"

"So naturally Stauffenberg was forced to postpone the attempt."

"I always thought we were being greedy. We should content ourselves with killing Hitler, not the whole triumvirate."

"Yes, well, why didn't you say so when we were planning this thing?"

"I did, but nobody was listening."

"Well, never mind, Franz, we've learned our lesson. We won't make the same mistake on Friday."

"Do you mean to say the Führer has called another conference for the fourteenth of July?"

"He most certainly has." Quirnheim began to kick one heel against the other, which Epp knew was a sign that he was worried. "General Olbricht is anxious to know what effect this postponement will have."

"On what? The officer situation?"

"Yes."

"We shall lose the second in command of the tank training unit at Krampnitz on posting to Twenty-one Panzer Division and two company commanders from the School of Infantry at Döberitz."

"That's a bit of a blow."

"There's worse to come," Epp said grimly. "A certain Major Otto Remer has been selected to command the Berlin Guard Battalion of the Grossdeutschland Regiment."

"When does he take up the appointment?"

"On the thirteenth, which could be a very unlucky day for us because he's reputed to be a staunch Party man."

"Does Beck know about this?" Quirnheim asked in a sharp tone of voice.

"Yes, he suggested we arranged for Remer to be transferred to his home town of Königsberg."

"Well, why don't we do that?"

"Because Stauffenberg thinks it would look suspicious if we singled him out."

"But we're counting on the Grossdeutschland Regiment; damn it all, Franz, it's the only unit in Inner Berlin which we know we can rely on."

"You're wrong, Mertz; we're relying on the commanding officer and we're hoping the Regiment will obey his orders to the letter."

Quirnheim smiled ruefully. "You always were a pessimist, Franz."

"I know someone who would agree with you."

"Who's that?"

"Anneliese Ohlendorf." Epp pushed his chair back and stood up. "Come on," he said, "let's go to the club and drown our sorrows in a drink."

Wing Commander Upton was twenty-six but, like most fliers in Bomber Command who'd been through the mill, he looked considerably older. A regular officer, he was one of the few survivors from the intake which had passed out of Cranwell in June 1939. His first tour of operations had lasted from the outbreak of war to the end of May 1942, by which time he'd completed 175 missions in Hampdens and had collected a DFC and bar. After spending fifteen months as a briefing officer at Headquarters Number 3 Group, he had converted to Lancasters and returned to operations in August 1943 to face a different and more lethal kind of war.

The wastage rate among air crews was such that a normal tour had been reduced to thirty combat missions, but, even so, few men completed the cycle, and Upton was no exception. Early in January '44 he had been badly wounded, losing his left hand and the sight of one eye when his Lancaster was attacked by a Junkers 88 on the return leg from Magdeburg. Discharged from the hospital some three months later, he was subsequently medically downgraded and posted to Headquarters Bomber Command at High Wycombe as Staff Officer (Operations).

Within that huge and complex organization, he had become accustomed to planning raids on the scale of eight hundred plus, and it was therefore something of a novel experience for him to be considering one which would merely involve a single aircraft. It was also the first time he'd had anything to do with SOE.

Upton said, "Let's get this straight, Major Newstead. You're saying that the Germans will provide us with a perfect aiming mark?"

"I am," Newstead said cheerfully.

"You seem very positive. Am I allowed to know why?"

"Because they're under the impression that we shall be sending in a troop of SAS to reinforce the local Resistance. They've even chosen the DZ for us."

"They?"

"The Abwehr. German Intelligence has turned one of our operators, and we've been stringing them along." Newstead unfolded his map on Upton's desk. "The DZ they've suggested is about three miles northwest of Bouglainval and will be marked with eight red lights arranged like the cross of Lorraine." His index finger pointed to an area shaded green. "I imagine their reception party will be hiding up in this wood."

"That's a pretty big target for one aircraft."

"I thought we might try the forward edge opposite the markers. With any luck, the Wehrmacht will have at least one infantry company on the ground to meet our hypothetical SAS troop, so we'd like you to drop something big and nasty." Newstead smiled. "Like a blockbuster," he said aimiably.

Upton placed a ruler over the map and measured the DZ. "About a thousand yards," he mused. "To make a tight para drop, a Dakota would have to fly straight and level at six hundred feet. At that altitude a Lancaster would give the show away, so we'll have to plump for a twin-engined job."

"How about a Mosquito?" Newstead suggested helpfully.

"Yes, we could give the job to Five Group. A high-capacity bomb would do the trick nicely, but I wouldn't like to drop one from low level. On the other hand, a four-thousand-pound general-purpose fitted with a short delay pistol would give the pilot time to get away before it went off."

"How effective is this general-purpose bomb?"

"Oh, it'll make quite a bang." Upton tilted the chair back onto its hind legs and wedged a knee against the desk. "Do you think we'll get a hostile reception?" he asked abruptly.

Newstead smiled wryly. It was a difficult if not impossible question to answer. A lot would depend on whether or not the Abwehr were anxious to prolong the spoof. He thought it would serve no useful purpose to point out that they would certainly tip their hand if they opened fire on the Mosquito. Upton wanted an informed opinion, not a wild guess.

"I really don't know," he said.

"Well, at least you're honest." Upton removed his knee, allowing the chair to regain its former equilibrium. "All right," he said, "we'll do it. Give me a date and I'll get a warning order off to Five Group."

"I was going to suggest Thursday; that should give us plenty of time to set it up."

Upton opened his desk diary. "The thirteenth?" he said dubiously.

"Why not? You're not superstitious, are you?"

Upton had yet to meet a pilot who wasn't. The more ops you completed the more superstitious you became, but that was something a "Brown Job" would never understand, especially one who was desk-bound.

"I suppose it could be worse."

"If it fell on a Friday?"

Upton smiled. "Now who's being irrational?"

"Not me. I'm a realist."

"In that case, tell me what happens if the pilot has to abort?"

"I've also learned to be flexible," said Newstead. "If it's necessary to postpone the mission, the BBC will simply broadcast the alternative date in a coded message."

The house in the rue des Loges was far too big for one person and difficult to run without any domestic help, but Holbrook could understand why Gabrielle hadn't put it up for sale after her father died. Situated in an exclusive neighborhood, it lay within easy walking distance of the Jardin Anglais, a local beauty spot, and the forest of Saint-Germain. Real estate agents might laud the view in their brochures, but as far as the established residents were concerned it was something of a mixed blessing. The rue des Loges was the kind of locality that attracted every thief in town, and any burglar lurking in the forest would know exactly when it was safe to effect a break-in.

Holbrook stood up and flexed his leg muscles. The sun had disappeared below the horizon and the house no longer stood out in sharp relief. To reach the back gate and enter the garden, he had to cross a strip of heathland and a narrow lane which served as a firebreak. Satisfied that the place was not being watched by the opposition, he moved cautiously out of the wood.

The back gate had sagged on its hinges and was difficult to budge at first, until, lifting it up, he managed to force an opening wide enough for him to squeeze through sideways. Avoiding the open expanse of lawn, he stayed close to the overgrown hedge, which, running the full length of the garden, afforded a more covered approach to the house.

Holbrook tried the back door and, discovering it was locked, pushed the bell. The clockwork mechanism gave a dull whirr and then stopped. Taking a clasp knife out of his pocket, he inserted the blade into the jamb and by dint of probing disengaged the lug from the housing. The door swung back slowly on its hinges and he stepped into the kitchen. Somewhere in another part of the house a radio was playing softly.

He traced the sound to what used to be the music room on the first floor and found Gabrielle curled up in an armchair nursing a glass of brandy. A loose floorboard creaked under his weight and, turning her head swiftly in his direction, she stared open-mouthed at him standing in the doorway; the goblet slid through her fingers and rolled across the carpet.

"My God," she whispered, "you frightened the life out of me."

"I'm sorry, I didn't mean to startle you." Holbrook retrieved the glass and set it down on the nest of tables by her armchair. Leaning over Gabrielle, he raised her chin toward his mouth and for the first time noticed that her bottom lip was swollen. "How did that happen?" he asked softly.

"One of your compatriots turned nasty."

"Compatriots?" He turned down the volume on the radiogram and dropped into a chair. "What the hell are you talking about?"

"Two Englishmen." She poured herself another brandy and drank it eagerly. "They were in Mantes last Friday."

"Yes?"

"They mean to kill you, Holbrook."

"Really?"

"Look, you'd better believe it," she snapped. "Dufoir says—"

"Dufoir?"

"Goddamn it, Holbrook," she said angrily, "will you please shut up and listen to me for a change? Dufoir was here on Saturday; he said that you had some sort of fixation about Rommel and were determined to assassinate him despite the fact that you had been officially warned off. For reasons which he doesn't even profess to understand, London is equally determined to stop you. It's as simple as that."

"And you believed him?"

"Yes, I did. Dufoir wants to help you."

"Help me?" Holbrook shook his head. "How can you be so naïve?"

"He said that if you gave yourself up he would see that you came to no harm."

"Oh, for God's sake, Gabrielle, he's been after me like a tiger."

"Then why isn't he waiting for you? He knew you would come back."

Holbrook rubbed his eyes. Gabrielle was right. If Dufoir had wanted to take him, he would have kept the house under surveillance. And if he accepted that premise, he had to go along with the supposition that London had signed his death warrant. But that was impossible; Newstead would never do a thing like that. Newstead wouldn't, but then again Parker might; Parker was ruthless enough for anything.

"Dufoir said that if all else failed I should try and persuade you to forget the whole idea and lie low."

"Did he now?" he said absently.

"But of course he wasn't to know that you would never listen to me."

"You never really knew my father, did you?"

"Your father?" Her eyebrows met in a bewildered frown. "What has he got to do with it?"

"Everything or nothing, depending on your point of view." Holbrook found a glass and poured himself a generous measure of brandy. "When Chamberlain announced that we were officially at war with Germany, my father rushed off to Paris and virtually lived on the doorstep of the British embassy until the military attaché pulled a few strings and got him back into uniform. The army turned him into a liaison officer and sent him off to the base supply depot at Rouen, which was a long way behind the lines, or at least it was until June 1940. Rommel was commanding the Seventh Panzer Division in those days, a major general out to make a name for himself, which indeed he did. His division bounced the Meuse, took Le Cateau, brushed aside a local British counterattack near Arras, and pushed on to reach the coast west of Dieppe in under a month. He then turned south and entered Saint-Valéry to receive the surrender of Fifty-first Highland Division before continuing to advance down the coast. Of course, the supply depot withdrew from Rouen and tried to set up shop in Normandy, but the front was collapsing like a pack of cards and the staff were putting ad hoc units together in a desperate attempt to plug the holes. That's how my father became a front-line soldier for the second time in his life."

She listened to him without once interrupting because he told it simply, and she had a vivid picture of the twenty-five reluctant soldiers who'd been hauled out of their familiar stores, handed a rifle and fifty rounds of ammunition apiece, and sent off under a middle-aged captain to keep the panzers from reaching Cherbourg. They had felled several trees, hoping they would make an effective antitank obstacle, and had dug slit trenches on either side of the road. Twenty-six men waiting under a broiling hot sun and watching for the first tank to nose its way out of Thiberville, knowing that they were just a tiny island of resistance, a small insignificant stumbling block.

"The tanks could have bypassed them"—Holbrook swallowed the rest of the brandy—"God knows they had plenty of room for maneuver, but this was the Seventh Panzers hell-bent for glory, and they rode right over them. The War Office received an account of the action some nine or ten months later from the next of kin of the only survivor—he'd been badly wounded and taken prisoner—and that's how I got to know about it."

Holbrook broke off and helped himself to another brandy.

"I don't expect you to understand," he said quietly.

Gabrielle understood only too well. It was a vendetta, pure and simple, a kind of family feud nurtured by the war.

"I think I do understand," she said sadly. "It's this war, it's changed everything and everyone. But I'll help you if you want me to."

"You're a remarkable woman, Gabrielle." Holbrook reached for her hand and squeezed it gently. "But even so, we can't work miracles. For one thing, I'm unarmed and, without Gilbert, I'm like a blind man with no stick or guide dog. I've got to know exactly where I can find Rommel in the forest of Moisson and how many people go shooting with him and what patrols I'm likely to encounter in the area. Only Gilbert can give me that kind of information, and there's no way I can get in touch with him."

"You're forgetting one thing," she said. "We still have the gold."

The gold would buy money and the money in turn could buy Gilbert's address from Cheval. It would be a hell of a risk but one which he thought was worth taking.

"We'd have to find a buyer first," he said.
"I know a man who would give us a good price for it."
"When can you arrange an introduction?"
"Tomorrow."
"Good."
"And this time, Holbrook, I'm coming with you." She leaned forward and kissed him. "No arguments," she said firmly. "From now on, where you go, I go."
"I can't let you."
"I'm not pleading with you, Holbrook. Dufoir won't be able to stall your compatriots for much longer, and I don't intend to be here when they come visiting." She kissed him again. "Have you had anything to eat?" she murmured.
"I could do with a bowl of soup."
"My God, you are an unromantic bastard."
Holbrook placed the glass on the nest of tables and pulled her into his arms. "If it's like that," he said, "the soup can wait."

Clare Russell-Jones had no idea what the message was about, but she checked the flimsy carefully to make sure the jumble of letters were correctly arranged in groups of five. From experience she knew how easy it was for an overworked cypher clerk to make a simple mistake in the grouping, and she always blamed herself whenever an out-station asked for a verification. Satisfied that there was no obvious error, she called the Foxhound station and got an acknowledgment of signal strength.

Conditions were perfect and the absence of static meant that she would not be requested to repeat any groups, for which blessing she was grateful because this signal was longer than most. She rapped the Morse key again, sending a message to Chartres which read:

DROP ARRANGED FOR 132100 ZULU. CONFIRMATION BBC 12 JULY QUOTE THE QUEEN OF HEARTS SHE MADE SOME TARTS UNQUOTE. STANDARD PROCEDURE IN EVENT POSTPONEMENT ALTERNATIVE DATE 24 HOURS AFTER TRANSMISSION QUOTE KEEP UP YOUR BRIGHT SWORDS FOR THE DEW WILL RUST THEM UNQUOTE. MESSAGE ENDS. ACKNOWLEDGE.

15

The first strident note was enough to wake Holbrook and he reached for the clock, stopping the alarm before it disturbed Gabrielle. Satisfied that she was still asleep, he slipped out of bed and crept toward the door. Opening it stealthily, he crossed the landing and entered the adjoining bedroom. First light was beginning to show, but although he could just make out the summerhouse at the bottom of the garden, the forest of Saint-Germain was hidden from view by a swirling blanket of ground mist.

Holbrook moved a high-backed chair up to the window and straddled the seat. In the poor light, it was easy to mistake every stunted rosebush for the figure of a crouching man, but experience had taught him not to depend on one sense alone and he listened intently, straining his ears to catch the slightest sound of movement. He thought that if there was anyone out there watching the house, the drawn curtains in Gabrielle's room might well engender a feeling of complacency. Overconfidence invariably led to some little carelessness, like a sudden desire to flex a cramped limb or to smoke a furtive cigarette.

The light began to improve; the back gate, sagging on its hinges, was no longer a vague blur but stood out boldly. The mist swirled, eddied, and gradually lifted, revealing first the narrow lane and then the strip of heathland beyond and the stunted rosebushes which were just rosebushes, not crouching figures.

Holbrook left the room to check the front of the house. The blackout curtains were still drawn across every window that he could see, and apart from a stray cat padding along the pavement there was no sign of life in the rue des Loges. Although it was beginning to look as if Dufoir was on the level, Holbrook knew there was at least one other way the inspector could keep tabs on Gabrielle. Provided the Gestapo didn't get wind of it, arranging a wire tap wouldn't be difficult for a man with his connections.

He remembered a post office supervisor once saying that you could always tell if you had an eavesdropper on the line because there would be an unmistakable click a split second after the incoming or outgoing call was answered. It had never been necessary for him to put this gratuitous piece of information to the test before, and on reflection he decided that this was not the opportune moment to do so either. There was no way he could find out if the line was being monitored without arousing their suspicion, and that was the last thing he wanted.

Gabrielle was still sleeping peacefully when he returned to the bedroom and he saw little point in waking her just yet. Collecting his razor, he went into the bathroom, shaved in water that was barely lukewarm, and then stood under the shower, which functioned in fits and starts, wheezing asthmatically. Alert now but also very hungry, he wrapped himself in a bath towel and ran downstairs.

There was a fine collection of herbs and spices in the larder but not very much in the way of food. Rationing was tight but not so tight as to make life impossible for an enterprising housewife. Although Gabrielle had never been exactly domesticated, he couldn't help wondering how she managed to keep body and soul together. Rummaging through the shelves, he found a tin of ersatz coffee, a pat of butter, and a jar of strawberry jam. Yesterday's loaf in the bread basket was like a teething rusk but it was better than nothing, and he wolfed down a couple of slices while he waited for the coffee to percolate on a slow gas. Even the porcelain cups and saucers which he discovered in the dresser couldn't disguise the fact that the coffee looked foul, smelled foul, and tasted foul.

Balancing the cups and saucers and a bowl of coarsely refined sugar beet on a tray, he returned to their room and found Gabrielle sitting on the bed in her underwear. She was examining a pair of silk stockings for runs, and he noticed that the inevitable cigarette was smoldering in an ashtray.

"Coffee?" she said. "Well, this is a pleasant surprise; I was beginning to wonder if you'd run out on me again." Her nose wrinkled. "What did you use, the tin of ersatz?"

"Yes."

"I thought so. I can smell the acorns."

Holbrook moved the alarm clock, stubbed out her cigarette, and placed the tray on the bedside table. "I couldn't find anything else."

"You should have looked in the tin marked RICE."

In the rice tin. Well, that figured. Gabrielle never did have any method. He padded barefoot across the room and picked up the grubby-looking shirt which was draped over a chair.

"There are lots of Papa's in his dressing room, if you want a clean one. They might not fit you too well but they'd look better than that thing." Gabrielle rolled a stocking carefully up her leg and fastened it to the garter. "Didn't you hear what I said?" she asked.

"No, I was thinking."

"Try Papa's dressing room. There are plenty of shirts in the closet."

"They'd never fit me."

"Oh, well, please yourself, Holbrook." Gabrielle stood up, straightened the seams on both stockings, and then, having smoothed the satin slip over her thighs, opened the wardrobe and chose a blue linen suit. "I think I'll wear this," she said. "What do you think?"

The suit was smart and looked very, very expensive. It might not seem out of place on the Champs-Élysées but it would cause a few raised eyebrows in the thirteenth arrondissement.

"You'll be overdressed."

"Overdressed?"

"It's fine for the George Fifth, but we'll be staying in a one-night hotel off the Place d'Italie where the management isn't too fussy about identity cards."

"But that's where all the tarts hang out."

"Exactly." He sat down on the bed and pulled on a pair of socks. "Are you sure you want to go through with this?" he asked. "I mean, you could find yourself in serious trouble."

"Oh, for God's sake, Holbrook," she said wearily, "the local

Resistance have my name in their black book, and I know what will happen if your friends catch up with me again. Selling a few bars of gold on the black market is the least of my worries."

She was right. Dealing on the black market wasn't a serious offense. Three months was the most she'd get if the magistrate happened to be in a bad mood. Prison would be an unpleasant experience for Gabrielle, but for the immediate future she would be much safer behind bars. There, at least, nobody would be able to put a bullet through her head.

Holbrook laced both shoes and stood up. "All right," he said, "we won't argue about it. I'll be looking for you in the Flea Market at twelve."

"You're going now?"

"Well, I do have to slip out the back way before anyone else is up and about."

"Yes," she said slowly, "I can see that."

He bent forward and gave her a hurried kiss, the sort of absentminded peck which passes between a wife and a husband who is late for the office, except that Holbrook wasn't catching the seven fifty to town.

Fletcher spotted Vallin striding along the rue Keller and drew back from the window. It seemed to him that the Frenchman was in no hurry to reach the safe house, which confirmed his opinion that the Albert circuit was giving them the runaround. Denise Jeanney hadn't been able to tell them a damn thing about Holbrook, and he suspected that Vallin had known it all along. They had spent the last four days cooped up indoors, getting on each other's nerves while the French supposedly pursued their inquiries with Roland de Neury and Gabrielle Marsac, inquiries which he thought had gone on long enough. Jackson was partly to blame for the mess they were in; if he hadn't agreed to hand over their transmitter, they'd be in direct touch with London instead of having to go through the French. London, he thought, wouldn't hesitate to put the boot in if they thought de Gaulle's people were dragging their feet.

Jackson said, "Suppose you let me in on the secret?"

"What?"

"You were muttering to yourself."

"Vallin's coming."

"So?"

"So I think we ought to lean on him. I mean, we just can't sit here twiddling our thumbs."

Fletcher was right—the French were taking their time—but there was a right way and a wrong way to prod them into action. Leaning on Vallin wasn't the answer; he was only a courier, a messenger boy without any influence. Diplomatic pressure would have to be exerted in London if they were to break the deadlock. There was no time, however, to discuss tactics with Fletcher now; hearing Vallin's gruff voice in the hall, Jackson decided he would have to play it by ear.

The Frenchman greeted them cheerfully and made a determined effort to steer the conversation along neutral lines. Jackson thought he must have sensed the atmosphere as soon as he walked into the room and was anxious to postpone the inevitable confrontation. Like a noisy magpie, he chatted about the weather until, meeting with a blank wall of silence, he suddenly dried up, his confidence completely evaporated.

Fletcher said, "I've met some bullshitters in my time but you're in a class of your own." He moved closer and tapped Vallin on the chest. The gesture wasn't entirely playful. "Let's forget the weather and talk about de Neury instead."

"What is there to say?" Vallin shrugged his shoulders. "We are proceeding with our inquiries."

"We've heard that one before."

"De Neury is being difficult; he refuses to answer any questions."

"You're a policeman, aren't you?" Fletcher said coldly.

"You don't understand." Vallin swallowed nervously and glanced toward Jackson, hoping the American might come to his aid. "This man has influence, he could make life very difficult for us. You see, he's on friendly terms with Stülpnagel, the Military Governor of France."

"And Gabrielle Marsac?" Jackson asked quietly. "Is she also acquainted with the Colonel General?"

"It's possible; after all, she moves in the same circle."

"As de Neury?"

"Yes."

"In that case, one of them is hiding something." Jackson snapped his fingers. "You know what?" he said. "I think we ought to call on Gabrielle Marsac."

"That's out of the question."

"Why?"

Vallin shifted his weight from one foot to the other. "I've already told you, these people have influence."

"They're not the only ones. What do you suppose will happen if our people don't hear from us? One thing is certain, it won't be long before somebody over there comes to the conclusion that the Albert circuit is being uncooperative." Jackson managed to look as if he were reluctant to mention it. "I don't imagine de Gaulle will be any too pleased with you if he finds himself caught in a vice between London and Washington."

Vallin was out of his depth. The American had shown him the rapier and was obviously the kind of man who wouldn't hesitate to use it if the necessity arose. He tried to think what Dufoir would do in his place.

"It's no use threatening me," he said belligerently. "I'm only a small cog in a very large machine."

"But you can turn a few wheels," Jackson said cheerfully. "Dufoir is a reasonable man, and I'm sure he will be only too anxious to meet us halfway after you've explained the situation to him."

"Of course he will," said Fletcher. "You just tell him that we're prepared to let bygones be bygones so long as we get to see Gabrielle Marsac." He clapped Vallin on the shoulder. "You might remind him that he can't talk to London unless we give him the key phrase for the day."

Vallin licked his lips. They weren't fencing with him now; the button had been removed and the naked rapier was pointing at his throat.

"I'll see what I can do," he said hoarsely. "It may take a little time; there are various arrangements to be made."

"That's all right. We're not in too much of a hurry, are we, Harry?"

"No," said Fletcher, "any time this afternoon will suit us."

There was a peculiar, lopsided smile on the Englishman's face which made Vallin uneasy.

The Flea Market had always attracted the bargain hunter, and if anything the war had increased its popularity. Among other things, it was the only place in Paris where it was still possible for a man to acquire a good pair of secondhand shoes which had leather instead of wooden soles, and a woman might be lucky enough to find a packet of needles there. The street traders, however, were not the only people who had a good thing going for them; inevitably, the crowded market was a favorite stamping ground for every pickpocket in town. As he edged toward her, Holbrook was relieved to see that Gabrielle was keeping a tight hold on her handbag.

The stall was doing a brisk trade in ribbons, shoelaces, buttons, and imitation leather goods. Holbrook spent a few minutes browsing through a collection of cheap-looking wallets and then moved on. Although no word or look of recognition had passed between them, he knew that she was following close behind. Leaving the Flea Market, he turned into a narrow side street and waited outside a snack bar until Gabrielle caught up with him.

The Métro was only a short distance away but he chose a circuitous route which crisscrossed the neighborhood. Like grasshoppers, they moved in fits and starts from one shop window to the next, heading first in one direction and then in another before doubling back on their tracks. By the time Holbrook was satisfied that no one was following them, they had covered the best part of two miles.

Gabrielle wished that she had worn a pair of low-heeled shoes. Her feet felt as if they had swollen to twice their normal size and the stitching had raised a blister on her right heel. Each step was agony, but now that the Métro was finally in sight she gritted her teeth and forced herself to push one foot in front of the other.

Limping inside, she waited for Holbrook to collect their tickets and then, latching onto his arm, she leaned against him and descended the long flight of steps to the platform. The atmosphere was moist and humid like the inside of a greenhouse on a hot summer's day, only worse. The sweat gathered in the roots of her hair and trickled down into her eyes. A warm breeze billowed the hem of her skirt, lifting it above her knees, and then the train roared into the station and squealed to a halt.

Holbrook opened the door of the nearest compartment, ushered Gabrielle inside, and steered her to a box seat at the far end. The carriage was almost empty. There were just six other people: a blind man, a woman with two fractious children, and a young couple holding hands. Certain that no one could see her, Gabrielle kicked off both shoes and wiggled her toes.

Holbrook glanced at her stockinged feet. "You'll regret it," he said cheerfully.

"I don't care, my shoes were killing me."

The train pulled out from the platform and clattered into the tunnel, the wheels settling into a rhythmic click as it gradually picked up speed.

Gabrielle leaned back against the seat and closed her eyes. "You didn't tell me we were going on a route march."

"You should thank your lucky stars that no one was following us."

"You're getting paranoid, Holbrook."

"I don't trust your friends, that's all."

"Not all of them are like Roland."

"I'm relieved to hear it. Did this other friend give you a good price?"

"My God," she breathed, "there's no peace for the wicked." Turning sideways, she opened her handbag and dropped a thick oblong-shaped envelope into his lap. "Ten thousand francs in hundreds and fifties."

"I thought we agreed you'd sell him four ounces?"

"That's right." Gabrielle closed her handbag. "I thought I did rather well."

"You were rooked."

"What did you expect," she whispered furiously, "the official exchange rate? Obviously you don't know the black market."

He did, but that was beside the point. Gabrielle had done the best she could, and it was no use bemoaning the fact that she'd been taken for a ride. Ten thousand francs was still enough to buy Cheval and keep a roof over their heads for several weeks.

"You did all right."

"Yes?"

"Well, I don't suppose I could have done any better."

"I never thought I'd live to hear you say that, Holbrook."

He grinned. "There's always a first time for everything," he said.

The train slowed, swayed across the points, and rolled into the station. The harassed-looking woman with the two fretful children got out; a nun, three schoolgirls, and a somberly dressed middle-aged man carrying a briefcase got in.

"What happens now?"

"I get off at the next stop." Holbrook pushed back his shirt cuff and glanced at his wristwatch. "Provided Cheval is still working the same shift, I'll meet you at six."

"Where?"

It was a good question. A crowded department store was the safest bet, but not if he was late. He tried to think of a rendezvous where a woman on her own would not look out of place.

"Le Dôme."

"Where's that?"

"In Montparnasse. A number ninety-one tram will drop you right outside the door."

"A number ninety-one tram," she repeated.

"And don't get in a sweat if I'm late."

Gabrielle closed her eyes again and wondered what she was going to do with herself for the next four and a half hours.

Heat waves danced and shimmered, creating the illusion that the road was undulating like an oily sea. Vallin looked to his left, saw that they were opposite number 28, and drifted across onto the wrong side of the road. Easing his foot off the accelerator, he edged into the curb and touched the brakes. The engine coughed, spluttered, and then finally died almost a minute after he'd switched off the ignition.

"This is it," he said.

Jackson leaned forward to take a closer look at the house and whistled softly. "A little ostentatious," he said, "but I could live with it."

"It's decadent," Fletcher said tersely, "like the French upper class."

He opened the door and scrambled out of the car, eager to get on with it. Society women like Gabrielle Marsac made him want to vomit: collaborators who sold France short and sucked up to the Germans, rich bitches in fancy creations besporting themselves at the Auteuil racetrack while a hundred and fifty hostages were executed in the prison yard at Abbeville. He jammed his thumb on the doorbell and held it there long enough to wake the dead.

Vallin said, "It doesn't look as if there's anyone at home."

Fletcher removed his thumb and stepped back. "We'll see about that," he said in a smug voice.

Jackson saw the smirk on his face and felt dismayed. Fletcher reminded him of a large overgrown schoolboy, the sort of creep who would enjoy pulling wings off butterflies.

"What are you going to do, Harry?" he asked quietly.

"I'm going to break in."

"I don't want any trouble," Vallin said nervously. "We don't have a search warrant."

"Fuck the search warrant." Fletcher jabbed him in the chest, a habit of his that was beginning to annoy Vallin. "If anybody complains, just show them your police identity card. That ought to shut them up."

Pushing Vallin aside, he followed a paved path which led around to the back. A few moments later, Jackson heard a loud crack and the tinkle of falling glass. The Frenchman closed his eyes and mouthed a string of four-letter words under his breath.

The door opened slowly. Fletcher smiled and crooked a finger, beckoning them to come inside. Jackson walked into the hall, took one look at the Persian carpet on the oak floor, and instinctively stepped back a pace to wipe his feet on a sunken doormat.

"All right," said Jackson, "what happens now?"

"You can take a look upstairs while Vallin and I go through the rooms on the ground floor."

"What are we looking for?"

"You mean who, don't you?"

"Holbrook?" Jackson snorted derisively. "You must be crazy."

"He's been here; I can feel it in my bones."

"Fifty dollars says you're wrong."

"You're on," said Fletcher.

The bet was just two hours old when Vallin discovered a snapshot of Holbrook in the family album.

Holbrook loosened his tie and unbuttoned the neck of his shirt. The ice had melted in the Pernod, and the small electric fan anchored on the wall above his head merely circulated a current of warm air. The heat had obviously rattled the barman, whose surly manner suggested that he would be glad to see the back of his one and only customer. Holbrook thought that if looks could kill he'd be dead on the spot, but he was determined that nobody, least of all an undersized, nose-picking bartender, was going to hustle him out onto the street. The Chez Armand would never find its way into a guidebook, but it was the only bar in the neighborhood with a commanding view of the bus depot.

The single-decker from La Roche-Guyon was already ten minutes late, but he managed to convince himself that there was nothing unusual about that. Buses were often halted or diverted off their route to make way for a military convoy, so it was just a question of waiting. Cheval was bound to turn up sooner or later. Or was he? Perhaps he'd met with a serious accident, or was sick, or had taken the day off, or had changed shifts?

Holbrook swallowed the Pernod and tried to think positively. He wondered if five hundred francs would be enough to buy the information he wanted. On second thoughts, he decided that a thousand would clinch it; a thousand would seem like a small fortune to Cheval, but unless there were safeguards he might try to palm him off with a false address. It occurred to him that he could always tear the notes in half and make it a cash-on-delivery sale.

A single-decker bus crawled past the window, a wisp of steam escaping from the radiator cap. Grinding away in low gear, it made a wide sweeping turn and entered the depot. After what seemed an eternity, Cheval punched the time clock outside the traffic office and walked out of the garage.

Holbrook waited until he'd turned the corner into the rue Saint-Denis and then went after him.

Sergeant Hugo Burghardt twiddled the dial and searched across the waveband until he found the BBC Overseas Service. A dance band was playing "American Patrol," and recognizing the familiar sound of Glenn Miller he picked up the beat and drummed his fingertips on the table. Burghardt, whose taste in music ran to swing, also liked the Dorsey brothers, Goodman, and Count Basie but rated Miller the best of them all. Miller, he thought, was something rather special.

The music faded out and there was a moment of complete silence before a base drum hammered the opening bars of Beethoven's Fifth. The V signal went on and on—di di di dah . . . di di di dah—swelling in volume until the speaker on the Grundig was vibrating. Burghardt felt his pulse begin to race; glancing sideways, he saw that Church was sweating.

The tattoo ceased abruptly and the personal messages began: "Silence alone is great, all else is feebleness"; "Dick sends his fond regard to Anne Marie"; "Jack and Jill went up the hill to fetch a pail of water"; "Throw out the lifeline across the dark wave"; "Uncle Henri is going on a long journey" . . .

Burghardt felt the moisture on his palms and dried his hands with a handkerchief.

. . . "If you have tears prepare to shed them now"; "Old King Cole was a merry old soul"; "Peter wishes to be remembered to Jean-Claude"; "The Queen of Hearts she made some tarts"—

Burghardt was sure that his pulse had stopped beating. "The Queen of Hearts she made some tarts." They were coming tomorrow, Thursday the thirteenth of July, at 2100 hours Greenwich Mean Time.

THE QUEEN OF HEARTS SHE MADE SOME TARTS.

Church retched, clapped a hand over his mouth, and ran out of the room.

16

A shrill voice drifted up from the courtyard below their room. Holbrook stirred and slowly opened his eyes. The window had been open all night but the pungent smell of cheap scent was still present, a reminder that this seedy hotel off the Place d'Italie was little better than a brothel. Reaching under the pillow, he was relieved to find that his wallet had not been stolen while he was asleep.

It was somewhat thinner now that Cheval had taken his cut, but he reckoned that the remaining nine thousand francs would be enough to tide them over for a month or two. They could keep on running while the money lasted, but in the end everything hinged on Marcel Gilbert. It was an unpalatable thought but he could see that they were finished if the Frenchman ignored his letter or failed to show up at the rendezvous in Vernon on Saturday. Saturday, however, was forty-eight hours away and he had been around long enough to know that it was best to live one day at a time.

Holbrook turned over onto his back and stared at the maze of hairline cracks in the ceiling. Vernon was less than eight miles from La Roche-Guyon, and he wondered if the town would be crawling with troops. If it was, they would be safer staying on in Paris until the last minute, but on the other hand the trains were unreliable these days. Vernon or Paris? It was a difficult choice, the sort of decision that could only be settled by tossing a coin.

Gabrielle yawned and stretched her arms above her head. "What is the time?" she asked drowsily.

"Almost seven."

"I don't think I've had a wink all night."

"You were sleeping like a log until a few moments ago."

"I wasn't snoring, was I?" She rolled over on top of him. "Tell me I wasn't snoring, Holbrook."

"You weren't snoring," he said dutifully.

She snuggled closer and nibbled at his ear. "A penny for them."

"What?"

"Your thoughts."

"They're not really worth it. I was trying to make up my mind whether we should stay here in Paris or go to Vernon."

"Do we have a choice?"

"You call it," he said. "Heads or tails?"

"Heads."

"That settles it, we go to Vernon."

"When?"

"Oh, sometime tomorrow afternoon."

She smiled and then moved against him, forcing a knee between his legs. "I love you, Holbrook."

"I love you too," he said absently.

"Yes?"

"You know I do."

She searched his face, seeking the assurance that his words had failed to convey. "I wish I could believe that."

"You can."

"No." She shook her head. "No, he will always be there between us. I can see it in your eyes."

"Can't you ever forget your bloody German?" he said angrily.

"Can you ever forget yours?" she countered.

He couldn't, for one very good reason. Killing Rommel before the hunters from SOE caught up with them was perhaps the only chance they had of staying alive, but he doubted if he could make her see that now, or even if it was wise to tell her.

Parker eyed the cigar between McCready's fingers and wished he would refrain from smoking in his office. Cigarettes were bad enough, but the aroma of an Havana persisted for days afterward. Hoping that he might take the hint, Parker placed the ashtray which he kept for visitors within easy reach of the American; McCready, however, had a hide like a rhinoceros.

"This cigar doesn't bother you any, does it, James?" he asked affably.

"Good Lord, no." Parker stretched his face in a glassy smile. "Whatever gave you that impression, George?"

"I just thought you looked a mite uncomfortable."

"Well, if I seem uneasy, it's not on account of your cigar."

McCready jammed the Havana between his teeth and shoved both hands into his pockets. "I guess things aren't going too well, right?"

"It's early days yet," Parker said cautiously. "We must be patient; after all, Paris is a pretty large city."

"I know that. I lived there from '34 to '40, remember?"

Parker closed his eyes. As if he could forget; McCready, a self-appointed expert on French affairs, was forever reminding him that for six years he'd been a foreign correspondent for the *Herald Tribune.* "I have every confidence in Jackson and Fletcher," he said patiently. "I'm sure they can pull it off but we must give them time."

"Time?" McCready scowled. "Time is one thing we don't have, James. We can expect Valkyrie any day, but the coup d'état will be a busted flush if Holbrook puts a bullet through Rommel in the meantime. Rommel is the cornerstone, the key man."

"Really?" murmured Parker. "I was under the impression that everything depended on Colonel Stauffenberg."

McCready studied him thoughtfully. "You've never been in favor of Valkyrie, have you, James?"

"Well, to be quite honest, I think it stinks. If it does come off, we'll be asking for trouble if we make a separate deal with the Germans. I can just imagine the sort of hostile reaction we'll get from the Russians."

"So what?" McCready removed the cigar from his mouth and mashed it in the ashtray. "We're going to have trouble with those people sooner or later anyway. I can see it coming a mile off. If we've got any sense at all, we'll make damn sure that we shake hands with the Russians as far to the east as possible. Preferably in Warsaw."

Parker suppressed a wry smile. He thought McCready ought to try voicing his opinion to Washington instead of preaching to the converted. Churchill was of a like mind but Roosevelt was insistent that Anvil, the invasion of southern France, should go ahead as planned. Unless the President could be persuaded otherwise, generals Alexander and Mark Clark would lose seven precious divisions to that sideshow just when they were on the verge of achieving a major breakthrough in Italy, a breakthrough which could take the Allied armies into Austria and the Balkans before autumn.

"Anyway, what makes you think that we've given Beck a definite commitment?"

"I thought—"

"Well, then, you thought wrong, James." McCready grinned. "We're just waiting to see which way the cookie crumbles. If Stauffenberg does hit the jackpot, we'll move in and pick up the pieces."

"My God," said Parker. "Who said you Americans weren't devious?" There was a note of unconcealed admiration in his voice that McCready found pleasing.

"Okay, let's both be perfidious and turn on the French."

"The French?" Parker repeated parrot fashion.

"Hell, they're practically running the show, aren't they? We can't get in touch with Fletcher or vice versa unless we go through them, right?" McCready left his chair and began to pace up and down the room. "They're in the driver's seat and we're getting nowhere." He stopped in mid-stride and whirled around to face Parker. "You know what? I think it's time we lit a fire under those guys in Duke Street."

The French did appear to lack a sense of urgency, but Parker thought that was understandable. Both he and McCready had been less than entirely frank with de Gaulle's Central Bureau.

"Perhaps we ought to take them into our confidence?" Parker suggested mildly. "After all, they're not in possession of all the facts."

"We've told them as much as they need to know. I'm not prepared to risk Valkyrie. We don't have to go down on our knees to them. Look, if de Gaulle wants to make a triumphant entry into Paris, it's up to them to keep us happy." McCready pointed to the green telephone on Parker's desk. "I've already spoken to the State Department; I suggest you do likewise with your people and then maybe we'll get some action."

Parker hesitated for a moment and then lifted the receiver. McCready's approach might be a little crude but he thought it would work.

There was a confident smile on Stauffenberg's face, but Epp couldn't help wondering if he was simply trying to bolster their sagging morale. Judging by their serious expressions, it was evident that Colonel General Olbricht and Mertz von Quirnheim were appalled by the news that the Führer had suddenly decided to move his headquarters from Berchtesgaden to Rastenberg in East Prussia and had postponed the conference scheduled for tomorrow. Of course it was typical of Stauffenberg to make light of the situation, but he wasn't fooling anybody; they had suffered yet another reverse and they would only be deluding themselves if they pretended otherwise.

It wasn't enough that the Führer had the devil's own luck, they had also to contend with the fact that he was completely unpredictable. Rastenberg; how could they possibly have foreseen that Hitler would return to the Wolf's Lair? Epp stared at the war map behind Olbricht's desk and was at a loss to understand why they had never considered this possibility when all the pointers were there right in front of their eyes. Twenty-seven divisions of Army Group Center had virtually ceased to exist; the Russians were already on the East Prussian border, and any day now OKW expected them to launch an even more massive offensive in the south than the one which had overwhelmed von Busch. With the enemy at the gates, it was only natural that a megalomaniac like Hitler would return to Rastenberg to direct the battle from close quarters.

"We mustn't lose our sense of proportion," Stauffenberg said cheerfully. "After all, the meeting has only been postponed for twenty-four hours. We should also remember that the conference room at Rastenberg is in a bombproof chamber—bombproof, that is, from an external explosion." He paused briefly to let the implication sink in. "Inside is an entirely different matter. I think it's no exaggeration to say that the blast effect of our device will be twice as deadly within a confined space."

There was no doubt that Stauffenberg's optimism was infectious, even though Epp noticed that he had omitted to mention that Rastenberg was extremely well guarded. To reach the Wolf's Lair he would have to pass through four checkpoints, one beyond the minefield, the second just inside the inner perimeter wire, and a third at the junction of the approach road and the horseshoe-shaped one-way circuit which encompassed the administrative area. The fourth lay inside another belt of wire surrounding the conference bunker and map room. Berchtesgaden had been well guarded too, but there was a subtle difference about this new venue; the Russians were now less than a hundred miles from Rastenberg and therefore the sentries would be a damn sight more alert.

"I hear Fromm is going with you," Olbricht said in a quiet tone of voice.

Stauffenberg nodded. "That's right. Your task should be much easier with him out of the way." He glanced toward Epp. "And yours too, Franz," he said, "though I daresay you would have enjoyed arresting the army commander."

"You won't see me shedding any tears," Epp said dryly.

Olbricht removed his glasses and pinched the bridge of his nose between forefinger and thumb. "I was wondering if we should take the risk of putting the troops on full alert from eleven hundred hours. What do you think, Claus?"

Stauffenberg pursed his lips and looked thoughtful. Epp held his breath and hoped he would veto the suggestion. It would be madness to put the garrison on full alert two hours before the Führer's conference had actually assembled.

"I don't see why you shouldn't issue Valkyrie Phase One," he said calmly. "As I see it, this would bring the outlying troops into Berlin without the unit commanders having to break open their sealed orders. I suggest you don't issue Phase Two until you've heard from me that the Führer is dead."

Olbricht and Quirnheim nodded in agreement. Epp merely raised a quizzical eyebrow. Issuing Valkyrie I was all very well, but he wondered how they would explain their action if Stauffenberg was forced to abandon the attempt.

The Opel trucks were parked nose to tail along a track deep within the wood, the rifle company was in position, and the DZ had been marked with eight red lights in a cross of Lorraine. Although he was satisfied that everything had been done that could be done, Burghardt was far from happy. The infantrymen were a scratch lot, eighty percent Ukrainian, and their discipline and standard of training did not impress him. Few of them had more than a smattering of German and he thought their commander, a nineteen-year-old lieutenant, would have the devil's own job to control them if they became involved in a fire fight with the SAS.

Burghardt was also worried that the British might have an ace up their sleeves. Turning Church had been child's play but the Funkspiel had always been in jeopardy so long as Holbrook remained unaccounted for, and he had a niggling anxiety that the Englishman had somehow managed to get in touch with London. Yet, looking back over the past few days, he was quite sure that SOE had not given him any cause to suspect that they knew the Foxhound station was working for the Abwehr. Of course he could be deluding himself, but it was a comforting thought to hang on to for the next ten minutes. In ten minutes it would be 2100 hours Greenwich Mean Time; in ten minutes he would finally know whether the ruse had succeeded or not. Burghardt glanced at the luminous face of his wristwatch again and decided it was time he collected Church. Turning about, he moved back into the forest.

Burghardt despised all traitors, but he couldn't help feeling sorry for Church. Church was a good linguist and a first-class wireless operator, but he had no business to be in the SOE. He was too immature and too weak a character to withstand pressure, deficiencies which Burghardt thought should have been spotted by his training instructors. If anyone was to blame for his defection, it was the selection board who'd accepted him in the first place.

Church heard a sharp crack and looked up quickly. For a

moment he thought a pistol had been discharged accidentally, but then the portly sergeant loomed up out of the darkness and he guessed that Burghardt must have stepped on a dry twig. It also dawned on him that if he was going to throw a spanner into the works, this was the time to do it. The guards wouldn't expect him to make a break for it at this juncture, and with any luck he might steal as much as twenty yards before they thought to open fire. Bracing his feet against the floor of the truck, he measured the distance to the tailboard. He would have to go out head first, break his fall with a forward somersault, and then move off quickly to a flank to get out of the line of fire. Church half rose from the bench seat, hesitated, remembered that his hands were still manacled, and sat down again. Feeling like a condemned man, he watched Burghardt remove both cotter pins and lower the tailboard.

"I won't do it," said Church. His voice rose to a shrill note. "You can't make me."

"You're quite wrong," Burghardt said quietly, "but don't worry, I don't intend to use force."

"No, you leave that to the SD, don't you?"

"Look around you, Captain Church, there are no SD here, only a rabble of trigger-happy Ukrainians who are going to kill a lot of your fellow countrymen unless you help me."

"You do your own dirty work." Church licked his lips. "I'm not going out there to lead them into an ambush."

"There will be no ambush, you have my word on it."

"Your word isn't worth a damn thing."

"I'll be with you," Burghardt said earnestly. "We'll walk out to the DZ together and lead them back."

"Into what?" snarled Church. "A fucking trap."

"Yes, a trap, but not an ambush. Don't you see I'm risking my life too? If anyone squeezes a trigger, I'll be right in the line of fire."

Burghardt leaned inside the truck to reach Church and then froze, one arm outstretched like a signpost. The aircraft was still a long way off but he was quite sure that it was heading in their direction.

"Well, captain," he said softly, "what is it to be? Twenty-five dead men or twenty-five live prisoners of war?"

Without saying a word, Church rose to his feet and climbed down from the truck. Burghardt sighed with relief and unlocked the handcuffs.

The plane roared over the DZ, turned through 180 degrees, and then came in at six hundred feet to release a four-thousand-pound general-purpose bomb fused with a short delay pistol. Burghardt saw a cylindrical object strike the ground and assumed the dispatcher had free-dropped a supply container ahead of the SAS. Craning his neck, he stared up into the night sky, hoping he would spot their parachutes in the ambient light of the stars. He thought the engines sounded too high-pitched for a transport, and then the pilot opened the throttles and, as the aircraft climbed away, he realized it was a Mosquito.

Burghardt turned to Church and opened his mouth to speak but the words never came. There was a blinding flash of white light as the general-purpose bomb exploded, and then the blast wave gutted both men from crotch to throat.

17

Dufoir left the Métro at Les Sablons and headed toward the Bois de Boulogne. Crossing the Boulevard Maurice Barrès, he turned right, following a narrow footpath which skirted the ornamental lake in the Jardin d'Acclimation to join the rue de Madrid at Neuilly. Ten minutes later he entered the Villa Michelet through a side gate set in a tall privet hedge.

The villa was regarded as a safe house, one of several in outer Paris which served as a meeting place for the Central Committee. Crossing a wide expanse of lawn, Dufoir walked into the conservatory and rapped on the communicating door, tapping out the recognition signal for the day. He was admitted by an elderly manservant and shown into the breakfast room overlooking the rose garden on the south side.

Paupal was waiting for him, seated at the head of a mahogany dining table as if he intended to chair a board meeting. An elegant silver coffeepot, sugar bowl, and matching cream pitcher were set on a tray in front of him, but Dufoir noticed that the staff had only allowed for two cups and saucers.

The lawyer waved a plump hand indicating the coffeepot. "Help yourself," he said, "and then perhaps we can get on with it."

"I think I'll pass."

"I wouldn't if I were you; it's Brazilian, not the usual ersatz rubbish that you and I have to put up with."

Dufoir leaned across the table and filled a delicate Limoges cup. The coffee had been made with freshly ground beans, a commodity which had long ago disappeared from the shelves.

He thought it must have cost their host a small fortune on the black market, but a hundred francs was obviously neither here nor there to someone who could afford a place like the Villa Michelet.

"It's nice to know that the other half can still afford to keep up appearances," he said dryly.

"Appearances can be deceptive. I always thought you were a very efficient policeman, but it seems I was mistaken." Paupal took out a silk handkerchief and blew his nose. "I'm afraid the Central Bureau in London is not very pleased with you."

"I'm doing my best."

"Unfortunately your best is not good enough. You've deliberately allowed Holbrook to slip through your fingers time and time again."

"Deliberately?" Dufoir flushed angrily. "What the hell do you mean by that, *maître?*"

"Gabrielle Marsac. Do I need to say anything more?"

Dufoir avoided the lawyer's icy stare. He wondered if Vallin had been talking out of turn but then dismissed the idea as nonsense. Vallin was not even aware of Paupal's existence, let alone the fact that he was a member of the Resistance Council. Paupal knew precisely when Gabrielle Marsac had first come to their notice and was quite capable of putting two and two together.

"I thought she might be able to help us."

"How?"

"By persuading Holbrook to give himself up."

"Are you his keeper?"

Dufoir longed to wipe the sneer off his face. As of that moment, nothing would have given him greater satisfaction, but he knew that it would be foolish to make an enemy of Paupal. Paupal was one of the leading advocates at the Court of Paris and a close friend of the Commissioner of Police. He was also a man to harbor a grudge; one word from him in the right quarter and there would be no more promotion. The war couldn't last forever and he had his career to consider.

"I don't see why I should be responsible for his death, *maître.*"

"He's got to be apprehended one way or the other. Whether

you like it or not, those are the orders we've received from the Central Bureau. I suggest you widen the search and try to anticipate his next move."

"What am I supposed to do? Circulate his description to every prefect of police in France?"

"I don't think you need go any farther afield than Vernon."

Paupal was sharp, very sharp. Vernon was just eight miles from La Roche-Guyon. Holbrook might well see it as a convenient place to meet Gilbert.

Dufoir leaned forward, resting both elbows on the table. "Look, why should we care what happens to Rommel?" He kept his voice even, hoping that by so doing he could make Paupal see reason. "Is he a friend of ours? I mean, if he's that important to us perhaps we should call in the Gestapo."

"I hope it won't come to that."

"I was joking."

"Really? Well, it may be necessary to drop a friendly word of advice in the right quarter."

Dufoir stared at him. He wondered what the lawyer meant by a friendly word of advice in the right quarter. Was he seriously suggesting that they should warn Rommel that his life was in danger?

"Roland de Neury is on good terms with General Stülpnagel, isn't he, Dufoir?"

"So I'm led to believe."

"Good. I imagine the Military Governor of France can persuade Rommel to exercise a little caution. I know how much the Field Marshal enjoys his private shoot in the forest of Moisson, but everyone has to make sacrifices in wartime. Of course we can't be sure how Stülpnagel will react to this gratuitous piece of information. It would be most unfortunate if he referred it to the Gestapo, but that's a risk you will have to take."

"Me?" Dufoir said blankly.

"Oh, didn't I tell you?" Paupal looked astonished that he should have been guilty of such a careless oversight. "Well, naturally the Central Committee came to the conclusion that a man of your experience would know exactly how to handle de Neury."

"I see."

"Do you?"

"I can see which way the wind is blowing," Dufoir said grimly. "Don't worry, *maître,* I'll deliver Holbrook to them on a platter."

"Splendid." Paupal rubbed his hands. "I knew we would reach an understanding. There is just one other thing."

"Yes?"

"Find somebody who can repair the radio set for Fletcher. After all, we must keep our friends in SOE happy."

Dufoir thought the sudden about-face could only mean one thing: London had found a way to grab de Gaulle by the short hair, and the Albert circuit had been told to get him off the hook.

Cheval placed a foot on the hub cap and, turning in the direction of the café, raised his hand in a farewell salute before climbing up into the driving cab of the single-decker bus. Gilbert saw the gesture and didn't know what to make of his curious behavior. He had become accustomed to Cheval treating him like a leper, but now it seemed he'd had a change of heart and was anxious to renew their friendship. There had been no explanation; Cheval had simply walked into the café and sought him out as if nothing whatever had come between them.

Gilbert pushed the cup of coffee to one side and took out his pipe and a tin of tobacco. He thought Cheval had been acting a part; he'd been too effusive, too hail-fellow-well-met, which was out of character. He had chattered away nineteen to the dozen about everything under the sun except the one subject which was obviously uppermost in his mind. On at least two occasions during their conversation he'd seemed ready to bring it out into the open, but each time his courage had failed him at the last minute. Although there was nothing he could definitely put his finger on, Gilbert had a funny feeling that Cheval's strange demeanor had something to do with the letter he'd received that morning.

The letter was supposed to have been written by Foxhound, but Gilbert wondered if it was genuine. The franking on the envelope showed that it had been mailed in Paris on Wednesday evening, whereas the Englishman was known to be operating in the area of Chartres. On the other hand, the writer was in possession of certain information which indicated that the letter might be authentic. Couched in veiled language, he'd referred to their intended RV in Mantes on the seventh of July which he believed had been canceled by the Albert circuit at the request of SOE. Without actually naming him, it was also apparent that he knew Cheval was the link between Paris and La Roche-Guyon.

Yet, despite these pointers, a nagging seed of doubt remained. Like Cheval, the Englishman struck him as being a shade too anxious. Gilbert frowned, narrowing his eyes. Why hadn't he thought of it before? Cheval was the key, the one man who could have supplied the information to the SD. Cheval had been turned by the Gestapo; he was a V Mann—a *Vertrauensmann*—a trusted informer. If the Germans had smashed the Albert circuit, it would explain why he hadn't heard from the Central Committee. Cheval had avoided him like the plague for more than a week, but now that the dust had settled after the mass arrests in Paris he had been ordered to get in touch with him again.

Everything fitted together like the pieces of a jigsaw puzzle. Or did it? If Cheval was working for the SD, they would already know that if he wasn't actually the leader he was certainly a prominent member of the Resistance cell in La Roche-Guyon. There was no need for them to play cat and mouse; he was an old man of seventy-three and they could break him whenever they liked.

Gilbert chewed the stem of his pipe. He wasn't thinking straight. That was the trouble with old age; the arteries to the brain had a tendency to harden. In the final analysis, he was faced with a choice: either he met the Englishman in Vernon tomorrow or else he stayed at home. It was as simple as that.

Thérèse put a book of matches on the tray beside the glass of cognac and moved around the counter. Monsieur Gilbert was obviously worried about something, and she thought a drink might help to cheer him up. Smiling warmly, she approached his table in the window and placed the glass in front of him.

Gilbert looked up with a puzzled expression on his face.

"Why, Thérèse," he said, "there must be some mistake. I didn't order a cognac."

"It's on the house," she said quickly. "I thought you needed a little something to cheer you up."

"How very kind of you, Thérèse, but really you shouldn't have bothered."

"You looked so preoccupied that I couldn't help wondering if you'd had some bad news."

"Bad news?" Gilbert shook his head. "I was just deep in thought."

She hovered, uncertain what to say to him. Monsieur Gilbert certainly looked as if he wanted to confide in someone, but he was a very independent old man, the sort who kept his troubles to himself.

"The matches," she said brightly. "I almost forgot to give them to you."

"Matches?"

"To light your pipe." She frowned. It was most unlike him to be so vague. Perhaps it had something to do with his daughter; maybe she had heard that her husband was ill. "How is Yvette?" she asked softly.

"She's in good health." Gilbert smiled wryly. "She misses Jean, of course."

"Has she heard from him recently?"

"Not since Christmas."

"Not a word since Christmas." Thérèse looked thoughtful. "And he's been a prisoner of war since 1940. It must be very hard for her."

"Yes."

"She is wasting the best years of her life. Sometimes I wonder if it is ever going to end."

"What?"

"The war."

Gilbert struck a match and lit his pipe. Whether she was aware of it or not, Thérèse had helped him to see things in perspective. Perhaps the Gestapo had laid a trap for him, but what did that matter? He'd had the best years of his life. Tomorrow he would go to Vernon and meet the Englishman. If he existed, then maybe, just maybe, they might be able to end the war a little sooner.

Anneliese Ohlendorf entered the Brandenburg apartment building and heaved a sigh of relief. She had only to climb the spiral staircase to her apartment on the third floor and then she would be able to cool off under the shower. It had been a mistake to walk all the way home from the Unter den Linden station in this heat, even though it had seemed a good idea at the time. The trams were running few and far between, and because there had been a long line at the stop she had thought it would be quicker to go on foot. One, two, three, four, five, she counted the steps silently to herself, six, seven, eight . . .

A voice behind her said, "Frau Ohlendorf?"

Anneliese turned around. "Yes?" she said inquiringly.

The man was tall, good-looking, and blond, a carbon copy of her husband, Ulrich.

"Permit me to introduce myself." He smiled. "My name is Hans Winklemann."

"Do I know you?"

"I work in Amt Four."

She clenched her hand, digging the nails into the banister. Amt IV, the Gestapo, one of Heinrich Müller's subordinates. Looking past him, she saw that the door to the supervisor's apartment was ajar and guessed that Winklemann had been talking to the janitor.

"May I take up a few minutes of your time?"

"Yes." She cleared her throat nervously. "Yes, of course. Shall we go upstairs to my flat?"

"If it's not putting you to too much trouble."

He was very polite, but she'd heard that they always were to begin with. It was a different story once you put foot inside their headquarters down on Prinz Albrechtstrasse.

"Have you had far to walk?"

"What?"

He caught up with Anneliese and fell in step beside her. "You look tired."

"I am," she said with feeling. "It's been a long day."

"Yes, I imagine it has. Things must have been pretty hectic at the Air Ministry."

Anneliese caught her breath. How did Winklemann know that she worked in the Air Ministry unless the Gestapo were watching her?

"No more than usual," she said faintly. "Have you been waiting long?"

"About two hours."

"I'm sorry. Usually I'm home by six at the latest, but this afternoon I stopped off to see an old friend."

No apology was necessary and Winklemann hadn't asked for an explanation either; all the same, she had felt constrained to show that she had nothing to hide.

"I'm used to waiting." Winklemann smiled disarmingly. "As a matter of fact I only popped in on the off chance, but then the janitor grabbed me and I couldn't get away. You know what it's like."

"Yes, he does tend to go on a bit." Anneliese opened her handbag and found the doorkey. "Sometimes I think he invents most of his gossip."

"Allow me." Winklemann relieved her of the key and opened the door. There was an envelope of a reddish-brown color on the mat and, stooping, he picked it up and handed it to her. "I'm afraid it's only the telephone bill." He laughed. "I know because I received mine this morning."

He was so very friendly and neighborly too, it seemed. She thought Heinrich Müller must have formulated a new technique for the interrogation of suspects, on the lines of first-win-their-trust-and-then-apply-the-thumbscrew.

Winklemann followed her inside, glancing about him and sizing up the room like a prospective tenant. "The janitor tells me that you were very lucky," he said.

"Lucky?"

"It seems you escaped the blast."

"Oh, you mean the air raid a week ago last Monday." Anneliese shrugged her shoulders. "Yes, I suppose I was fortunate. The blast caught the front of the building; my apartment happens to be at the rear."

"It would have been a pity if this room had been damaged." He smiled again for the second time in as many minutes. "If you will allow me to say so, I admire your taste."

"Why, thank you, Herr Winklemann."

"And this must be your husband," he said, pointing to a photograph on a rosewood table.

"Yes, that's Ulrich."

"A magnificent pilot and an exceptionally brave man." Winklemann frowned. "I believe he scored eleven victories over the British and a further one hundred and four on the Eastern Front before he was reported missing in action. Am I right?"

"Yes." It was all too evident that Winklemann had done his homework. "He was awarded the Knight's Cross, but I expect you already know that."

"You must be very proud of him."

"I am." She hesitated briefly. "Can I get you a drink?"

"Oh, no. It's very kind of you to offer, but I've already taken up far too much of your time as it is. Actually, the reason I'm here is that I thought you ought to know that we are a little worried about Colonel General Ludwig Beck. I'm told you visit him quite frequently?"

"Yes." Anneliese moistened her lips. "We're distantly related."

"Quite. I understand he's a third cousin on your mother's side of the family or something like that. Anyway, we think he is behaving rather foolishly, mixing with the wrong kind of people. Of course, I hasten to add that we don't include you in that category."

"But you would advise me not to see him again?" Anneliese was horribly aware that her voice was little more than a whisper.

"Nothing of the kind; we have no desire to interfere in your personal affairs." He stared at the photograph of Ulrich Ohlendorf. "As a matter of fact, we hope that you might be able to help us."

"What do you want me to do?" she asked huskily.

"Just keep your ears and eyes open. We're interested in all his visitors."

"Am I to be a spy for the Gestapo?"

"My dear lady," he said smoothly, "your husband was an

ardent National Socialist and a war hero. Surely there is no need for me to labor the point?"

"No," she said quietly. "I'm aware of my obligation to the Führer."

"Good. I knew we could rely on you." Winklemann moved toward the hall and then suddenly turned about. "By the way," he said, "doesn't Major Epp live in this building?"

"Yes, he has an apartment on the floor below."

"Are you acquainted with him?"

Anneliese felt her stomach sink. Winklemann had been talking to the janitor and would know that she and Franz were seeing a lot of each other. "Yes." She clenched her hands, crumpling the telephone bill which she was still holding. "Is he in some sort of trouble?"

"Good heavens, no. I must remember to look him up sometime; we have a mutual friend. Perhaps you would give Franz my best wishes?"

"Certainly." Her throat was dry and she had difficulty in swallowing. "Actually, I know his wife, Sophie, much better than I do Franz. I've missed her an awful lot since she went to stay with her parents in Bavaria." Anneliese frowned, trying to recall exactly where in Bavaria Sophie had fled to so that she could lend substance to the lie. "They live in Kempten," she said brightly.

"Quite so." Winklemann stepped out into the hall. "If anything should come up," he said idly, "you will remember to call me, won't you?"

"Of course I will," she said gravely. "You'd better give me your telephone number."

"It's Potsdam Central three-one-nine-two."

"Potsdam Central three-one-nine-two. And the extension?"

"Four-oh-four."

"I'll make a note of it." She reached past him and opened the front door. "How very foolish of Ludwig," she muttered. "I mean you'd think he would know better than to get mixed up with the wrong kind of people."

"Well, I daresay he's in his dotage." Winklemann bowed and kissed her hand. "I'm delighted to have made your acquaintance, dear lady."

"And I yours, Herr Winklemann."

She closed the door behind him and leaned against it. Franz, she thought, I must warn Franz. No, that would never do; the janitor, the damned janitor would be watching her like a hawk from now on. Better and safer for Franz if she were to avoid him.

For the first time in her life, Anneliese Ohlendorf knew what it was like to be paralyzed with fear.

Holbrook walked out of the Église Notre Dame in Vernon satisfied that, although he had been forced to pick the spot from a guidebook, the church would make a good rendezvous. If Marcel Gilbert showed up tomorrow, he would be there waiting for him in the third row down from the back on the left-hand side of the nave. He glanced at his wristwatch, saw that it was after seven thirty, and decided it was time he met up with Gabrielle again. They were supposed to be two lovers snatching a night together in a strange town. It wasn't much of a cover story but it was the best he could do, and he thought there was a fair chance that the desk clerk would swallow it. The French had always had a proper regard for an affair of the heart.

18

Epp placed the checklist on the desk and drew the telephone toward him. His eyes went to the clock again and he watched the minute hand jump forward to cover the hour. Lifting the receiver, he dialed 9 to bypass the exchange and, having obtained an outside line, followed it with 82411. The call was answered promptly by the Wannsee Military Exchange and he asked the operator to put him through to the Orderly Room. There was just a brief pause before a deep voice said, "Extension three-thirty-one, adjutant speaking."

Epp wiped a tiny bead of perspiration from his upper lip and cleared his throat. "Major Epp," he said curtly, "General Staff One-B Headquarters Reserve Army. Operation Valkyrie Phase One with effect from eleven hundred hours."

"Operation Valkyrie Phase One, eleven hundred hours."

"Correct," said Epp. "Follow standard operating procedures and authenticate. This message timed at ten-oh-two hours."

He hung up and placed a large tick against the Luftwaffe Parachute Training School, realizing as he did so that there was no way out now because he had committed himself to an irreversible course of action. The adjutant at Wannsee would turn to the Reserve Army staff list, look up his name and office extension, and then ring back. The incoming call would be routed through the telephone exchange in the basement, and in all probability the operator would hear at least part of their conversation. If the coup d'état went off half cocked, it was more than likely that the duty signaler would remember that on Saturday the fifteenth of July, Major Franz Epp was one of several officers in the Bendlerstrasse who had been responsible for initiating Operation Valkyrie.

He picked up the telephone again, obtained an outside line, and dialed the School of Infantry at Döberitz. The exchange was quick to answer but the adjutant wasn't. A minute passed, then two, then three. Finally a breathless voice said, "Thadden, second in command."

Epp frowned, his eyebrows meeting in a straight line. "I wanted the adjutant."

"Well, you can't have him," said Thadden. "He's out on the training area with the commanding officer. You'll have to make do with me. Anyway, who wants him?"

"Major Epp, General Staff One-B Reserve Army. You'd better warn them both that Operation Valkyrie Phase One is effective from eleven hundred hours."

"I'm new here. What the hell is Valkyrie?"

Epp closed his eyes and mouthed an obscenity. "Get hold of your chief clerk and tell him to look up Internal Security Instruction four dash six dash alpha of twenty-one January 'forty-four. He'll know what to do."

"Right."

"One other thing," said Epp. "There are sealed orders for Valkyrie Phase Two in the adjutant's safe. You are not, repeat not, to open these until you receive the appropriate code word."

"Which is?"

"Gneisau."

"Gneisau," Thadden muttered vaguely.

"This message timed at ten-oh-seven hours."

"What's all that mean?"

"It means you've got fifty-three minutes to pull your finger out and get the unit rolling."

Epp dropped the phone on Thadden and ticked the School of Infantry off his list. Two down and three to go: the tanks at Wünsdorf, the Artillery Training Battalion at Jüterbog and the Panzer Grenadiers at Krampnitz. The tankers could prove awkward; they were at the disposal of Colonel General Guderian, the inspector of armored troops, and their commanding officer might jib at the idea of taking his orders direct from Reserve

Army. In the circumstances, he thought it would be advisable to deal with the other units first.

The telephone buzzed and he stretched out his right hand to answer it.

"Neurath," boomed a hearty voice, "Adjutant Luftwaffe Parachute Training School Wannsee. Is that Major Epp?"

"It is."

"Good; suppose you authenticate?"

"Valkyrie Phase One," said Epp, "your message timed at ten-oh-two hours."

"All right, what gives?"

"The natives are getting restless."

Neurath laughed rather too heartily. "Don't tell me that a mob is trying to burn our beloved Reichsmarshal Hermann Göring out of house and home?"

"Not yet, but it's a distinct possibility."

"Great. We'll bring a few cans of petrol with us to stoke up the fire."

"You're wasting time," Epp said coldly.

"Yes?"

"It's now ten-twelve; you'd better get moving."

"Oh, God," said Neurath, "to hear you talk, anyone would think there was a war on."

Epp smiled in spite of himself. "Good-bye, Neurath," he said cheerfully. "I'll buy you a drink when it's all over."

Neurath said, "I've heard that one before," and hung up.

In the space of the next thirty minutes, Epp rang Jüterbog, Krampnitz, and Wünsdorf. In each case, the tankers, the artillerymen, and the Panzer Grenadiers returned his call to verify that Valkyrie was authentic. The coup d'état, he thought, was proceeding smoothly, very smoothly thus far. He wondered if Mertz von Quirnheim had met with an equally satisfactory response from the units stationed in inner Berlin.

Apart from the Grossdeutschland Regiment, Quirnheim would have alerted the Weapon Training School and four Home Service battalions of dubious quality. Against these forces, the SS could muster their own Panzer Grenadier establishment at Saarow, the Totenkopf Training Center at Oranienburg, and the officer cadets from Lankwitz and Gross Lichterfelde. At Friedental they also had Otto Skorzeny's Special Service battalion, the elite unit which in September 1943 had rescued Mussolini from the mountaintop hotel at Gran Sasso where he was being held captive.

Epp thought it was fortunate that the Reserve Army was not responsible for these units which were part of Himmler's empire. Thanks to this divided chain of command, they were under no obligation to alert the Waffen SS, and the Wehrmacht would therefore have a head start on them. If it came to a showdown between the opposing forces, the Totenkopf and the officer cadets from Lankwitz and Gross Lichterfelde would probably make mincemeat of the four Home Service battalions. The Grossdeutschland Regiment, however, would be able to hold its own against the best of the SS unless Otto Remer, who had just taken over command of the Berlin Guard, became suspicious and refused to comply with the orders he received from the Bendlerstrasse. Whatever happened, it was going to be a close-run thing and the tanks from Wünsdorf could tip the balance either way.

The telephone interrupted his train of thought. Answering it, he heard a harsh voice say, "Thank God, now we're getting somewhere at last. Who am I speaking to?"

"Major Epp," he said acidly, "General Staff One-B."

"Oh, you're the General Staff, are you? Well, my name's Dollmann and I want to know what the hell's going on."

Epp frowned. Dollmann was the acting commandant of the Tank School, a fire-eater if ever there was one. "What can I do for you, colonel?" he said calmly.

"Do for me? I've already told you: I want to know what the hell you people in the Bendlerstrasse think you're playing at? I've just returned from Zossen to find twenty-five of my panthers sitting on the tank park with their bloody engines ticking over."

"That's because Valkyrie Phase One was passed to your unit at ten-twenty-three hours, colonel."

"Are you trying to teach me to suck eggs? I know we're at Condition Amber, but does Colonel General Guderian?"

"I assume he's been informed."

"Oh, you assume he's been informed," Dollmann said with

heavy irony. "Well, I'll tell you something, Epp, you'd better make damn sure he has, because I'm not moving from here until I hear something definite."

Give me strength, thought Epp, for God's sake give me strength; this bloody-minded individual is going to wreck everything.

"We are trying to get in touch with Colonel General Guderian," he said patiently, "but so far we haven't been able to reach him."

"That's your bad luck."

"Sir, this is an emergency; we haven't got time to go through the recognized chain of command."

"An emergency, you say?"

"Yes, sir." Epp played his trump card. "If you don't believe me, I suggest you speak to Colonel General Olbricht."

"Don't think I haven't tried already; his bloody telephone is permanently engaged." Dollmann clucked his tongue as if in two minds to leave it at that. Curiosity finally got the better of him. "Where's the Army Commander?" he rasped.

"On the way to Rastenberg with Colonel Stauffenberg."

"How very convenient."

In the silence which followed, Epp could hear a rhythmic click on the line. For a moment he thought they were in danger of being cut off, but then he realized that Dollmann was probably beating time with a ruler while he mulled over the situation.

"You are sure this is an emergency, Epp?"

"Yes, colonel."

"All right, we'll comply with your orders, but God help you if this turns out to be a training exercise."

Epp replaced the telephone and dried his sweating palms on a handkerchief, conscious that as of now there was nothing more he could do. In ten minutes' time the outlying units would leave their barracks to converge on Berlin; by noon, a ring of steel would encircle the Gestapo Headquarters in Prinz Albrecht-strasse, the Air Ministry in the Potsdamer Platz, and the Foreign Office, Reich Chancellory, and Department of Propaganda on Wilhelmstrasse.

Marcel Gilbert dismounted stiffly, leaned his bicycle against the railings in the rue Carnet, and padlocked the rear wheel to the frame. The eight-mile cycle ride from La Roche-Guyon had taken more out of him than he had bargained for; his calf muscles felt like lumps of iron but it was the pain in his chest that worried him more than anything else. It would, he thought, be a cruel stroke of fate if his heart should give out just when he was within spitting distance of the rendezvous. Squaring his shoulders back like a soldier on parade, he walked into the Église Notre Dame.

Black spots danced in front of him but he told himself that this was only to be expected; his eyes needed time to become accustomed to the stygian gloom inside the church. There was no need to rush things; the Englishman had said he would wait for him in the third row down from the back on the left-hand side of the nave, and he had underlined the word wait.

Gradually the mist cleared and he was able to see the altar at the far end of the nave. His pulse raced faster than ever; Foxhound was there, just where he had said he would be, in the third row down. Without noticeably turning his head, he glanced around the church and saw that it was practically deserted. There was nothing to fear; there were only ten other people, six of them women, and they were all elderly.

Gilbert walked slowly forward, spotted the prayer book lying on the chair next to Foxhound, and noted that it had been opened and placed face down with the spine pointing diagonally toward the aisle. His face still impassive, he stepped into the fourth row and sank down onto his knees. The Englishman had said to wait five minutes before he attempted to make contact with him, and he had to resist the temptation to keep looking at the watch in his waistcoat pocket. Five minutes was three hundred seconds, but he thought he would count up to three hundred and twenty to be on the safe side.

Holbrook watched the old man anxiously. He had caught a glimpse of him before he'd turned to face the altar and had been disturbed by the deathly pallor of his face. His back was ramrod straight now but the silver hair at the nape of his neck was still damp with sweat. It was a hot day, yet the old man, apparently determined to ignore the weather, was wearing a black suit, waistcoat, collar, and tie. Holbrook thought it was small wonder that he had almost fainted.

The old man rose to his feet and turned to face the aisle, his right hand gripping the back of the chair for support. Holbrook saw his index finger move, watched it tap out the Morse V signal and knew he was Gilbert. A brief flicker of recognition passed between them and then he was gone. Holbrook allowed a full minute to pass before he left his seat in the third row.

Gilbert stopped in front of the Virgin Mary, dropped a few coins into the collection box, and lit a candle. A hand brushed against his arm and, knowing what was expected of him, he turned away and walked out into the bright sun. He felt a gentle pressure on his elbow and was grateful to see that the Englishman was steering him toward a bench seat in the shade.

Holbrook said, "Are you feeling all right, Marcel?"

"I'm a little dizzy, but I'll be fine in a minute." Gilbert sat down on the bench and loosened his collar. "I expect it's the heat."

"It's good to see you."

"And you." Gilbert took out a large handkerchief and mopped his face. "What do I call you?"

"André," said Holbrook, "André Beauvais; it's a name I've been traveling with for some time. I ought to warn you that I'm not very popular with my people."

"So I gathered from your letter." Gilbert smiled to himself. "I don't imagine mine will be very pleased with me either after today."

"I still think we ought to go ahead, Marcel."

"So do I. What is it you wish to know?"

"Let's start with the shooting party."

Gilbert nodded. "There are usually six of them: the Field Marshal, his ADC, a lieutenant colonel in the Engineers, a fat little corporal who's in charge of the assault boat, a signaler, and the gamekeeper, Gustav Rudelatt. Rudelatt lives with his wife and two small children in a cottage on the other side of the river from La Roche-Guyon, opposite the demolished suspension bridge. He is connected to the château by a field telephone so that the Germans are able to warn him in advance when to expect

Rommel—usually about seven thirty in the morning at this time of the year." Gilbert paused and chewed his lip thoughtfully. "The Field Marshal has been known to miss a day, André."

"Yes?"

"It depends on the situation at the battlefront. If things are quiet, it seems he is content to stay in La Roche-Guyon."

"We'll just have to keep our fingers crossed." Holbrook scratched the rash of prickly heat that had developed under his chin. "What about this man Rudelatt?" he asked quietly. "Can he be trusted?"

"No. He bends with the wind like a reed; today he is a collaborator, tomorrow it might be a different story." Gilbert shrugged his shoulders. "I daresay the Resistance will multiply in leaps and bounds once artillery fire is heard in the distance." He wiped his face again. "Do you have a firearm?" he whispered.

"No, I plan to steal one. There must be plenty of dispatch riders on the road."

An old woman, her shoes down at heel, approached their bench and sat down with a sigh of relief. Gilbert stared at her with unconcealed loathing and slowly rose to his feet. There was nothing for it but to move on, preferably toward the river where they might be able to find a sheltered spot under the trees.

"Bonnières would be your best bet," he said when they were out of earshot. "Do you know it at all?"

"No."

"It's a small village between here and La Roche-Guyon. There's a very narrow bridge about half a mile outside Bonnières which the dispatch riders from Seventh Army use as a shortcut." Gilbert caught his breath; the pain in his chest was back again, stabbing like a knife. Gritting his teeth, he tried to ignore it. "You will find plenty of cover to spring an ambush, but if all else fails you can always dig up my carbine."

"What carbine?"

"An 1898 Berthier. I buried it in 1940 together with nine rounds of ammunition. Don't smile, it still works."

"I'm not smiling." Holbrook shot him an anxious glance. "Are you sure you're feeling all right?"

"Of course I am," Gilbert said irritably. "I keep telling you, it's just the heat. It was stupid of me to wear a suit."

"Perhaps we should find a café?"

"No, no, that wouldn't do at all; somebody might overhear us and there is so much I have to tell you."

His jaw was set in an obstinate line, and it was obvious to Holbrook that he was determined to have his own way. If he couldn't persuade the old man to rest, at least he could make sure they strolled along at a leisurely pace.

It took them twenty minutes to reach the river and Gilbert kept up a nonstop monologue, describing La Roche-Guyon in such detail that Holbrook could picture every house, every twist and turn of its narrow streets; the Château Rochefoucauld was as real to him as if he had seen it every day of his life, and by the time Marcel had finished, he felt he knew every track and clearing in the forest of Moisson as well as any of the villagers.

"Is there anything else I can tell you, André?"

"I don't think so." Holbrook squeezed his shoulder and smiled. "If half our people were as good as you, Marcel, this war would have been over long ago."

Of course the Englishman was exaggerating, Gilbert thought, but it was nice of him to say so. "What will you do now?" he asked quietly.

"We'll have to move on until we find somewhere to lie up."

"We? You have a companion?"

"A girl who's been helping me. It's a long story, but we're stuck with each other."

"I have a niece who owns a farm not far from here. . . ."

Gilbert leaned forward, resting both arms on his knees. He was tired, very tired, but it would only take a few minutes to tell the Englishman how to find Anne-Marie's place, and then he could go home to Yvette.

The bluebottle flew aimlessly back and forth, changing orbit with maddening inconsistency. Dufoir clenched the tightly rolled newspaper and waited for it to come within striking range. He had tried to ignore it, but the monotonous buzz of the insect's wings was a constant reminder of its presence and he was determined to kill it. Occasionally the fly would land on a wall, the ceiling, or a windowpane and there would be a moment or two of silence, but then, as if to deliberately provoke him, it would take off again.

Avoiding the drifting smoke from Vallin's cigarette, the blowfly described a figure eight in front of his face before spiraling in to land on the pen and inkstand. The insect rubbed its front legs together until, attracted by the odor of sweat, it left its relatively safe perch and settled on the blotting pad. Dufoir allowed the insect to develop a fleeting, false sense of security and then destroyed it with a vicious swat.

Vallin said, "I bet you wish you could do that to the Englishman, patron."

Dufoir dropped the newspaper into the wastepaper basket. Vallin had put his finger on a sore spot. He didn't like being reminded that Holbrook was a damn sight more elusive than any blowfly.

"I think you'd better watch your step, sergeant," he said coldly.

Vallin hastily looked the other way and wished he'd kept his mouth shut. He had known the patron long enough to read the warning signs. The downward slant of his mouth and the perpetual scowl were obvious indications that he was in a foul mood, and it had been stupid of him to ignore these omens.

The telephone broke through the wall of silence. It jangled once, lapsed, and then rang again. Dufoir answered it lethargically, convinced that the exchange operator had flashed the wrong extension.

A nasal voice said, "Inspector Dufoir?"

"Yes?"

"This is Inspector Kiffer; I'm calling from Vernon. I understand that you are interested in the whereabouts of a certain André Beauvais?"

"That's right."

"Well, it has just come to my notice that an André Beauvais from Rouen is staying at the Poste Hotel."

Dufoir glanced at the clock and raised his eyebrows in disbelief. The morning had gone and this bovine idiot on the other end of the telephone would have him believe that his men had only just finished wading through the hotel registrations. He wondered what sort of police department Kiffer was running in Vernon.

"The room was booked by a Madame Gabrielle Marsac. Does that mean anything to you?"

"Yes, it does. Look, I'd take it as a personal favor if you picked her up as well."

"It's as good as done."

"Do you know where they are at this present moment?" Dufoir asked casually.

"Not exactly, but don't worry, they won't get very far. Believe me," Kiffer said pompously, "I've got this town sewn up."

Dufoir cupped a hand over the mouthpiece. "All right, Vallin," he said wearily, "get the lead out. With any luck they might still be in Vernon."

"What about Fletcher and Jackson, patron?" Vallin saw the expression on his face and got the message. "I was only asking," he said plaintively.

Dufoir waited until his sergeant had left the office and then uncovered the mouthpiece. "Look, Kiffer," he said, oozing charm, "I hope you won't take this the wrong way, but I think you're going to need all the help you can get."

19

Marcel Gilbert mounted his bicycle and rode off down the rue Carnet. He would arrive home much later than Yvette had expected, but he was glad that he had listened to the Englishman and taken a rest. He was feeling much better; the pain in his chest had vanished and even his calf muscles had loosened up. Of course he would have to hide it from Yvette; she would only worry herself silly if she knew that he had had a mild heart attack, and she already had enough problems to cope with as it was.

He turned into the rue de Albufera and narrowly missed a pedestrian who had chosen the wrong moment to step off the curb. The woman shouted something after him but he didn't catch what she said, because suddenly the pain was back again, stabbing at his chest and spreading now to his left arm. Another hammer blow struck him and it was just as though he were falling into a dark, bottomless pit. Losing all sense of direction, he swerved across the road, mounted the pavement, and plowed into a fruit and vegetable stall outside a greengrocer's. The impact lifted him out of the saddle and he went over the handlebars, his arms and legs flailing like the vanes of a windmill. His head struck the plate glass window a glancing blow and he rolled over onto his back and lay there among the overturned crates, staring up at the sky through eyes that were sightless.

The shopkeeper was the first on the scene, but within the space of a few seconds a small crowd had gathered. A young woman, trying to be helpful, suggested that they ought to move well back so that the poor old man could get some air, but she was standing on the fringe and couldn't see his face. The greengrocer could;

he took one look at his open mouth and wide staring eyes and returned to the shop to call the hospital.

The ambulance men could see that the old man was dead, but in compliance with hospital regulations he was taken to the casualty department, where he was officially pronounced dead on arrival. From documents found in his possession, it was established that the deceased was Marcel Gilbert of 66A rue du Docteur Duval, La Roche-Guyon, and the police were notified accordingly. Subsequently, the body was transferred to the mortuary to await a post-mortem after formal identification by the next of kin.

Epp rested both arms on the ledge and leaned out of the window. A cloud of brick dust floated in the still air, making the heat haze over the Friedrichshain district thicker than elsewhere in the city. Somewhere beyond the massive flak towers which dominated the skyline it was evident that a party of workmen were busy demolishing the huge complex of tenement buildings which incendiaries had gutted earlier in the year. The Bendlerstrasse, however, was an oasis of calm and, but for the fact that he could just hear a Panther tank maneuvering into position in the vicinity of the Potsdamer Platz, it was difficult to believe that they were now poised to launch Phase II of Operation Valkyrie.

It seemed to him that they were still woefully unprepared to launch the coup d'état. They had to rely on a land line to communicate with the Grossdeutschland Regiment, and they were completely out of touch with the Panzer Grenadier company which was supposed to have cordoned off the radio stations at Königswusterhausen and Zossen. Anyone could see that it was vital to establish a wireless net to command the units which had moved into Berlin, but it appeared that Olbricht was reluctant to take this step yet, even though Stauffenberg had telephoned him at thirteen hundred hours to confirm that the conference was about to begin. He supposed Olbricht was worried in case the duty signals officer, a staunch member of the Nazi Party, became suspicious, but that didn't make a lot of sense. The die had been cast when he'd summoned the Military Commandant of Berlin to his office.

General von Hase had arrived shortly after eleven o'clock to be informed that in all probability Hitler would be killed that day and had departed half an hour later, after having given Olbricht an assurance that he would obey any order issued by the Bendlerstrasse. Epp reckoned that if the cat wasn't already out of the bag by now, its head was certainly showing.

He stared at the staff car which was parked in the shade of the trees on the opposite side of the road and envied the driver, who was fast asleep. There was one man, he thought, who obviously didn't have any problems on his mind. He looked a typical infantryman, tough, durable, and uncomplaining; Epp hoped he was not the sort of man to question an order from a superior officer, because very soon now he would have to collect Colonel General Beck from his house at Number 9 Goethestrasse.

Epp wondered what Anneliese Ohlendorf was doing at this moment. Preparing lunch? No, that was unlikely; she rarely had more than a sandwich and a cup of coffee at midday. Perhaps she was spending the weekend with her cousin whose apartment in Wilmersdorf overlooked the Dianasee? It would certainly explain why he had been unable to get an answer when he'd rung the bell of her apartment yesterday evening, but all the same he thought it was most unlike Anneliese to go off without leaving a message.

A voice behind him said, "The Colonel General would like to see you in his office, Herr Major."

Epp withdrew his head from the window and turned to face the chief clerk. The warrant officer's face was expressionless; either he didn't know what was going on or else he was very good at hiding his thoughts.

"Now?" he said unnecessarily.

"Yes, sir."

Epp collected his clipboard and limped out into the corridor, filled with a sense of deep foreboding.

Olbricht's office was only next door but one, yet it seemed more than a million light years away. As soon as he entered the room, it was obvious that something was terribly wrong. Mertz von Quirnheim looked as if he had seen a ghost, and the general seemed equally distraught although he was better at concealing it.

Olbricht looked up and greeted him with a nervous smile. "I've just had another telephone call from Rastenberg."

"From Claus?"

"Yes. It appears the meeting had barely got under way when, for no apparent reason, the Führer simply got up and walked out of the conference room. In these circumstances, Colonel Stauffenberg was left with no alternative but to abandon the attempt."

For the second time, thought Epp. First Berchtesgaden, now Rastenberg.

"That bloody man must suffer from Saint Vitus's dance," Quirnheim said dejectedly. "Sometimes I get the feeling that Hitler is indestructible."

"He's certainly unpredictable," Olbricht said calmly, "but all men are mortal. Our luck is bound to change soon."

"I hope you are right, general." Quirnheim leaned against the wall and folded his arms. "Anyway, what happens now? Do you want me to stand the units down?"

Olbricht pursed his lips and then nodded his head. There was nothing else they could do, but for a moment he had seemed reluctant to accept defeat

"What do I tell them, sir?"

"Nothing. I'll spend the rest of the afternoon visiting each commanding officer in turn to explain that Phase One of Operation Valkyrie was a training exercise."

Epp frowned. As soon as he returned from Rastenberg, Fromm was bound to ask on whose authority the exercise had been ordered. Epp could just picture him reminding them all that there was only one commander of the Reserve Army and his name was Fritz Fromm, not Friedrich Olbricht. There was, however, just a chance that the unit commanders might swallow it; Dollmann, the acting commandant of the tank school, certainly would because he had suspected that it might be an exercise from the word go.

"I shall want you to accompany me, Franz."

Epp looked at Olbricht and nodded dumbly.

"Of course, after this fiasco, the units may not respond with quite the same alacrity on the twentieth."

"What's happening on the twentieth, Herr General?"

"Oh, didn't I tell you?" Olbricht said casually. "That's the date of the next Führer Conference."

Jackson got out of the car and followed Fletcher and Vallin into the Poste Hotel. Kiffer, the officer in charge of the police station at Vernon, had said that it wasn't much of a place, and Jackson thought that if anything this was an understatement. The whole façade needed repointing before the bricks crumbled away, and there was a peculiar musty smell about the interior as if the wooden floors were infected with dry rot. The lobby, which included a poky little bar and sitting room at one end, was painted dark green to harmonize with the jungle of potted ferns and mother-in-law's tongue in the windows.

Vallin glanced around the lobby and frowned. Kiffer might like to think that he had the town sewn up, but there was no sign of the gendarme who was supposed to be keeping an eye on the place. If this was a typical example of the Vernon police department in action, it didn't give him a lot of faith in their ability to find the stable door, let alone close it after the horse had bolted.

"Don't tell me you're surprised," Fletcher said acidly. "I mean, you must know what these provincials are like. They're just a bunch of cabbages."

Vallin ignored him and rang the bell to summon the receptionist. Meeting with no response, he pressed it a second time. Eventually, a sour-faced young woman dressed in black appeared from the office. Vallin placed his ID card on the desk; the receptionist peered at it, squinting her eyes as if shortsighted, and then raised the counter flap.

"You'll find a gendarme waiting in the office."

The tone of her voice matched the expression on her face; Jackson couldn't help thinking it was a good thing the hotel didn't depend on her for its trade.

"André Beauvais and Gabrielle Marsac?" Fletcher leaned both elbows on the desk and hunched his shoulders. "What's their room number?"

The woman stared at him for a moment and then turned to Vallin, her lips compressed in a thin straight line. "I suppose this man is a police officer?" she said coldly.

Fletcher reached out and grabbed her by the wrist. "You want to watch your step," he said unpleasantly. "If you'd asked me nicely, I might have shown you my warrant card, but I don't like people who talk through me as if I didn't exist." He twisted her wrist just enough to make her grimace with pain and smiled sadistically. "Now, what did you say their room number was?"

"Two-oh-four."

"Two-oh-four." Fletcher released her and snapped his fingers impatiently. "Now be a good little girl and give me the passkey."

The woman massaged her wrist and glared at him with loathing. "You can have the key to their room," she snapped. "They won't be back until this evening."

"How long have they been gone?"

"Since nine o'clock."

Fletcher grunted and looked at Jackson. "What do you think?"

"I think seven hours is a very long time."

"So do I, but we'll take a look anyway."

"Maybe Vallin should cover the lobby while we go through their room?"

"Why not?" Fletcher moved toward the staircase. "He can always hold the gendarme's hand or hers."

Holbrook's room was at the far end of the corridor, facing the street and next door to one of the two bathrooms on the second floor. A large double bed crowned with brass knobs took up most of the available space, leaving just enough room for a washstand, a chest of drawers, and a hanging cupboard. There was a stick of shaving soap by the washbasin and a couple of toothbrushes in a tumbler on the shelf, but apart from two suitcases, both of which were locked, there was only one cheap-looking dress hanging in the cupboard.

Jackson turned the covers back, looked under the pillows, and then searched the chest of drawers. "You know something?" he said. "I get the impression that they left a few props behind to fool the management."

"I'd say that was pretty obvious." Fletcher dumped both fiber suitcases on the bed and forced the locks with a jackknife. "More stage props," he said.

"Don't tell me; they're stuffed full of newspapers and old magazines, right?"

"Clever," said Fletcher, "very clever. Now look into your crystal ball again and explain to me why Holbrook checked one of these suitcases into the left luggage office at the railway station in Vernon?"

"I don't know. Perhaps Gabrielle Marsac went on ahead to make the hotel reservations while he looked the place over?"

"What place?"

"Some sort of rendezvous. Look, I'm sure he came here to meet somebody, probably somebody who lives in La Roche-Guyon."

It was pure conjecture but it made sense. Holbrook was stalking a specific target, and he would want to know exactly how many standing patrols he was likely to encounter in the area of La Roche-Guyon and the pattern of their activity.

"I think you've hit the nail on the head," Fletcher said thoughtfully. "I can't see how Holbrook did it, but I've got a nasty feeling that he's bypassed the Albert circuit and is in touch with the local Resistance."

"And now they could be hiding him. Have you thought of that possibility?"

"I have, and I don't like it."

"Perhaps Dufoir can help us?"

"How?"

It was a good question, one that Jackson found it impossible to answer off the cuff. "Your guess is as good as mine," he said lamely. "Couldn't Dufoir ask the Central Committee in Paris to use their influence? They ought to be able to get some cooperation out of the local Resistance."

"And just what do we do in the meantime?"

"We can always hang around the police station for a bit." Jackson shrugged his shoulders. "Something might turn up."

"You sound like Mr. Micawber."

"Well, if you've got a better idea, let's hear it."

Fletcher smiled sourly. "That's the trouble, I haven't."

He still thought it would be a complete waste of time but, as it turned out, he was wrong. At twenty minutes past five, a slim dark-haired girl walked into the police station in Vernon and asked to see Inspector Kiffer. Her name, she said, was Yvette Lemmonier and she had come at the request of the police in La Roche-Guyon to identify a body which might be that of her father, Marcel Gilbert. It took Vallin less than half an hour to contact Dufoir and establish that Marcel Gilbert commanded the Resistance group in La Roche-Guyon. It took Jackson and Fletcher just two minutes to decide that if they were going to find Holbrook in time they could say good-bye to Paris.

Holbrook stared at the farm, which lay well back from the lane, and wondered if this was the place they were looking for. It matched Gilbert's description, but he'd seen three other farms in the neighborhood which were very similar. He thought they had covered the best part of seven miles, which ought to put them well beyond the village of Blaru, but he couldn't be sure. Once clear of Vernon, he had made a wide detour through the forest of Bizy to avoid the road leading south, and it was possible that he had veered too far to the east.

"Are we lost?" Gabrielle asked anxiously.

"I'm not sure."

"I can see a hamlet in the distance, if that's any help."

"Where?"

"Behind you." Gabrielle sat down on the grass verge and stretched her legs, grateful for the respite to take the weight off her feet.

Holbrook turned about. There was a hamlet in the distance, but it was the double line of poplar trees which interested him more. Where there were poplar trees, there was almost certain to be a main road, and if that was so, this one happened to run in a straight line from east to west.

"That must be National Route Thirteen," he muttered.

"What does that mean?"

"It means I know where we are." He grabbed hold of her hand and dragged Gabrielle to her feet. "Come on," he said encouragingly, "it's not much farther now."

"I wish I could believe that," she said with feeling.

A dog heard them coming while they were still some way off

and started barking. By the time they reached the farmhouse, a little girl of five or six, a tough-looking young man, and a very stout middle-aged woman with iron-gray hair were waiting for them. The young man was holding a pitchfork and looked as if he was prepared to use it. Holbrook thought it was quite a reception committee.

"Madame Anne-Marie Lebrun?" he asked tentatively.

"Who wants to know?"

"Marcel Gilbert said you would shelter us."

"Marcel Gilbert?" Her eyes narrowed to pinpoints. "I don't know any Marcel Gilbert."

The young man raised the pitchfork and pointed it at him like a bayonet.

"He said that if there was any doubt in your mind, I should remind you of a scar."

"A scar?"

"On your right leg above the kneecap. You were thirteen years old, and you got it trying to climb over a barbed wire fence."

Her eyes grew bigger, a broad smile creased her plump face, and then she embraced Holbrook and the young man lowered his pitchfork.

Nine hundred miles to the east, Anneliese Ohlendorf was seeking a different kind of haven, one that was far removed from the Gestapo Headquarters in Prinz Albrechtstrasse and where people like Heinrich Müller and Hans Winklemann would never be able to reach her. She looked at the sleeping pills in her hand and smiled. A kindly doctor had prescribed them for her when Ulrich was reported missing in action, little knowing that she had no need of them. Swallowing the pills, she hastily washed them down with a large glass of schnapps and then climbed into bed. Putting her head into the gas oven would have been a more certain way of ending her life, but she was anxious that the coroner should record a verdict of accidental death. The Gestapo might suspect that she had committed suicide but they would have no proof, and Franz would be safe. She wondered if Franz Epp would understand that she had chosen this way out for both their sakes.

20

Anneliese Ohlendorf opened her eyes and raised an arm to shield her face from the glare of the sun. The inside of her mouth felt as if it had been coated with a thick paste, and her head was splitting. The black despair which came with the realization that her attempt at suicide had failed swiftly disappeared and was replaced by a profound sense of relief that she was still alive. Suddenly aware that a bell was ringing, she rolled over onto her side and instinctively reached out to shut off the alarm.

The bell refused to stop, and above its strident peal she thought she could hear someone calling her name. For several seconds she lay there convinced that the disturbance must be a figment of her imagination, but then the caller started pounding on the door, and above the din she recognized the voice of Franz Epp.

Throwing the bedclothes to one side, Anneliese slipped her feet into a pair of slippers and, grabbing her dressing gown, staggered out into the hall. Her legs felt as if they were made of cotton wool, and in her anxiety to reach the door before he succeeded in arousing the whole apartment house she slipped and fell on the polished floor, bruising her head against the corner of the hall table. Still dazed from the blow, she struggled to her feet and opened the door.

Epp caught her as she was about to fall again and helped her into the sitting room. It wasn't easy for him with his damaged pelvis but he managed somehow to lower Anneliese onto the couch, put her feet up, and place a cushion behind her head. It was then that he noticed the film of white mucus around her mouth. Taking out a handkerchief, he gently wiped her lips.

"I'll get you a drink," he said huskily.

Anneliese waved a hand in feeble protest. "No." She cleared her throat and tried again. "No, a drink is the last thing I want."

"Coffee then?"

She nodded and smiled wanly. "Dear Franz," she whispered, "what would I do without you?"

"I often ask myself the same question about you. I can't imagine what life would be like if we never saw each other again."

"I can't take much more of this, Franz."

Take much more of what? he wondered. Their hole-in-the-corner affair? Well, she was right; it was time he faced up to the situation and did something about it.

"We need each other, Anneliese," he said quietly. "Look, as soon as I get the chance, I'll go to Kempten and explain things to Sophie."

"No." She shook her head vehemently. "No, you don't understand. It has nothing to do with Sophie; I just can't go on, that's all, I just can't go on." Her voice tailed away and died in a whisper.

"I'll make the coffee." Epp patted her hand and awkwardly rose to his feet. "And then we'll talk about it, all right?"

"If you say so."

Epp left her reluctantly and went into the kitchen. He was no psychologist, but he'd spent a year on the Russian Front and could recognize the symptoms of acute anxiety neurosis when he saw them. Anneliese had been on edge for some time, but he'd never seen her looking so distraught before. He had a nasty feeling that something traumatic must have happened to her in the last forty-eight hours. Scarcely aware of what he was doing, Epp filled the coffeepot and, leaving it to percolate on a low flame, returned to the sitting room.

"Coffee in ten minutes," he announced in a cheerful voice.

"That's nice."

She was still listless and withdrawn. Somehow he would have to find a way to get past the barrier without disclosing that he was worried about her.

"You've had me running around in circles," he said teasingly. "I thought you were trying to avoid me. I even rang your cousin in Wilmersdorf to see if you were staying with her."

"What time is it?"

The question threw him completely. Epp stared at her for several moments and then, recovering, he said, "It's eleven thirty. Obviously you must have overslept."

"I tried to kill myself."

Epp thought there must be something wrong with his hearing. Anneliese was a practicing Catholic; she would never dream of doing a thing like that. "What did you say?" His voice sounded as if it were coming from a long way off.

"I tried to kill myself with an overdose of sleeping pills."

"For God's sake," he said hoarsely, "what on earth possessed you to do such a stupid thing?"

"Hans Winklemann."

"Winklemann?" he repeated blankly.

"A Gestapo agent. He asked to be remembered to you; it seems you have a mutual friend."

"I'm quite certain we haven't."

Anneliese inclined her head in a manner which suggested that she had always known that Winklemann was lying. Her eyes began to cloud over. As the silence between them lengthened, he feared that Anneliese had retreated into a protective shell where no one could reach her, but then suddenly the dam gave way and she couldn't stop talking.

It wasn't a very coherent story, but he could follow it well enough and even anticipate the ending. Ever since the day Anneliese had told him that she thought a Gestapo agent had shadowed her from Beck's house in Goethestrasse, he had had a premonition of impending disaster, and now it was upon them. Apparently, Winklemann had as good as said that the SD suspected Beck was involved in some sort of conspiracy; they were probably watching Stauffenberg, Olbricht, and Quirnheim too. He wondered if, like Fromm, the Gestapo were sitting on the fence biding their time while they waited to see which way the cat would jump.

Fromm certainly knew that something was in the wind. Any other commander in chief who discovered that his staff had ordered Valkyrie Phase I to be implemented without his authority would have raised one hell of a stink, but not Fromm. On his return from Rastenberg, the army commander had asked Quirnheim for his report on the exercise and then, having expressed an opinion to the effect that it had obviously been a complete foul-up, had merely warned him to be more careful in future.

Whether or not it was intentional, Fromm had definitely succeeded in making things a damn sight more awkward for them. Mindful of his veiled warning to Mertz von Quirnheim, Olbricht had decided that it would be foolish to place the garrison on full alert before the Führer's conference had assembled. They had learned a valuable lesson, he'd said, and therefore on Thursday the twentieth of July they would do nothing, absolutely nothing, to set the wheels in motion until they heard from Rastenberg that Adolf Hitler was dead.

"You do understand, don't you, Franz?"

Epp smiled to cover his confusion. This was the second time that Anneliese had caught him woolgathering. He wished he'd paid more attention to what she had been saying.

"I had to do it." She chewed her thumb, nibbling at the nail. "You see, I knew that if the Gestapo interrogated me for any length of time, I was almost bound to betray you and Ludwig and all the others."

Her question made sense to him and he knew she was right. If the Gestapo turned nasty, she would snap like a dry twig. He would have to get her out of Berlin on some pretext or other, because all hell could break loose on Thursday.

"You need a rest, my girl," he said cheerfully. "A holiday in the country."

"A holiday." Her head slumped forward on her shoulders. "There's nothing I'd like better, but how can I possibly leave Berlin at a time like this? There's still so much to do."

"Nonsense," Epp said firmly. "Everything is cut and dried. It may seem brutal but we don't need you any more."

"You don't?"

Her voice sounded doubtful but he could tell that she was eager for him to reassure her. "Look, Beck knows that we will send a car for him as soon as we hear that Stauffenberg has sent our glorious Führer to kingdom come. You've done your bit. It's over—finished."

Her lips parted in a tentative smile but it didn't last. "You've forgotten one thing," she said dejectedly, "my job at the Air Ministry."

Epp rubbed his eyes. Anneliese was a great one for making difficulties. "Who's your doctor?" he asked.

"Zeitzler, Erhard Zeitzler."

"How long have you been going to him?"

"Three years." She frowned. "No, it's more like four. He was very kind to me when Ulrich was reported missing in action."

"Well then, I daresay he will be only too happy to give you a sick note. I want you to telephone him now and say that you are feeling very poorly and could he please come and see you as soon as it's convenient."

"I can't do that, Franz."

Epp ignored the interruption. "And then I'll call Sophie to let her know when you will be arriving."

"Sophie?" Anneliese pushed a hand through her tousled hair. "You must be out of your mind. How can I possibly stay with Sophie?"

"Sophie likes you. She's always thought of you as one of her dearest friends."

"Oh, I'm a very dear friend," Anneliese said bitterly. "The moment her back is turned I can't wait to climb into bed with her husband. She's bound to ask me all sorts of embarrassing questions about you. What am I going to say to her? 'My dear Sophie, you don't know what you've been missing all these months; Franz has been humping me like mad and I've enjoyed every minute of our lovemaking'?"

"All right, all right," he said desperately, "if you can't bear to face Sophie, where will you go instead?"

"I don't know, Franz. Does it matter?"

"It matters to me." He leaned over the couch and gently squeezed her shoulder. "Sophie doesn't have to know; you could keep it from her if you really tried. You must go to Kempten, if not for your sake, then for mine."

"I'll think about it."

"We're running out of time," he said quietly. "When I leave for La Roche-Guyon tomorrow, I want to know that you will be on the train for Munich."

"La Roche-Guyon?" Her voice was a dull echo. "Why are you going there?"

"Oh, it's just routine. Army Group B is screaming for reinforcements and Fromm wants me to soft-soap them."

The lie rolled off his tongue with practiced ease, but Epp was glad that she couldn't see his face. The reinforcement situation was just a means to an end; the real purpose of his visit was to reassure Rommel that, contrary to what he might have heard on the grapevine, everything was going smoothly. The foul-up on the fifteenth of July? My dear Field Marshal, you know how it is with a dress rehearsal, but rest assured it will be all right on the day.

"When are you leaving, Franz?"

"At oh-one-hundred hours." Epp smiled. "Can you think of a more ghastly time?"

Anneliese swung her feet off the couch. "The coffee will be boiling over."

"What about Dr. Zeitzler?"

"I'll call him after I've seen to the coffee."

"Do it now."

"Don't push me, Franz," she said. "I've said that I will telephone him, and I mean to in my own good time."

Dufoir walked into the elevator, closed the gate behind him, and pressed the button for the fourth floor. He thought it must be nice to be someone like Paupal who could afford an apartment on the rue de Rivoli with a view of the Tuilerie Gardens. It was ironic but, in a way, Paupal owed much of his affluence to him, in that a large part of the lawyer's income stemmed from prosecuting or defending the people whom he arrested and charged. Dufoir reckoned that if he could have his time over again he knew which profession he would choose.

The elevator shuddered to a halt, jarring his spine. Opening the gate, Dufoir stepped across the corridor and rang the bell to the lawyer's apartment. Paupal didn't seem at all pleased to see him, not that there was anything unusual about that; offhand, Dufoir could not recall a single occasion when he had received a cordial welcome from him. On a social level they were poles apart, and Paupal seemed determined to keep it that way. This was his first visit to the apartment on the rue de Rivoli, and it looked as if the study was all that he was going to see of it. For a moment Dufoir wondered if the lawyer was even going to invite him to sit down, but then a plump hand waved vaguely, which he took as an indication that he should make himself comfortable in one of the leather armchairs if he so wished.

"I hope you've got some good news for me this time," Paupal said, frowning.

"I only wish I had, *maître.*" Dufoir pinched the lobe of his right ear, an unconscious habit which only came to the fore when he felt ill at ease. "Unfortunately, Vallin thinks that Holbrook and Gabrielle Marsac must have left Vernon before the road-blocks were in position."

"So you've lost them again?"

"Temporarily."

"Temporarily." Paupal snorted in disgust. "I've heard that one before. What about Gilbert's daughter? Doesn't she have any idea where they might have gone?"

Dufoir shook his head. "Madame Lemmonier wasn't even aware that her father was connected with the Resistance."

"I find that incredible."

"Well, you don't have any children, do you, *maître?* I mean, it simply wouldn't occur to you that Marcel Gilbert would want to protect his daughter. As far as he was concerned, the less Yvette knew about the Resistance movement in La Roche-Guyon, the better it was for her. Still, we can be sure of one thing: Hollbrook won't have strayed far from the area."

"I didn't know you had a crystal ball, Dufoir."

"I'm a policeman," he said coldly. "I deal in facts, not flights of fancy. Gilbert will have told him everything he wants to know except the one vital piece of information which he was not in a position to supply anyway. All the intelligence data in the world can't alter the fact that Rommel has a mind of his own; he's the man who decides whether or not he can spare the time to go shooting. If Holbrook is determined to assassinate the Field Marshal, he'll have to keep the château under observation. My guess is that he will build himself a hide on the opposite side of the river."

Paupal thought Dufoir was probably right, but he couldn't see where it was leading them. It would take Vallin and the two SOE agents several days, if not a week, to search the forest of Moisson, even supposing they could enter this prohibited area.

"If I were Holbrook, *maître,* I'd also want to keep an eye on the gamekeeper. It won't be easy to arrange, but if we could get both SOE agents into Rudelatt's cottage, I think they would then be well placed to intercept him."

It was not a wholly impracticable idea, but in Paupal's opinion the risks were unacceptably high and the end result too uncertain. There was an alternative: they could use de Neury to warn the German High Command that Rommel's life was in danger. Much as he found it distasteful to deal with a collaborator, he was now convinced that this was the only solution which stood any chance of success.

"I think you had better recall Vallin," he said quietly.

"When?"

"As soon as possible."

"That's what I thought you would say, *maître,* but it can't be done; at least, not until things blow over." Dufoir could see that Paupal didn't like it, nor did he appreciate the complications. "Look," he said forcefully, "we've told the Vernon police department that Holbrook and Gabrielle Marsac are wanted for questioning in connection with a series of burglaries committed in Paris. Now, whether we like it or not, Inspector Kiffer has got the bit between his teeth and we've got to go along with him. You take it from me, he'll think it very strange if we pull Vallin and the others out before he's positive that our two suspects are no longer in his area. I know what you've got in mind, *maître,* and I'll warn Vallin to stay well clear of La Roche-Guyon, but that's the best I can do. Even then I can't guarantee that the other two will take any notice of me. The American might, but not the Englishman."

"That's quite a speech," Paupal said coldly.

"I'm sorry, but I thought you ought to know just how many problems we're up against."

The lawyer stared at him, the expression on his face a mixture of resentment and grudging respect. Dufoir got the impression that perhaps for the first time in a long and distinguished career,

Paupal found himself unable to think of an argument to rebut the facts.

"All right," he said reluctantly, "we'll handle it your way. But I want you to see de Neury today, without fail. Is that clear?"

It was only a partial surrender and there was a nasty sting in the tail. Unless he did something about it, Paupal would leave him holding the shitty end of the stick.

"Would you accompany me?" Dufoir said slowly. "You see, I'm only a police inspector but you're a man of considerable influence, *maître,* and I think de Neury would listen to you." He waited expectantly, hoping the lawyer was not averse to a little flattery.

"Do you happen to know his telephone number?"

"It's Trinité nine-eight-six-two-oh."

"I can see I underestimated you." Paupal smiled fleetingly and reached for the telephone. "I have a feeling that I have been out maneuvered."

Dufoir leaned back in his chair and heaved a quiet sigh of relief. It was a pity about Holbrook, but he'd done the best he could for him and that was it: finis, kaput, over. Nobody could save Holbrook from himself, except perhaps SOE. They should never have sent him back to France again. Twice was enough for any man; giving him a third mission was just asking for trouble.

Paupal replaced the phone and swore. "De Neury," he said tersely, "is spending the weekend in Versailles."

"Yes?"

"So I've left a message that I want to see him tomorrow morning at nine."

Dufoir nodded. Holbrook, it seemed, had been granted a short reprieve; Dufoir just hoped that he would use the next twenty hours to advantage.

Holbrook pumped the foot pedal and held the kitchen knife against the grindstone, honing it until he was satisfied that the blade was as sharp as a razor. He remembered one of his instructors at the Special Training School saying that even the most innocent-looking object could be turned into a lethal weapon with a little ingenuity. His favorite example had been the handle of a lady's hair comb which had been shaved to a needle point and which he claimed was as good as six inches of cold steel. The instructor had been a great one for breathing fire and brimstone, but Holbrook wondered if he'd ever even seen a German soldier, let alone getting close enough to sink a knife into him.

Holbrook tested the point against his thumb and then placed it down on the workbench. The knife was a standby weapon and with any luck he wouldn't have to use it. He ran an eye over the rest of the equipment: a fishing rod, a spare reel, a homemade knife sheath, a pair of pliers, and a length of wire attached to an earphone belonging to an old crystal set. With the exception of the earphone and the knife, it looked innocent enough, but if he was stopped and searched for any reason, he knew that he would have a hard time trying to explain why he needed those two items. Holbrook glanced at the rusty bicycle propped against the wall. He could always hide the earphone in the small tool bag behind the saddle, but the knife was a different matter altogether. No inquisitive German was likely to believe that this murderous weapon formed part of his fishing tackle.

The door behind him opened inward, scraping against the floor of the lean-to shed, and instinctively he grabbed the knife and whirled around to face the intruder. Gabrielle Marsac stared at the blade pointed at her stomach and backed away.

"For God's sake," she whispered hoarsely, "it's only me."

Holbrook pushed the knife into the homemade sheath and put it back on the workbench. Conscious that his hands were shaking, he hid them behind his back in the hope that she wouldn't notice. "I thought it was someone else," he said lamely.

"Who? Anne-Marie Lebrun? Are you frightened of a woman now?" Gabrielle shook her head sadly. "Take a good look at yourself, Simon, you're wound up like a spring. One more turn of the key and you'll snap."

Simon, he thought; well, that was one for the book. Gabrielle had stopped calling him Simon the day she announced that she was going to marry Charles Marsac. "Have you quite finished?" he asked softly.

"Not by a long sight, but I know I'll be wasting my breath. I doubt if there is anything I can say which will make you change your mind."

"You don't understand . . ."

"Oh, I understand better than you think," she said vehemently. "This childish vendetta is all because of your father." She clenched her hands, digging her nails into the palms. "And your father never was and never could be worth dying for. Behind that ready smile and superficial charm, he was nothing, a nobody, a sponger who lived off your mother's people."

She saw his eyes narrow and braced herself, expecting him to strike her.

"Don't you think I'm aware of that?" He cupped her face in the palm of his hand. "There's nothing you can tell me about my family that I haven't seen with my own eyes. Maybe there was a time when I saw this as an opportunity to settle an old score, but that hasn't been so for quite a while now."

"No? Then why not give it up?"

The question was purely rhetorical. Holbrook dropped his hand and leaned against the workbench, knowing that it was pointless to interrupt her until Gabrielle had finished whatever it was she wanted to say.

"Look, Simon, can't you see that we're safe here? We can stay in hiding until the Allies arrive and then you can explain everything. Perhaps that sounds despicable to you, but you've done more than your share. Let someone else do the fighting for a change."

It was an age-old argument, one that dated back to time immemorial. He thought it probable that throughout history, in countless millions of homes, countless millions of women had said much the same thing to countless millions of men.

"You're not listening to me." Anger showed in her eyes.

"You're wrong," he said quietly. "Don't think I'm not tempted, but I can't forget that out there, somewhere, there are two men looking for me and they won't give up searching. Sooner or later they will catch up with us, and when they do, they won't be in a mood to listen to any explanations from me. If I shoot Rommel before they get to me, then we stand a chance."

He turned his back on Gabrielle and placed his left foot up on the workbench. Hiking the trouser leg up to the knee, he picked up the sheathed knife and strapped it to his calf.

"Besides, there's another reason."

"I don't want to be reminded that it's your duty," she said wearily.

"It has nothing to do with duty. I'm tired of this war; I want it to end so that I can go home."

"Home, Simon? And just where might that be?"

"Home is where you are," he said.

Gabrielle stared at him, her eyes blinking rapidly. "Oh, God," she said, "I think I'm going to cry."

Lieutenant Josef Udet was one of a tiny handful of officers and men who had served with the 21st Panzer Division from the day it had first appeared in the Wehrmacht Order of Battle. He had been right through the North African campaign with the division from May 1941 until March 1943, when he was evacuated from Tunisia after being severely wounded at Medenine; and now he was back with the same old outfit in Normandy, except that it wasn't quite the same old outfit. What was left of the old 21st Panzer Division after the long retreat from El Alamein to Tunis had gone into the bag when von Arnim surrendered, and the character of this phoenix which had risen from the ashes of defeat was entirely different. It was still a division to be reckoned with, stubborn and tenacious in defense, but it had lost its old fire and élan in attack.

It was also under strength; Lieutenant Udet's company consisted of exactly five Tiger tanks which were deployed in an orchard outside Saint-Pair. From this position he had a commanding view of the railway embankment beyond the sunken road which ran from Troarn to Mondeville on the outskirts of Caen. Udet had fought the British at Tobruk, Sidi Rezegh, Knightsbridge, Alam-el-Halfa, El Alamein, and Medenine, and he had thought that he knew them so well that they were incapable of springing a surprise on him, but he had been mistaken. Under cover of darkness, the British had erected a huge canvas screen which stretched from a small copse on the forward slope of the high ground beyond the railway embankment to a group of farm buildings on the skyline.

Udet had spent the whole day staring at the canvas screen and the columns of dust which rose into the air behind it. The buildup of armored vehicles which had continued on and off since first light had now started up again, after a lull lasting all afternoon. Udet lowered his field glasses and thought it was about time he sent another sitrep to Regimental Headquarters.

Dropping back inside the turret of his Tiger tank, he adjusted his headset and called control. His was just one of a thousand sightings which flowed back through regiment, division, corps, and 7th Army to La Roche-Guyon, just one of a thousand sightings which confirmed Rommel's opinion that the British were about to launch a major offensive from the salient east of the Orne River with the aim of seizing the Caen–Falaise plain.

The offensive was code-named GOODWOOD, and that was about the only thing which was secret about it. Into the tiny salient held by the 6th Airborne and 51st Highland divisions, Montgomery had moved the 11th, 7th, and Guards armored divisions, and despite the most elaborate camouflage and deception plan it was impossible to conceal this fact from the Germans. Rommel's assessment of the situation was correct in every detail except one; he was convinced that the attack would open on Monday, July 17, whereas it was scheduled for Tuesday.

21

The twilight had faded rapidly, and now that it was dark the wood came alive with the sound of movement. The undergrowth rustled, an owl hooted, and somewhere in the distance a fox barked. A squirrel in search of food paused to stare at a clump of ferns, only to dart away again as if alarmed by what it had seen. Making as little noise as possible, Holbrook removed the camouflage screen of bracken which covered his body from head to foot and climbed out of the shallow ditch where he had been lying on his back for the past four hours. For some moments he stood there in the clearing, flexing his cramped leg muscles to remove the stiffness, and then, picking up the fishing rod, he moved stealthily toward the road.

National Route 13 resembled an old Roman road. From Évreux, with the exception of a kink south of Pacy, it ran dead straight through open country until, reaching the forest sandwiched between the crossroads outside Bonnières, it snaked through a series of S-bends. This particular stretch of road was a known accident black spot, and the military police had posted warning signs on both approaches to the hazard. In choosing this site for an ambush, Holbrook had thought it reasonable to assume that a dispatch rider from 7th Army was unlikely to observe the speed limit, since he would know the route to La Roche-Guyon like the back of his hand.

Leaning the fishing rod against the tree, Holbrook removed his shoes and walked across the road in his stockinged feet. The plan which he had in mind was simple enough and was based on a tip he had picked up from one of his instructors who had served with the International Brigade in Spain. Taking both reels out of his jacket pocket, he tied the hooks and married the separate catguts by weaving the lines together in a crude splice. The fir tree which he selected as an anchor was roughly eighteen inches in diameter, but to be on the safe side he used six feet of line to make a firm lashing around the trunk at chest height. Satisfied that it would take the strain, he then walked backward, unreeling and twisting the lines to form a single strand of trip wire across the road to the wood on the opposite side, where he looped the other end of the cord over a low-hanging branch. Needing a toggle to spring the trap, he broke the fishing rod in half and tied both pieces onto the line. In theory there was no reason why it shouldn't work, but to reassure himself that the line would run smoothly he gave the toggle a savage jerk and was exalted when the wire, which was almost invisible to the naked eye, whipped into the air. Releasing the toggle, Holbrook relaid the trip wire across the road and then, having collected his shoes, sat down to wait, resting his back against the tree to make himself as comfortable as possible.

There was no telling when a victim might come his way, but he knew that soon after last light every field unit would have sent a strength-and-casualty return to its parent formation headquarters. Sooner or later, some harassed staff officer would produce a consolidated return for the whole of 7th Army in such detail that it couldn't be sent over the air by the wireless rear link to La Roche-Guyon. Sooner or later, therefore, this return would end up at the signals center for onward movement by a dispatch rider. It was exactly 0155 hours when Holbrook heard the snarl of a motorcycle in the distance and knew that his hypothesis was correct.

The dispatch rider ignored the speed limit and went through the first S-bend doing fifty. Veering across to the wrong side of the road, he negotiated the next curve and opened the throttle as he entered the straight. The beam of light from the masked headlamp was too faint to pick up the trip wire, and he only saw it a split second before it sliced into his chest and lifted him out of the saddle. The line snapped under the strain and, whiplashing, stripped the foliage from the branch above Holbrook's head. The BMW, meanwhile, flipped over onto its side and slewed toward the verge, the footrest gouging a jagged furrow in the road surface. The throttle was still open and the 500cc engine screamed like a banshee as it continued to drive the rear wheel.

Holbrook took one look at the German, saw that his neck was broken, and ran toward the motorcycle. Stalling the engine, he lifted it up, put the gearshift into neutral, and pushed the machine into the wood. Without pausing to catch his breath, he then doubled back to the dispatch rider and dragged him behind a clump of bushes before returning once more to retrieve the all-important Schmeisser machine pistol, which had parted company with its owner.

The motorcycle and the uniform were only useful accessories because, in the end, everything hinged on the weapon; unless it was in working order, the ambush could be written off as a total failure. Moving deeper into the wood, Holbrook stripped off his jacket and, kneeling down, made a thorough examination of the Schmeisser, taking it apart to inspect the barrel, the magazine housing, and the breech block. The leather sling had been ripped out of the forward swivel, which explained how the weapon had come adrift, and he also noticed that the body had been dented near the pistol grip but fortunately not deep enough to interfere with the return spring mechanism. Satisfied that it would function, he reassembled the Schmeisser and knotted the leather strap around the forehand grip so that he would be able to sling the weapon over his shoulder.

Placing the machine pistol down on his jacket, he then returned to the German and stripped off his uniform. Although they were approximately the same height, the dispatch rider was a good deal slimmer and the tunic was a tight fit. Not surprisingly, he had to let the web belt out a couple of notches before he could buckle it around his waist, and the boots were also a size too small, but with some discomfort he managed to squeeze his feet into them.

It meant taking a risk, but there was no time to bury the dead man. Dawn would break in a little over two hours and it was vital that he tap Rudelatt's telephone while it was still dark. Rolling the body under the clump of bushes, Holbrook covered it with bracken and then, moving back into the wood, he collected the Schmeisser and dumped the civilian clothes he'd been wearing.

The BMW refused to start at first because the carburetor was flooded, and he was forced to shut off the gas until he had cleared the cylinder. Starting from scratch again, he primed the pump and, straddling the bike, kicked the engine into life. There was a slight grating noise as he put the gear into first, but there was no drag when he let the clutch in, and that was all that mattered. Five minutes later, he swept through the peaceful village of Bonnières, unaware that a second dispatch rider from 7th Army was only a short distance behind him.

The foot patrol tramped past the mayor's office in single file and headed toward the lower courtyard of the château. Not one of the four men, including the NCO in charge, could really understand why it was necessary to check the village every two hours after the curfew had been enforced, but of all the guard duties they were called upon to perform in La Roche-Guyon, this was the least irksome and therefore the most popular. Rumor also had it that there was a very attractive young woman living in the rue Vieille Charrière who was in the habit of appearing undressed in the window of her bedroom, but despite the fact that this street was visited more frequently than any other, no one had ever laid eyes on her. Yet the myth persisted and the lurid stories multiplied, even though there was a growing body of opinion among the infantrymen of the defense company that it was just a huge confidence trick perpetrated by the clerks.

So far as the infantrymen were concerned, the clerks were on to a good thing. They were excused all guard duties, they didn't know the meaning of hard work, they kept regular office hours, they always had their meals on time, and they could count on at least eight hours of sleep every night. Like the young woman of the rue Vieille Charrière, this was also a myth. Since the D-Day landings on the sixth of June, the clerks of the logistics, operations, and intelligence staff branches were lucky if they had one unbroken night in three.

The clerks in the Ops Room would willingly have swapped

places with the town patrol. They had been on duty now for nearly nineteen hours, and the way things were shaping up it was beginning to look as if they would have to work right through Monday as well. Although the traffic on the wireless nets had noticeably slackened, they were still busy sorting out the backlog of conflicting situation reports which had been pouring in all day from the formations watching the Orne bridgehead. Routine returns arriving by dispatch rider from 7th Army were therefore accorded a low priority, and it was after 0300 hours before one of the clerks noticed that the strength-and-casualty return was missing. Unable to understand why the citations for honors and awards had already arrived when they had been dispatched at a later time than the operational return, he referred the matter to the duty officer.

The hunt started in a leisurely fashion with a telephone call to the signals center, but the pace hotted up once it was known that a dispatch rider from 7th Army was missing. At first, no one seriously believed that he had been ambushed because there were security patrols operating on all the main supply routes and it was assumed that he had had a mechanical breakdown. However, this complacent opinion was discredited when it was established that, although the dispatch rider had passed through the traffic control post outside Pacy, he had failed to arrive at either the Vernon or Mantes checkpoints. In accordance with standing orders, the provost marshal was therefore alerted and a search organized for the missing signalman.

Holbrook switched off the ignition and put the gear lever into neutral. According to the reading on the speedometer, he had clocked up seven miles, which he reckoned would put him about a thousand yards from the river. So far, the topography seemed to tally with Gilbert's description of the area and he was pretty confident that the track which stretched before him was the one he had been told to look out for after leaving Bonnières. Holbrook went over the route again in his head and then, positive that he had followed Gilbert's instructions to the letter, he dismounted and wheeled the motorcycle off the track.

Finding a hiding place for the BMW in the forest of Moisson

was not as easy as he'd thought, however, and the longer he was forced to push it, the more he was convinced that the machine weighed a ton. Just when he was beginning to think that he would have to leave it in one of the innumerable clearings and trust to luck that no one stumbled across it, he found a clump of bushes in a deep hollow. Content that he couldn't have chosen a better spot, he left the BMW in the hollow and returned to the track, where he hacked off a branch and obliterated the tire marks.

First light was beginning to show as Holbrook set off for the river, and, anxious to save time, he kept on the track where the going was easier. Some ten minutes later he saw the blurred outline of Rudelatt's cottage. Branching off into the forest, he circled the gamekeeper's lodge, looking for the signal cable which linked it with the château. Gilbert had led him to believe that the telephone line from the Wehrmacht headquarters ran through the orchard opposite the château and was then strung across the river above the site of the suspension bridge which had been demolished by the French Army in 1940, but he could find no sign of it downstream of the cottage. Retracing his steps, he eventually found the cable, which had been connected to the house via a junction box nailed to a tree on the right-hand side of the track.

He thought it would be a simple enough job to tap into the line, providing he found a place somewhat less exposed. Moving two hundred yards upstream from Rudelatt's cottage, he discovered that the field telephone cable had been carelessly looped over the branch of an oak tree some nine feet above the ground. The sun was already beginning to appear above the horizon and it was obviously going to be a race against time, because Gilbert had warned him that the defense company at La Roche-Guyon always sent a patrol across the river half an hour after sunrise to check out the far bank.

The branch seemed tantalizingly low but he couldn't reach it from a standing jump, and, backing off, he ran at the tree, slamming the toe of his right boot into a knothole to give himself that extra bit of leverage so that he was able to grab the branch with both hands. For a moment he hung there suspended in midair until, swinging like a pendulum, he managed to hook a heel over the bough, and then, straining every muscle, he heaved himself up and twisted over onto his stomach.

The telephone line was within easy reach now, and with the aid of a pair of pliers he stripped off the insulation, baring the wires. Somewhere on the other side of the river an engine suddenly coughed and spluttered into life. Within the space of a few seconds, the note changed to a high-pitched whine as the outboard motor picked up speed, and he could hear the water slapping against the flat bottom of the assault boat.

His fingers were all thumbs and he was thankful that the earphone from the crystal set was already wired up so that he was able to connect it straight to the field telephone cable. It wasn't exactly a sophisticated listening device, but it would work. Twisting sideways, he held on to the branch, lowering himself to the full extent of his arms before dropping to the ground.

Although he'd been told that the patrol never strayed far from the bank, Holbrook moved deep into the wood and then went into hiding. He hoped Rommel's ADC wouldn't call Rudelatt in the meantime, because he would have to wait at least an hour before it was safe to return.

Fletcher was a light sleeper and, although the communicating door deadened most of the sound, the faint clatter of footsteps in the adjoining room was enough to wake him instantly. At first he thought it was only a gendarme returning from beat duty, but then somebody with a harsh guttural voice spoke to the desk sergeant in bastardized French. As he lay there listening intently, a spring creaked as Vallin turned over onto his back; within moments his loud snores, coupled with Jackson's deep breathing, made it impossible for Fletcher to hear more than one word in five. Throwing the blankets aside, he slipped out of bed and crept over to the door.

The German was shouting now, banging a fist on the desk to emphasize what he thought of France, the French people, and the inhabitants of Vernon in particular. It was the other face of the Occupation, brutal and loud-mouthed as opposed to the well-mannered and courteous approach favored by the Military Government. The tirade rose to a crescendo and then ceased abruptly; a different voice shouted "Heil Hitler!" and a few moments later a door slammed, rattling the front windows of the police station. The desk sergeant was still mouthing obscenities under his breath when Fletcher walked into the room and asked him what all the fuss was about.

The sergeant looked up, his face contorted with anger. "The Boche have lost one of their bloody dispatch riders." Leaning over the desk, he hawked into a waste bin as if to show what he thought of the Wehrmacht. "I hope somebody has killed the bastard."

"Is that what they think?"

"Who knows?" The sergeant gesticulated with his hands and shrugged his shoulders. "They said the Town Major would seize fifty hostages if he didn't turn up in the next hour, but it could be a bluff."

"You hope."

"I tried to tell them that Pacy was a long way from here but the pigs wouldn't listen to me."

Fletcher walked past the sergeant and stared at the map pinned to the wall. "Where's Pacy?"

"Near Évreux." The sergeant took out a handkerchief and blew his nose loudly. "It seems he was on his way to La Roche-Guyon."

Flether found Évreux on the map, and suddenly everything fell into place. It wasn't necessary to be a military genius; anyone who wasn't a complete idiot could see that National Route 13 had to be the main supply line for 7th Army. Anyone who wasn't a complete idiot would also know why this simple, obvious fact was so important to Holbrook. The forest of Moisson was a prohibited area, but not to a man in uniform; somewhere between Pacy and Bonnières he had lain in ambush and killed the first dispatch rider who was unlucky enough to come his way.

Holbrook was close to the target now and he was armed. Fletcher thought it was about time they did something about it. Returning to the interview room which had been set aside for their use, he roused Jackson and Vallin.

22

Holbrook felt himself nodding off. Fighting to stay awake, he pinched his thigh viciously, but the pain soon wore off and his head lolled forward again; enveloped in a warm, pleasant glow, he gave up the unequal struggle and closed his eyes. He was floating on cotton wool now, his body light was a feather, and Gabrielle was stroking his face and she was murmuring something to him and he was slipping an arm around her waist, wanting to hug her close. Like a reed bending with the wind, he swayed from side to side and then suddenly he was falling into an abyss. His hands flailed the air and found a hold. For several moments it seemed as if the world was upside down, but then the adrenaline flowed and he realized that he was staring up at the sky above his head. Straining every muscle, he hauled on both arms, twisted over onto his stomach, and sat up, his legs astride the branch.

Everything looked strange, especially the veil of mist hanging above the river, which he couldn't recall seeing before, and he wondered how long he had been asleep. According to his wristwatch it was twenty past seven, but the light was gray enough to suggest that it was evening. The possibility that he had slept right through the day set his pulse racing until he noticed that the light was still coming from the east. With a sigh of relief, Holbrook leaned forward and retrieved the earphone, which was dangling below the branch.

At first, he associated the low puttering noise with the cranking handle of a field telephone, but when he listened in there was only a low-pitched hum on the line. The noise gradually became louder and he glanced anxiously toward the river, wondering if the defense company in La Roche-Guyon was sending another patrol across, before it dawned on him that it was only a spotter plane. Craning his neck, he peered up at the sky, trying to catch a glimpse of it, but the foliage was too thick.

Epp broke into a cold sweat as the Feisler Storch hit an air pocket and dropped like a stone. For a while he thought he was going to be sick again, but the feeling of nausea slowly subsided and he mopped his face with a handkerchief. Quirnheim had always maintained that air sickness was largely psychological, a malady which could be conquered if the mind was kept fully occupied. Like most theories, it sounded very convincing until it was put into practice, for although he had boarded the JU-52 in Berlin with any number of problems on his mind, the remedy hadn't worked for him. Minutes after the plane had taken off for Paris, he had succumbed as usual.

The pilot touched him on the shoulder and pointed ahead with a gloved hand. Responding to the gesture, Epp leaned forward and stared through the Perspex windshield. A thin veil of ground mist hung above the Seine, masking the landing field, but it wasn't dense enough to hide the treetops and the pilot seemed unconcerned. Above La Roche-Guyon, the Château Roche-foucauld looked clean and sharp in the early morning sunlight, and, despite the umbrella of camouflage nets, the wireless vehicles and Hanomag half-tracks in the lower courtyard were clearly visible.

Epp yawned. So much had happened following his previous visit to Headquarters Army Group B that it was hard to believe that only three weeks had gone by since then. His conversation with Field Marshal Rommel in the high-ceilinged room on the ground floor of the château seemed a lifetime ago, which in a way it was. The conspiracy had been in its infancy then, and it was still possible to believe that the Gestapo were unaware that the Bendlerstrasse was a hotbed of intrigue. In retrospect, they might have guessed the SD would keep an eye on Beck; the Colonel General had always been an outspoken critic of the regime and Hitler could never forget that the former Chief of the General Staff had resigned in protest over the Czechoslovakian crisis of '38. It was futile to be wise after the event, but all the same he couldn't help feeling that they ought to have avoided Beck like the plague until Stauffenberg succeeded in removing Hitler.

The Storch banked, dipped toward the landing field, and rapidly lost height. The trees raced by on either side and then, just when Epp thought they must be getting desperately close to the embankment at the far end of the meadow, the wheels touched down with a spine-jarring thump and the plane taxied to a halt. The pilot cut the switches and leaned back in his seat, frowning, as if he wasn't any too happy with their landing either.

Epp opened the door, dropped his walking stick and briefcase onto the ground, and climbed out, conscious of a nagging area of pain in his pelvis. Unlike the previous occasion, there was no Kübelwagen waiting under the trees, and he wondered if the staff expected him.

"How long should I wait for you, sir?"

Epp retrieved his briefcase and walking stick and straightened up. "I haven't the faintest idea, corporal," he said irritably, "it all depends on the Field Marshal. Do you have another detail?"

"No, Herr Major, but I ought to warn the air traffic control at Le Bourget when they can expect to see me again." The pilot removed his flying helmet and ran a hand through his tousled hair. "It's only a precaution in case something comes up in the meantime."

Epp glanced at his wristwatch. "It's almost seven thirty now, corporal."

"Yes, sir."

Almost seven thirty. In a little over an hour and a half, Anneliese would catch the train for Munich, where Sophie would be waiting to meet her. Sophie had been distant and withdrawn when he'd spoken to her on the telephone yesterday, and there had been a few awkward moments when she'd asked him point blank whether he was having an affair. It had been touch and go, but in the end he'd managed to persuade her that Anneliese was run down and had been advised to take a rest in the country, and Sophie, perhaps anxious to clutch at any straw, had swallowed her pride and said that of course she could stay with her parents.

"Is anything the matter, sir?"

Epp looked up with a startled expression on his face. "What did you say, corporal?" he asked curtly.

The NCO pilot swallowed nervously. "I thought you looked faint, Herr Major."

"Yes, well, I'm afraid flying doesn't agree with me." He smiled fleetingly. "As a matter of fact, I won't be too sorry if you are required for another detail. Perhaps you had better advise Le Bourget that your ETA will be twelve hundred hours. If I'm not back by eleven thirty, you may take off without me."

Epp turned away and stumped off, angry with himself because his mind had been elsewhere. Anneliese would be all right with Sophie in Kempten, and there was no longer any need to be concerned for her safety. Olbricht and the others were relying on him to reassure Rommel that everything was going according to plan, and he had no business to be preoccupied with his own affairs. He had a feeling that the next few hours could well be critical, and in a sense he was right, but not in the way he supposed. Leaving the meadow, Epp turned into the rue de l'Hospice and limped toward the château.

Vallin pulled into the side just short of the crossroads and slipped the gear into neutral. They could turn left for Bonnières or right for Pacy and Évreux, a simple enough choice in some ways except that they would be asking for trouble whichever direction they chose. Dufoir had warned him not to go anywhere near La Roche-Guyon and the forest of Moisson, but that was easier said than done. Vallin wished to God he was back in Paris and had never laid eyes on the crazy, fanatical Englishman who was sitting beside him, because he was going to do for them yet.

Fletcher said, "What are you waiting for?"

Vallin licked his lips. "I'm not sure which way you want to go," he said lamely.

"You can read, can't you?" Fletcher pointed to the signpost. "We want to go through Bonnières."

"Not yet we don't." Jackson leaned forward and pushed the road map under his nose. "We're not going near that god-damned forest until I'm satisfied that our man is in there."

"You want proof, is that it?"

"You bet I do, and we might just find it if we turn right at the crossroads."

Vallin shifted into gear and let the clutch in. National Route 13 was the lesser of two evils, but it was still the main supply line into Normandy and the military police were bound to be out in force looking for the missing dispatch rider. He hoped somebody was ready with a convincing story if they were stopped, since the Boche were unlikely to be overly impressed by their police identity cards. He also wished they weren't carrying sidearms, because he had a nasty premonition that the Englishman might well use his pistol if things got sticky.

The hazard warning signs prompted him to ease his foot on the accelerator before entering the first S-bend. Glancing at the woods on either side, it occurred to him that this was a pretty good spot to lay a night ambush, and then the road curved again and as they went into the straight before the next hairpin, he saw the long, jagged groove and the skid marks on the surface. Old habits die hard and Vallin was first and foremost a policeman. If he had thought about it, he would have acted differently, but instead instinct took over and he trod on the brakes.

Both SOE agents left the Citroën a split second after the car had stopped moving and it was too late then to have any regrets, but all the same he couldn't help feeling that he had stuck his head into a noose. If there was a connection between the skid marks and the missing dispatch rider, they would head back to Bonnières and that would be it.

Vallin looked into the rearview mirror. Both men were crouching in the middle of the road, but a few moments later they split up and disappeared into the woods on either side of him. Neither moved silently, and he could hear them beating the undergrowth as they worked their way forward, looking for any kind of evidence which would indicate that the missing dispatch rider had been ambushed. The minutes crawled by, stretching his nerves to breaking point, and then, just when he was beginning to hope that they had drawn a complete blank, the Englishman reappeared some distance ahead of the car, waving his arms and shouting. The American sprinted across the road to join him. Vallin wondered what was so special about the tree which obviously held such a fascination for them.

There was a faint whirring noise in the distance and an engine coughed into life; less than a minute later, a Kübelwagen rounded the bend and skidded to a halt and a heavily built corporal toting a Schmeisser submachine gun got out of the car and sauntered toward the SOE agents. Vallin, conscious that the other NCO was staring at him through the windshield, forced himself to meet his gaze with a bland smile.

It was one of those chance encounters and they had been caught napping. The MPs were obviously looking for the missing dispatch rider, and he supposed that they must have been searching the woods a hundred yards or so up the road.

This was one time when he wished he could lip read. The American was doing most of the talking and the corporal seemed less hostile. There was a lot of arm waving as they moved closer to the tree, and then the German stooped down and picked up a length of wire. The Englishman reached inside his jacket, and for one horrible moment it looked as if the idiot intended to draw his automatic and shoot the corporal in the back of the neck, but when he opened his eyes again Vallin was relieved to see that he had merely produced his identity card. The MP examined it briefly and nodded; turning about, he shouted to his companion and, raising one arm above his head, described a circle in the air. The driver waved back, maneuvered the Kübelwagen through a U-turn, and was inching forward in first gear as the corporal sprinted across the road and leaped into the vehicle. Trailing a thin plume of exhaust fumes behind them, they rounded the bend doing forty.

Jackson heaved a sigh of relief and leaned back against the tree. Fletcher was grinning at him in an inane sort of way, and Jackson noticed that his hands were shaking as he lit a cigarette. "That was close, Harry," he said.

"So what?" Fletcher drew on his cigarette and blew a perfect smoke ring. "We got away with it, didn't we?"

"We might not be so lucky next time."

"I know what you're thinking and it won't wash. We might not have found a body, but Holbrook was here and I'm not turning back now."

"Who said anything about turning back, Harry?"

Fletcher shrugged his shoulders. "Perhaps I got the wrong impression. You don't have to come with me. I can take Holbrook without any help from you."

"Maybe you can but you're stuck with me all the same." Jackson smiled lopsidedly "You see, I'm in the mood to be a hero."

"You know something?" said Fletcher. "I bet Vallin isn't."

He turned on his heel and walked toward the car. The same fixed, inane smile was still there on Vallin's face.

De Neury pressed his hands together and raised them to his lips. He had been puzzled to know why Paupal had wanted to see him, and even now he wasn't sure that he really understood the purpose of his visit. At first he had been under the impression that it had something to do with Gabrielle Marsac, an assumption which had not seemed unreasonable when the lawyer had introduced him to the police inspector. It was only after Dufoir had been talking for some length of time that it dawned on him that he'd been mistaken.

De Neury glared at Paupal and wondered what he was up to. The story Dufoir had told him was so fantastic, so unbelievable, that he was inclined to think it could be an elaborate practical joke. Perhaps in some obscure sort of way the lawyer intended to make him look a fool, but that didn't ring true because, from what he'd heard, Paupal was not exactly blessed with a sense of humor.

"This plot to assassinate Field Marshal Rommel," de Neury said abruptly, "why should it be of particular interest to me?"

"Because we are aware of your friendship with Colonel General Stülpnagel."

"We?"

"The Resistance," Paupal said coolly.

De Neury wasn't surprised; he'd never made any secret of his admiration for the New Order, and it was common knowledge that the Military Governor of France was a frequent guest in his house. The fact that the lawyer had openly associated himself with the Resistance movement didn't surprise him either. Now that the writing was on the wall, the FFI were becoming increasingly bold.

"We believe Stülpnagel would listen to you."

De Neury raised an eyebrow. "You must think I'm a complete fool. Why on earth should you want me to save the Field Marshal from an assassin's bullet?"

"That hardly concerns you."

"I thought you'd say that. I don't know what you hope to gain from this practical joke of yours but—"

"It isn't a joke," Paupal said coldly. "You really must be stupid if you seriously believe that one of the most prominent advocates in Paris and a senior police officer have nothing better to do with their time. I would have thought that you, of all people, would be anxious to help us. I need hardly remind you that times are changing."

De Neury smiled sourly. Times were indeed changing, and for the worse. He had heard a number of disquieting stories about the sort of rough justice the Resistance had handed out to collaborators in and around Caen after the city had been liberated, and he could just imagine what they would do to him if they got the chance. The more he thought about it, the more he was convinced that this was an opportune moment to establish a foot in the other camp.

"I'm sorry," he said contritely, "it's just that Dufoir's story seemed a little farfetched. Naturally, I'm only too happy to be of service to the Resistance."

Dufoir could feel the bile rising in his throat. As soon as this urbane, smooth-talking, fascist-loving aristocrat picked up the telephone and spoke to Stülpnagel at his headquarters in the Hotel Majestic, Holbrook would be a dead man.

23

Fletcher opened the side window and poked his head out of the car. Apart from a loose tappet which rattled intermittently as the engine ticked over, the forest was still, almost too still for his liking. The ground mist had lifted now and the sun, filtering through the overhanging branches, cast dappled patches of light on the unpaved track leading to the river where Holbrook would be lying in wait. It was obvious to him that from here on they would have to go on foot, moving stealthily like hunters dogging a wounded animal in the bush, or Holbrook would jump them first.

Stealth meant time, and time was probably running out for them. The MP corporal had been too excited to think straight, but it would be a different story when the provost marshal started to grill him. Under questioning, he would recall their conversation piece by piece, and inevitably somebody would ask why it was that two French policemen should connect a wanted criminal with the missing dispatch rider. Once that particular penny dropped, he thought Holbrook wouldn't be the only man who was being hunted.

Fletcher withdrew his head and closed the window. Nudging Vallin, he said, "We ought to park off the track. There's a clearing a little way behind us."

"Do you want me to back into it?"

"That's the general idea."

Vallin opened the ashtray in the dashboard, removed the cigarette which was stuck to his lower lip, and stubbed it out. Shifting into reverse, he looked over his shoulder and slowly backed up the track, locking the wheel over to the left as the Citroën drew level with the clearing. Maneuvering over the uneven ground, he tucked the car behind a clump of bushes and then switched off the ignition.

"What happens now?" Vallin knew that he sounded nervous but he didn't care. Every man was afraid at some time or other unless he was a maniac like the Englishman. "I mean, what am I supposed to do?"

"Well, I reckon you ought to come along with us. If nothing else, the walk will do you a power of good."

Funny, thought Vallin, oh, very funny. He'd heard that the English had an odd sense of humor but this man had to be in a class of his own.

"Maybe he should stay with the car, Harry," Jackson suggested.

"I don't think it's going to run away." Fletcher removed the ignition key from the dashboard and slipped it into his pocket. "But on the other hand, we both know somebody who might, don't we, Vallin?"

Nobody said a word after that. Like animated dolls responding to a hidden puppet master, they got out of the car and moved toward the river in an irregular arrowhead formation. They were, at one and the same time, the hunters and the hunted.

Epp was beginning to feel that he had outstayed his welcome at Army Group B. No one had said so outright but there had been a number of hints, ranging from the vexed frown of the lieutenant colonel in charge of Section Ib when he'd launched into a long-winded account of the difficulties besetting the Reserve Army, to the impatient attitude of the second- and third-grade junior staff officers, none of whom had been exactly pleased to see him.

There was an ominous sign outside the Ops Room which read, VISITORS—KEEP OUT. Glancing up and down the corridor, Epp wondered who else he could see. Logistics and Intelligence were out because there was no valid reason for him to visit either staff branch, and he was sure that no one would put out the welcome mat in the Signals Center. He had already spoken to every officer in Personnel and he could scarcely call on the camp commandant to ask for transport before the Feisler Storch had taken off for Paris without him.

He looked at the Ops Room again, where he knew Rommel was locked in conference with Speidel, the Chief of Staff. He thought it probable that both men were preoccupied with the war map, studying the host of colored pins which denoted the buildup of 2nd British Army in the Orne bridgehead. Everybody at La Roche-Guyon had been waiting for Montgomery to launch his expected offensive at dawn, and the fact that he hadn't had added to the air of uncertainty. In the circumstances, there was no telling when the Field Marshal would be available, but it would obviously be more than his life was worth to ignore the off limits sign on the door.

The defense company commander would probably think it very odd that a staff officer from Berlin should be interested in his sub unit, but there was nowhere else left for him to go, and no matter how lame the excuse might seem, he had to waste time. Stauffenberg, Olbricht, and Quirnheim were relying on him and he couldn't leave La Roche-Guyon without seeing Rommel. Leaning heavily on his walking stick, Epp limped out of the château.

The sun was a blast furnace and he could almost cut the humidity in the atmosphere. Keeping in the shade of the linden trees, Epp slowly made his way down to the Grande Rue and was about to turn into the lower courtyard when he remembered that there was a café beyond the mayoral offices where he could perhaps kill an hour over a cup of coffee. He was still dithering, unable to make up his mind, when the general alarm sounded and the defense company poured out of their billets.

He watched them, fascinated because there was the same air of professionalism about the unit that had been the hallmark of the battalion he'd served with in the Crimea. A civilian observing the milling throng in the lower courtyard would see only chaos, but to Epp the company was a precision machine with ninety-six separate working parts, each of which functioned smoothly. A few terse instructions and the camouflage nets were removed from the Hanomag half-tracks, the inflatable assault boats collected from the stores, and the ammunition broken out and issued to each man. Another sharp word of command and the company fell in by platoons, each soldier automatically dressing off in line with the next and then standing easy for the briefing.

The company commander matched their professionalism. His orders were a model, clear and concise and delivered in a quiet but authoritative voice. A veteran of the Polish campaign, the breakthrough at Sedan in 1940, and the Russian Front, he knew exactly what he wanted. As he spoke to them, Epp noticed that he used his hands to illustrate the pincer movement. One clenched fist became the platoon which was to cross the river in the assault boats, while the other hand, scything in a hook, represented the rest of the company in half-tracks, who would cross the Seine by the narrow bridge at Bonnières in order to cut off the terrorists lurking in the forest of Moisson.

There was a brief pause for questions and then they broke ranks, two platoons piling into the Hanomag troop carriers. Six engines whirred, caught, and thundered into life; tracks squealing on the cobbled surface, they moved off in single file, turning right outside the gates to head down the rue de l'Hospice toward Bonnières. The third sub unit waited until the noise of the half-tracks had faded into the distance before they picked up the assault boats and moved down to the river.

Epp had been looking for a way to kill time, and now fate had presented him with the means to do so. Dragging one foot like a spastic, he tagged on to the last section, confident that he could make himself useful. As he followed them into the rue du Docteur Duval, a Wanderer staff car sped down the avenue of linden trees, turned into the rue de l'Hospice, and roared off in the direction of Vernon. Glancing around, Epp was just in time to catch a brief glimpse of Rommel sitting bolt upright in the back. The habits of a lifetime die hard, and it was obvious to him that the Field Marshal was intent on overhauling the Hanomag troop carriers. When the pincer movement swept in behind the forest of Moisson, Rommel would be there, breathing down the neck of the company commander, just as he had always done in the desert.

Holbrook shifted into a more comfortable position. The clatter of tracked vehicles on the move was much fainter now and it was pretty obvious that they were heading downstream toward Vernon. He wondered if a training area lay in that direction and wished he'd thought to ask Gilbert. It was tiny details that counted and this was one he had overlooked, but only time would show whether or not it was an important omission.

The dull ache in his spine came back again and he could feel it spreading down below the pelvis to create a numbing sensation in both legs. Rocking backward and forward, he flexed his limbs, knowing from previous experience that this was the only way to gain a brief respite from the discomfort. The cramp was just beginning to disappear when the field telephone started clicking; reacting quickly, Holbrook grabbed the headpiece and held it to his ear.

A man with a gruff voice answered the call and the operator spoke to him in hesitant French. The wire tap wasn't very efficient and there was a considerable amount of induction on the line, but he caught the words "terrorists" and "forest" and suddenly it wasn't very difficult to put two and two together and come up with the right answer. Somebody had blown the whistle on him and the Wehrmacht was looking after its own, warning Rudelatt to stay indoors to avoid being caught in the crossfire. Common sense dictated that he should cut his losses and get the hell out. Swinging his legs out into space, Holbrook pushed himself off the branch. Breaking his fall with a shoulder roll, he staggered to his feet and started running. The assault boats were in the water now and he could hear the whine of their outboard motors as he plunged through the forest, making for the hollow where the BMW was concealed.

Fletcher saw the cottage through a gap in the trees and signaled Jackson and Vallin to stay where they were while he moved off to a flank and attempted to work his way forward to the river. Something very odd was going on because he could hear the high-pitched drone of several outboard motors, and he knew that nobody in wartime France was able to run a pleasure boat. Like a man walking on thin ice, he covered twenty yards and then froze, suddenly aware of another sound in the forest, that of a man running fast.

Guided by the noise, he swung around to face the line of trees beyond the track leading to the cottage, and in that instant the soldier broke cover. They were about forty yards apart, and although the man was in profile Fletcher recognized him instantly. All the years of training were lost in the heat of that moment, and reverting to his native tongue he called out to Jackson in English, screaming for him to look to his right.

Yet the old skills had not entirely deserted him and he snatched the MAS model 35 automatic from the shoulder holster, tripped back the hammer, and, swinging ahead of the moving target, squeezed off two shots in quick succession. The point of aim was too high, and both rounds, clipping a branch above Holbrook, ricocheted wildly, buzzing like angry wasps. Crouching lower, he realigned the blade foresight and fired again, double-tapping the trigger.

Holbrook threw himself sideways, rolled over twice, and came up into the crouch position. The gunman was between him and the BMW and there was nothing for it but to break contact and then try to outflank him. He could see one man near a large elm tree to his front, and there was obviously another lying somewhere farther back. Traversing the Schmeisser from right to left, he backed off, emptying the thirty-two-round magazine in short bursts in the hope that the suppressive fire would keep their heads down until he was out of pistol range. As the last case was ejected, the working parts slid forward with a dull clunk and, turning his back on the ambushers, he started running again. There was no question of trying to outflank them now because he could hear a line of beaters moving toward him and he knew that he would have to go to ground.

Jackson raised his head and saw a section of infantrymen advancing through the forest in extended line. It was apparent that Fletcher hadn't seen them because he was facing in the wrong direction and he shouted a warning, but his voice didn't carry above the crack of pistol fire. If their positions had been reversed, Fletcher would have simply left him in the lurch, but the thought never occurred to Jackson, and without any hesitation he opened up at extreme pistol range, trying to provide some sort of covering fire which would enable Fletcher to withdraw from his exposed position.

A rifleman on the right flank of the advancing section spotted a man standing by an elm tree and dropped to a kneeling position. He was one of the worst shots in the defense company, but the target was only seventy-five yards away and he couldn't very well miss. His finger curled around the trigger of the Mauser rifle, took up the first pressure, and squeezed. The bullet thumped into Fletcher's back and he embraced the tree, his arms folding halfway round the trunk as if he were hugging a woman to his chest. A ragged volley followed but he didn't hear it above the curious ringing noise in his ears. The pistol slipped from his grasp and he sank down onto his knees, and then a bullet punched into his skull, crushing it like an overripe peach.

Vallin was up and running as fast as his legs could carry him. Jinking in a zigzag pattern, he plunged through the forest, spurred on by the crack and thump of the bullets passing high above his head. The American was still returning their fire, but he would run out of ammunition before long and it was vital to reach the car before that happened. The sweat was pouring into his eyes and his lungs felt as if they were going to burst, yet nothing was going to stop him, not even the stitch which was knifing into his side.

Jackson looked over his shoulder, hoping that Vallin would be there to cover his withdrawal, but there was no sign of the Frenchman and he realized that he would have to go it alone. He had never been noted as a sprinter and the athletic track left him cold, yet this was different because his life was at stake and he made the first hundred yards in ten seconds dead. Twenty strides later, a chance shot caught him in the back of his right leg and, exiting through the kneecap, bowled him over like a rabbit. One look at the pieces of bone protruding through the ruptured skin was enough to convince him that he wasn't going anywhere, and pushing himself up into a sitting position he leaned back against a tree. There were just two rounds left out of eight in the magazine, and he knew he wouldn't have long to wait.

Holbrook lay face down in the dense bracken and held his

breath. The infantrymen were almost on top of him now but they were wheeling right, drawn to the sound of gunfire like homing pigeons returning to the loft. He could hear them crashing through the undergrowth, moving at the double, the section commander's voice hoarse with excitement as he urged them on. A boot landed within a few inches of his nose, somebody behind him reeled off a string of four-letter words, and then they were gone, heading deeper into the forest. Just when he thought it was safe to move, he heard someone else walking slowly toward him, swishing at the undergrowth with a stick. Placing the Schmeisser on one side, Holbrook reached into his boot and drew out the razor-sharp knife.

As soon as the section broke into a double, Epp knew that he hadn't a hope of keeping up with them and so he followed on at a more leisurely pace, hacking at the undergrowth now and again with his walking stick. He heard the Feisler Storch take off for Paris without him and smiled, because now he had yet another excuse for hanging on at La Roche-Guyon. The pilot, who was obviously a punctual fellow, had taken off on the stroke of eleven thirty, and he supposed that Anneliese must be halfway to Munich by now, assuming the train was running on time. Anneliese was well out of it; he couldn't see into the future but all the same he was glad that she wouldn't be in Berlin on Thursday the twentieth of July. Epp swung his stick again, flattening a clump of ferns, and then a soldier rose in front of him and a knife went into his rib cage. A hand closed over his mouth and the knife went in a second time and there was a terrible searing pain in his chest before he slipped into the dark, bottomless void.

Holbrook lowered the dead man on to the ground and backed away. He could still smell a faint odor of vomit on the major's breath and he gagged, thinking he was going to be sick, but the feeling passed and, collecting the Schmeisser, he moved off in the opposite direction. Later, when he judged it safe to do so, he would try to reach the BMW again.

Jackson saw the advancing infantrymen through a haze, and although he clasped both hands around the butt of the automatic to steady the aim, the barrel wavered up and down like a seesaw. There had been a bad smell about this particular mission from the very beginning and this was an opportunity to put things right; Holbrook was still out there somewhere, and if he could distract them long enough, there was a chance that he would be able to slip through the net. McCready wouldn't approve, but that didn't matter; Jackson had a hunch that if he lived through the day, Holbrook would never take a second crack at Rommel. He had lost a lot of blood and was close to fainting and the physical effort of squeezing the trigger taxed his strength to the limit. The first round plowed into the earth and the second embedded itself in a tree trunk some eight feet above the ground. There was a momentary pause before one man returned the fire, and then the rest of the platoon joined in.

Vallin reached the car, opened the door, and scrambled inside. As he searched through his pockets it suddenly dawned on him that Fletcher still had the ignition key and he started to pound the steering wheel, giving vent to a paroxysm of rage. Just when it seemed his luck had finally run out, something clicked and he remembered that morning in the rue de la Soussaye when Tambour and Herriot had been injured and Dufoir had told him to find someone who knew how to bypass the switch because the Englishman had stolen the key and he couldn't start the Citroën without it. It was almost too much to hope that this was the same car but the scratch marks on the dashboard looked familiar and, holding his breath, he opened the glove compartment. A feeling of trepidation gave way to one of triumph as his fingers closed around the piece of wire the mechanic had left behind.

The gunfire had died away and in the unnatural silence he could hear voices, but the forest magnified every sound and it was impossible to judge distance with any accuracy. For all Vallin knew, the advancing riflemen could be anything from one to four hundred yards away. Whether he had three or twelve minutes' head start on them, it was still going to be a race against time. Panic was just below the surface and he had to force himself to stay calm; raising the hood, he stared at the engine, trying to recall exactly what the mechanic had done. There was a moment of blankness before everything clicked into place and he was able to bypass the ignition switch.

The engine caught hesitantly and was only just warming up when he moved out of the clearing. Turning right on the track, he pushed the choke in and went up through the gearbox. Foot hard down on the accelerator, he took the first bend at fifty and was doing over sixty when he came to the next.

The pincer movement had suffered one setback after another. As the column was approaching the bridge at Bonnières, the leading troop carrier had shed a track, blocking the road, and it had taken the company the best part of half an hour to manhandle it out of the way. Less than half a mile beyond Bonnières a second half-track had burned out a clutch, delaying them even further so that they were forced to go flat out in an attempt to make up for lost time.

Vallin, rounding the bend on the wrong side of the road, met the leading Hanomag head on. The crash bar went into the Citroën with such impact that the car folded up like a concertina. The body members buckled, shearing the mounting bolts on the engine, which smashed through the forward bulkhead and crushed Vallin into a bloody pulp. Moving sideways now, the car slowly overturned, spilling gasoline from the ruptured fuel tank onto the red hot exhaust. There was a four-second delay before the vapor exploded, and then both vehicles were engulfed in a sea of flame.

Holbrook heard the explosion and, looking up through a gap in the trees above his head, saw a column of black smoke rising into the air. Although he couldn't even begin to guess what had happened, he had an intuitive feeling that the fire would cause a diversion, and leaving the clump of bushes where he had gone to ground he began to feel his way forward. As near as he could make it, the fire was roughly half a mile beyond the hollow where the BMW was hidden, and since it was also in line with the advancing infantry, he thought the conflagration would draw them on like a magnet.

The hunch that they were moving away from him grew even stronger when he crossed the track leading to Rudelatt's cottage and saw the spent cartridge cases lying in the grass. From then on it was easy to follow their trail, and, pausing frequently to observe and listen, he sprinted from one patch of cover to the next. There were a few uncomfortable minutes when it began to look as if their axis of advance must have taken them straight through the hollow where the BMW was concealed, but then their tracks veered farther to the right, where he could see the crumpled figure of a man lying in a clearing. Glancing around, he spotted an other body under the trees approximately a hundred yards away, and in that instant he was convinced that these were the two men whom Parker had unleashed. A long-term threat had been removed. Although he wasn't yet in the clear, Holbrook was quite sure that he would make it now because the hollow was there, right in front of him, just a short dash away.

His legs became pistons driving him forward and, plunging into the hollow, he dragged the BMW out of the bushes and kicked it into life. The road to Bonnières was obviously blocked but he aimed to go cross country, making a wide outflanking movement that would bring him out of the forest somewhere between Méricourt and Rolleboise, from which point he would head due west. Once across National Route 13, it would be necessary to ditch the motorbike and find a hiding place within an hour's walking distance of the Lebruns' farm, where he would have to lie low until nightfall.

The Hanomag was blazing like a torch now, and as he weaved in and out of the trees, drawing farther and farther away from the scene of the holocaust, the reserve small-arms ammunition in the troop carrier started to go off like giant-sized firecrackers.

Rommel looked at his wristwatch and frowned. The Hanomag troop carriers had held them up on the outskirts of La Roche-Guyon, but the defense company commander was in no way to blame for the fact that they would be late in arriving at the headquarters of the 12th SS Panzer Division. It had been a mistake to hang on in the Ops Room, a mistake to believe that the British would launch their offensive today merely because this was his assessment of the situation. The enemy rarely conformed with one's preconceived ideas, at least not in matters of specific detail. He glanced at the map spread across his knees and wondered if he would have time to inspect the defenses between Troarn Saint-Pair and the Colombelles factory area northeast of Caen. It would delay them even further, but his aide could always get on to 12th SS through 21 Panzer Division at Troarn Saint-Pair to advise them of their amended ETA.

The minor roads were behind them now and the Wanderer staff car was touching a hundred and forty kilometers an hour, hurtling toward Pacy on National Route 13, the main supply line to the 7th Army in Normandy.

Holbrook saw a gap in the hedgerow and went through it into the adjoining field. Riding through the standing corn, he swerved to the right and picked up a rough, narrow cart track which led straight to the line of poplars in the middle distance. His mouth was dry with excitement because he knew that National Route 13 was there, right in front of him, just beyond the trees. Forty, thirty, twenty yards to go; closing the throttle, he touched the footbrakes, slowing the motorbike to a halt.

For several moments he stared at the milestone across the road, scarcely able to believe that he was so near Pacy. The wide outflanking movement had also taken him far too close to the traffic control post on the outskirts, and there was a distinct possibility that he might bump into a mobile police patrol at any moment. Gazing at the farmland before him, it seemed to Holbrook that half the local population had been rounded up to harvest the crop of new potatoes. Much as he disliked the idea, it was obvious that he was stuck with National Route 13. Moving out of the cornfield, he headed back toward Bonnières, looking for a chance to leave the road and strike out across country. Holbrook had traveled less than a mile when, in the distance, he saw a car coming toward him.

At first he thought it was a Kübelwagen, but as the gap narrowed and the oncoming vehicle became more distinct he realized that it was a Wanderer staff car. It needed just one eagle-eyed brass hat to pull him up for being slovenly dressed and then the fat really would be in the fire. Bracing himself, Holbrook threw his shoulders back like a guardsman on parade and opened the throttle, hoping that he would flash past the car before any of the occupants had time to notice his appearance.

The slipstream from the Wanderer buffeted his motorcycle, and as he struggled to maintain his balance, Holbrook caught a fleeting glimpse of Rommel sitting in the back beside his ADC. It happened so fast that he had no time to think of the possible consequences and his foot went down on the brake pedal, to send the BMW sliding into a broadside skid which left globules of burning rubber on the road. The machine started to topple over, the footrest digging into the surface as he hurled himself out of the saddle and rolled over. Winded by the fall, he struggled to his feet and lifted the web sling over his head.

The Schmeisser was in his hands with a full magazine in the housing, and all he had to do was cock it, aim, and fire. It was a simple drill, something that could be performed mechanically, and his finger closed around the trigger, took up the slack, and squeezed. The gun fired just one round and then stopped with a separated case in the breech.

In almost total disbelief he watched the car draw farther and farther away from him until it was no more than a speck in the distance. There had been no reaction from Rommel, the driver, the escort, or the ADC, and but for the fact that the barrel was still warm to the touch, it would have been easy to dismiss the incident as a figment of the imagination. It was some minutes before Holbrook was able to accept that the long manhunt had ended, and then, as the sense of failure slowly gave way to one of release, he slung the Schmeisser over his shoulder and walked back to the BMW.

Five minutes later he turned off National Route 13 and headed northeast, riding cross country toward the Lebrun farm where he knew Gabrielle Marsac would be waiting for him.

Enemy aircraft had made the liaison visit extremely hazardous, but Rommel had insisted on visiting every division in the line from Troarn Saint-Pair to the Colombelles factory area northeast of Caen. Their last port of call had been the headquarters of the 12th SS Panzer Division, and they were now heading south from Livarot on the D579 in the direction of Vimoutiers, hoping that by sticking to this minor road they could avoid the marauding Spitfires. Transport was at a virtual standstill, and in whichever direction they looked columns of black smoke rose from the burning vehicles to mask the evening sun.

The eight fighter planes orbiting above Livarot presented an ominous threat but they pushed on through the town, believing the solitary staff car would not be spotted from the air. Some ten minutes later, however, the lookout observed two Spitfires heading in their direction and shouted a warning; urged on by Rommel, the driver put his foot down and the Wanderer picked up speed. They were looking for a side turning which might take them out of harm's way when the leading Spitfire leveled off a few feet above the road and opened up with cannon and machine-gun fire at a range of five hundred yards. The strike of shot raised puff marks behind them and then the driver slumped forward and the car spun off the road, mounted the bank, and overturned. One wheel was still gyrating slowly when the medical corpsmen dragged the unconscious Field Marshal from the wreck and carried him into the village of Sainte-Foy-de-Montgomery.

The précis had been put together by Lewis, who was very good at that sort of thing. An amalgam of the various signals which SOE had received over the past ten days, it also included reports from neutral sources and extracts from the news bulletins put out by the Deutschlandsender radio station in Berlin. Newstead had thought it would take Parker some time to digest the information, since it ran to six sheets of foolscap, but he was wrong, because Parker was already familiar with most of the facts and he finished reading it in ten minutes.

"You know," he drawled, "I always said this bomb plot McCready was so keen on would never amount to anything."

"Isn't that a little harsh?" Newstead said tentatively. "After all, they damn near brought it off."

"They failed, Dennis, and that's all there is to it."

They had failed, all right, and Stauffenberg, Quirnheim, Olbricht, and Beck had paid with their lives for it, and once Himmler got started Newstead thought that quite a few generals on the fringe of the conspiracy would be hanged in the bargain.

"And we lost a good agent for nothing."

"Oh, I believe you'll find that Holbrook will surface again, sooner or later."

Parker's lips met in a thin, straight line. "I wasn't referring to him," he snapped.

Newstead saw that he was thinking of Fletcher; Jackson had been excluded because he was OSS and therefore not one of their men.

"This Gabrielle Marsac. Was she a member of the Albert circuit?"

"I wouldn't know."

"I can't understand how they did it," Parker said in a vexed tone of voice. "They were up against us, the OSS, the Albert circuit, the Gestapo, and the bloody Wehrmacht, and yet they managed to disappear from the face of the earth."

"Well, I always thought Holbrook was one of the best agents we ever had."

"*Had* is the operative word," Parker said angrily. "I'll tell you one thing, Dennis, that man is never going to work for us again." His fist struck the desk to emphasize the point. "He's finished, you understand, finished."

Newstead had a feeling that Holbrook had already decided that for himself.